10/2

SPACE TEAM: THE TIME TITAN OF TOMORROW

BARRY J. HUTCHISON

ZERTEX
MEDIA LTD

Published worldwide by Zertex Books.

www.barryjhutchison.com

ALSO BY BARRY J. HUTCHISON

SPACE TEAM SERIES

Space Team

Space Team: The Wrath of Vajazzle

Space Team: The Search for Spurt

Space Team: Song of the Space Siren

Space Team: The Guns of Nana Joan

Space Team: Return of the Dead Guy

Space Team: Planet of the Japes

Space Team: The Time Titan of Tomorrow

Space Team: The King of Space Must Die

Space Team: A Lot of Weird Space Shizz

DAN DEADMAN SERIES

"Dial D for Deadman"

"Dead Inside"

EVERYTHING ELSE

The Bug

For Doc Brown

ONE

Draven Nostro was agitated. It had been almost a week since he had last killed someone and this, for him, was something of a record.

It wasn't his *all-time* record, of course. That had lasted five years and was unlikely to be challenged anytime soon as, in the decades following that fifth birthday party, his murder rate had continued on a steepening upwards curve. Nowadays, if he didn't slaughter someone every couple of days he started to get grouchy. He put it down to a combination of his increasing age, his decreasing patience, and the fact that he *really* – on a fundamental level – liked to kill people.

"Draven?"

The voice spat at him from across the table. Draven flicked the dark pools of his eyes over to his younger brother, Sliske, then down to the cards he held clutched in his own pointed fingers.

"Deflect," he said. He nodded to the bloated, toad-like figure who sat around the table on his right. "Target Musso."

Musso's tongue slapped across one of his bulbous eyeballs. Draven recognized it as one of the Gorf's more obvious tells. Musso was holding nothing. Whatever came out of his mouth next was a bluff. The knot of irritation that was coiled in Draven's gut slackened a little in anticipation.

"Uh, uh..."

"Take your time," urged Draven's sister, Esera. She sat on Draven's left, directly across from Musso. Her voice, like her face, was soft and sweet, and betrayed none of the dark urges that surged through her black and lifeless veins. "There's no rush."

"Speak for yourself," said Sliske, which brought a giggle from his sister.

Musso took a handkerchief from his breast pocket and dabbed at his sopping brow. His eyes, which always seemed to point in slightly opposite directions, swam independently as they took in the three waiting faces around the table, then stole a desperate glance at the door.

"Could I... Would you mind if I took a short bathroom break?"

"Yes," said Draven.

Musso half-sobbed in relief and began to stand. "Oh! Thank you, I won't be—"

"We *would* mind," Draven concluded.

Musso stopped halfway to his feet, one hand on the back of his chair, the other still clutching his cards.

"Sit down, honey," Esera told him, her smile now showing off far more teeth than it previously had been.

The chair creaked as Musso lowered himself back onto it. The waterproof plastic sheeting on the floor rustled beneath his feet.

Musso didn't bother to dab at his brow now. What was the point? He studied his cards. There was nothing he could play, no move left for him to make, but he couldn't bring himself to admit it. Not yet.

He looked up at the faces of the others. Draven was the eldest, and considered by many to be the worst of the three. It was Sliske who had always worried Musso the most, though. There was something disarmingly attractive about the man, with his porcelain white skin and immaculate eyebrows, but while all four members of the Nostro family were murderers, there was an air about Sliske that suggested he probably got more of a kick out of it than rest of them.

"I have a family," Musso pleaded. "I... I have four children."

"You should've thought of that, fat man," Sliske said. "Before you took your seat."

"No, I mean take *them*," Musso sobbed. "They are younger. Leaner. I mean *look at me*." He thudded himself on his chest, making his sagging breasts jiggle beneath his shirt. "You don't want me. You don't want *this*. I am old and fat and—"

Esera lunged across the table, her lips drawing back to reveal all her many teeth. Musso attempted to scream as she tore out his throat, but just sort of farted a couple of wet hiccups from his ravaged windpipe, instead.

"Hey! It was my turn to go first!" Sliske protested, grabbing his sister by the hair and wrenching her head back. Esera spat a half-chewed mouthful of Musso in his face, hissed loudly, then buried her face in the still-alive-but-rapidly-becoming-less-so Gorf's open throat.

Her weight toppled the chair backwards. By the time Musso hit the floor, Esera was straddling him, giggling as she played in his fountaining blood like a child in the spray of an open fire hydrant.

"I get the next one," Sliske said. "It should have been my turn."

"We'll see," said Draven. He gestured to the cards, cups and colorful balls now scattered on the table, then rose slowly and grandly. "Set up the next game. Tidy up. I shall see if any other challengers await."

Sliske protested, but Draven made it very clear he wasn't listening. He glided past the now very much dead Musso, paused to savor the coppery tang of blood that flavored the air, then continued to the door. It jerked sharply aside at his approach as if terrified he might touch it. A small but lavishly decorated bar area was revealed, with another door set into the wall opposite.

A blue-skinned cocktail waitress stood by the bar. She straightened at the sight of him, and nodded eagerly when he glanced her way. His smooth brow furrowed as he looked her up and down. "Where is the other one?"

"She's, uh, she's sick," the waitress said. "The agency sent me."

Draven waited, one eyebrow raised.

"Sir. The agency sent me, *sir*."

The eyebrow held steady for a while, before eventually dropping to join the other one. "We will require refreshments."

"Yes, sir. Right away," the waitress said, practically snapping to attention.

Draven held up a hand to stop her. "You may wish to wait a few moments. They're still cleaning up in there."

The waitress looked from Draven to the door and back again. She swallowed, then nodded slowly. "I'll do that. Thank you."

Draven had barely taken a step when the waitress spoke again.

"Uh, and anything for your father, sir?"

He stopped abruptly, then was on her at once, his slender fingers wrapping around her throat. He jerked her off the ground without any apparent effort and her blue skin tinged purple as she gasped and wheezed, her feet kicking at the air.

"My father is none of your concern," he said, his voice devoid of any emotion. "Is that understood?"

The waitress gargled out something unintelligible, but it seemed to do the trick. Draven released his grip, letting her slump to the floor. "Never mention him again," he warned, then he turned and swept onwards to the second door. Like the first, this one beat a hasty retreat, shunting sharply into the doorframe as Draven approached.

The room beyond this door was set out like a doctor's waiting area. But an expensive doctor who had probably never seen an ill person in their life, and who instead charged a lot of money to make the faces of the rich and famous incrementally worse.

There were two 'people' waiting – although that term applied only very loosely to one of them, who appeared to be primarily made of metal. Draven made no attempt to hide the way his nostrils flared in distaste. Cyborgs. Was there any crueler joke than a living creature without a drop of blood in its body? Such a waste.

The other person – the non-cyborg one – had been draped across one of the waiting room's leather sofas, his hands tucked behind his head. He jumped up as Draven entered, his utterly unremarkable humanoid face lighting up with a grin.

"Well, hey there, tall dark and spooky! I thought you were never going to come out."

Draven looked the man up and down, pausing just

briefly on his outstretched right hand. "Who are you?" he asked. "I was expecting a Gorf."

"The froggy guys? Yeah, I'm not one of them."

Draven turned away. "You should not have been let through. I do not know you. Be on your way."

"Yeah, the guys on the door, they weren't going to let us in," the man explained. "But then they found out who I was."

This made Draven hesitate. He turned his head to look back over his shoulder. "Oh? And who are you?"

"The name's Cal. Cal Carver," the newcomer replied. "I'm the King of Planet Earth." He jabbed a thumb back in the direction of Mech, the cyborg. "This here's my faithful manservant, Gunga."

Mech opened his mouth to say something, but Cal quickly jumped in. "He doesn't speak. Completely mute. Poor guy. Watch this."

He turned and addressed Mech directly. "I'm better than you, right? I'm the most awesome guy you've ever met. I'm better than you in every single way. Say absolutely nothing if you agree."

Mech's expression darkened, but his metal bottom jaw creaked slowly shut.

Cal turned back to Draven. "See? Not a word. Poor son of a bedge." He puffed out his cheeks. "Anyway, I'm here in town for a few days on business. You know, King stuff. I heard that you run some kind of card den here, or whatever, and I thought I'd swing by and check it out."

Draven shook his head, but only once. The desire to kill had lessened a little when he'd watched the Gorf die, but every moment in this man's company was making it grow. There was something about him. His face, probably. Or his demeanor. Whatever, the thought of tearing him apart made Draven's teeth hum pleasantly inside their sockets.

He turned crisply on his heels until he was facing the Earthman once more. "Very well. Follow me, *Your Majesty*," he said, bowing in a way that was roughly one third respectful and two thirds sarcastic. "Welcome to the game."

TWO

Cal pulled his chair in closer to the table, crinkling the pristine plastic sheeting beneath him. The whole room smelled lemon-fresh, although he was fairly sure there were no actual lemons involved. Space lemons, maybe.

"Is that in case of spillages?" he asked, gesturing to the floor.

"In a way," said Draven.

"Good idea," said Cal. "Speaking of which, any chance I could get a drink? I noticed a bar back there..."

"Refreshments are coming," Draven assured him. He nodded across the table to Sliske. "Deal, brother. Our guest is eager to begin."

Cal rubbed his hands together. "Yes, I am," he said, then he went to his belt and unhooked a leather pouch roughly the size of a water canteen. It *chinked* as he deposited it on the table. The three other players sitting at the table eyed it indifferently.

"What is *that*?" Esera asked, with the sort of tone that suggested Cal had placed a bag full of his own steaming hot excrement in front of her.

"It's my stake," said Cal. All three of the siblings visibly flinched at that last word. "You know, credits? Cash. Money. Moolah. Dough." His brow furrowed. "I can't think of any other... *Bones!*"

"What is he talking about?" Sliske asked.

"Bread. That's another one," said Cal.

"You misunderstand, Your Majesty," said Draven. "We do not play for money."

Cal raised his eyebrows. "Oh. I see." He looked around the table. "Just for fun, huh? Well – and I'm going to be honest here – that *is* refreshing. Everyone's so materialistic these days, don't you think? It's nice that four people can just sit together and play a game for the sheer fun of it."

Esera smiled, and Cal felt his eyes be drawn to her teeth. "Ooh, I like this one. He's funny," she said.

"I disagree," said Sliske. "I already find him tiresome."

"Oh... *you*!" said Cal, winking at the younger of the siblings. "Give it an hour and you'll love me. Or, you know, hate me. One of those. It can go either way."

"You misunderstand," said Draven with as much patience as he could muster. Which wasn't much. "*You* play for money. If you win, we shall make you stupidly wealthy."

"And if I lose?"

It was Sliske's turn to show his teeth. "Then we tear you open and gorge on your blood."

Cal blinked.

Then he blinked again.

He put a finger behind one ear and pushed it forward. "Sorry, you...?"

"We eat you alive," Draven said.

Cal nodded slowly. "Right. Right. I thought that was pretty much the gist of what he said, I just wanted to double check. I mean, that seems... Well, it seems..."

His voice faltered into a croak. Clearing his throat, he turned in his seat. Mech stood behind him, his back against the wall. "Did, uh, did you know about this?"

Mech nodded. It was taking an enormous amount of self-control to keep the smirk from his face, but he was managing somehow.

"You did? Why didn't you say something?"

"I thought you said he couldn't speak?" Draven interjected.

"What? Oh, yeah. Yeah, no. I mean no, but... He can mime! You couldn't have fonking mimed?"

Mech raised his metal shoulders in a nonchalant shrug.

"You're totally getting a pay cut for this," Cal told him. "I want you to know that. And kiss goodbye to your Christmas bonus."

The plastic wrap rustled beneath Cal's feet as he turned back to the table. Sliske and Esera were practically drooling as they eyed him hungrily, but Draven was demonstrating a somewhat greater level of self-control.

"Do you wish to retire from the game?" the oldest of the three siblings asked.

"I'll be honest, kind of," Cal admitted. "I mean, no offence – if I was going to be eaten alive by anyone, I'd want it to be you guys – but it isn't quite how I envisioned spending the afternoon."

"Retiring means you forfeit," said Esera.

"Forfeiting means you die," Sliske added. They exchanged glances and both giggled in a creepy kind of harmony.

Draven waved a hand vaguely. "But, it is your decision, of course."

Cal leaned back in his chair. "So, just to be clear - if I quit the game, you'll *definitely* kill me. If I play, you'll *prob-*

ably kill me. Unless I win, in which case, I'll be rich and you *won't* kill me. Have I followed that correctly?"

"You have," Draven confirmed.

Cal drummed his hands on the table. "Well alrighty, then. As long as we all know where we stand. Deal me in."

Esera clapped her hands together excitedly. "I knew I liked this one."

"I'm first," Sliske reminded her.

"Fair enough," said Cal. "And then... what? Does it go clockwise?"

"No, not the game. Eating you, I meant," Sliske said. "I'm first."

Cal swallowed. "Oh. Right. Gotcha. Well, you know... enjoy, I guess."

"I will."

"I suspect I'm pretty succulent," Cal boasted. "I mean, I don't want to overpromise or anything, but I don't think you'll be disappointed. In fact, I came very close to eating myself once. I mean, not by choice – that would be insane – but still."

The door jerked aside, revealing the blue-skinned waitress in the doorway. A tray floated above a metal cuff on her wrist, remaining perfectly balanced in the air. On it sat four drinks. Three of them were red and gloopy while the fourth was clear and sparkling.

Draven gestured impatiently for her to serve. Her eyes met Cal's as she deposited the clear drink on a small side table that unfolded from within his chair's arm rest.

"Why thank you, young lady," he said. "And what's your name?"

"Loren," said the waitress.

Cal's smile didn't falter. "Loren? That's... that's your name?"

Loren nodded.

"That's not exactly original, is it?"

Loren frowned. "What do you mean?"

"Well... I mean of all the names you could be called, 'Loren' seems a little obvious, don't you think?"

"And what's your name?" Loren asked, her voice clipped and short. "Hmm? Cal Carver, was it? That's what you said, right? That's not exactly new and original, is it?"

"That's different," said Cal.

"How?" demanded Loren.

"Because I'm the King of Earth."

Loren snorted. "Oh *please*."

Draven cleared his throat. It was a sound that suggested anything else currently going on should probably stop.

Cal and Loren both turned to the oldest of the Nostro siblings and smiled anxiously.

"Anyway, a pleasure to meet you, Loren," said Cal. "Great name. Great service. Thank you for the drink. I'd tip you, but I have no money."

The Nostro's all glanced down at the bag of credits still sitting on the table. Cal pretended not to notice.

"You're welcome," said Loren, nodding curtly. She placed the other glasses in front of the Nostros, then backed towards the door. "I'll be right outside."

Draven dismissed her with a wave of his hand, then raised his glass to his lips. He was about to take a sip when Cal interrupted.

"I'd like to propose a toast."

The Nostros all looked confused. "A what?" asked Esera.

"A toast. It's something we do back where I come from," Cal explained. "It's like this thing you say to mark a special moment."

"Very well. If you must," said Draven, making very little attempt to hide his displeasure.

Cal raised his own glass. "To family," he said. "Especially, and I hope you'll indulge me here, to my dad, the previous King of Earth. Kind. Funny. And he had this special room in the palace we all lived in where he spent most of his days. You know? A special place he liked to just go and be by himself that wasn't really public knowledge, but we all knew about."

He wiped an imaginary tear from his eye and raised his glass towards the ceiling. "Happy trails, Dad."

The others looked either confused or uncomfortable, it was tricky to say which.

"Can we drink now?" Draven asked.

"Sure, knock yourself out," said Cal, but Draven hadn't bothered to wait for an answer. He glugged a third of the gloopy red liquid, swirled it around in his mouth, then swallowed it.

"What is that?" asked Cal. "Tomato juice?"

"Would you like a taste?" asked Esera, her eyes wide and innocent. Cal watched Draven's black tongue catch a trickle of the stuff that was about to dribble down his chin, and slowly shook his head.

"Know what? I'm fine. I'll stick to whatever this stuff is," he said, raising his glass. He took a deep breath, then knocked the stuff back in one gulp. He smacked his lips together a few times, then failed to hide his disappointment. "It's water. It's fizzy water. Well, that's not going to take the edge off anything."

"One more thing, before we start," said Draven. His fingertips glided across the surface of the table until a pulsing red circle appeared. He tapped it lightly and the air seemed to shimmer. Behind Cal, Mech's arms fell limply to his sides. He tried to look down at them, but his head, like the rest of him, refused to move.

"A low-level electromagnetic pulse," Draven explained. "It temporarily blocks any hidden comm-devices and disables any weapons. Your manservant will remain alert, but physically immobile. This will prevent him trying to stop us devouring you if we win."

"*When* you win!" Cal corrected, then his eyes narrowed. "No, wait. I got that the wrong way around. If. If you win."

He glanced back at Mech, then looked round again as a small pile of cards was stacked on the table in front of him. Before he could reach to pick them up, two plastic cups were set on either side of the stack, one upright, the other upside-down.

"OK, so...?"

A white-painted wooden sphere was placed on the upturned bottom of the wrong-way-up cup. Cal picked it up, tossed it from hand to hand, then set it down again. He nodded, trying to convey the impression he fully understood what was going on.

"Well, that all seems in order," he said, before being interrupted by Sliske sliding a pile of rectangular metal chips in front of him, along with a small mirror, two stubby pencils and a breathtakingly detailed drawing of a horse. Or something not a million miles away from one, at least.

Cal watched the youngest of the Nostros expectantly, but no more game pieces seemed to be coming his way. "Well OK, then," he said, picking up his cards. He thumbed through them, his frown deepening. "Uh, these are all blank."

Draven and the others appeared momentarily confused. "Yes?"

"Of course they are," said Sliske. "What did you expect?"

"Well, I mean..."

"He doesn't know how to play!" Esera realized, her eyes blazing with excitement. "You don't, do you? You don't know how to play!"

Cal snorted. "What? No. This? Come on. With the ball and the cups and the little mirror? And the, you know, the drawing of a horse? Get out of here. I've played this a thousand times."

"Good. Then you can make the opening move," Draven informed him.

"Uh, what? No. It's fine. One of you guys can go first."

"Please," said Draven. "We insist."

"Seriously, it's fine," Cal said, then he jumped as Sliske slapped a hand down on the table.

"We *insist*."

Cal hesitated. He licked his lips, which were suddenly lacking in anything resembling moisture, and swallowed noisily. "Well then... *yay*. I love going first."

He looked from his cards to the assortment of items assembled on the table in front of him. Everyone else seemed to have the same set-up, although the balls were all different colors, and the space horses were striking a variety of quite unhorse-like poses.

"I'll be honest, I'm a little rusty," Cal said. "So..."

He reached for the ball, watching the others for their reaction. All three chairs creaked as the siblings leaned forward. Sliske's tongue darted hungrily across his lips.

Cal withdrew his hand. The sense of disappointment from the Nostros was palpable. He took that as a sign that he probably shouldn't touch the ball anytime soon.

He thumbed through his cards again and was disappointed, if not entirely surprised, to discover they were still blank. He glanced at the back of them to make sure he had them around the right way, but the other side was completely featureless, too, so he wasn't sure how anyone was supposed to tell which way they went.

"Just double-checking – which version of the rules are we playing?" he asked. "Because there are so many different variations, I'd hate to get the wrong one."

"The standard rules," said Draven.

"The...?"

"We're playing the standard rules," Draven repeated.

"Right," said Cal. "Right! Great! Standard. Just the standard, everyday rules. Nothing unusual or out of the ordinary. Just the run-of-the-mill bog-standard—"

"Hurry up!" Sliske barked. "We don't have all day."

"Or *do* we?" asked Cal, smiling hopefully.

"No. We don't."

"Right. Yes," said Cal. "Fair enough."

He looked at his cards again. Still blank.

Still fonking blank.

"OK," Cal muttered. He rolled the word around in his mouth for a while, then said it again. "OK. So I think I am going to..." He inhaled slowly through his nose. "Pass?" he said with an upward inflection that was one part confusion, two parts '*Oh shizz, I'm about to be eaten alive.*'

There was silence from the others, then Sliske banged his fist on the table, making the ball fall off his cup.

"Gah!" he spat.

Directly across from Cal, Esera nodded her admiration. "Well, well, well. It seems that you *have* played this game before after all, Earthman," she said. "Perhaps I misjudged you."

"What?" Cal squeaked. He closed his mouth, which

had dropped open, cleared his throat, then sat up straighter. "I mean yes. Yes, perhaps you did."

He watched as Draven made his move. It involved turning one of his cups over and moving it to the other side of his stack. Cal let out a low whistle of appreciation.

"Classic," he said. "Classic move."

He lifted his drink, remembered it was water, and set it back down again without taking a sip. Across the table, Esera was writing something on one of her cards.

"So *that's* why they're blank!" Cal said.

All eyes flicked to him. He shifted awkwardly and produced a grin from nowhere. "As we are all already aware," he said.

The scratching of Esera's pencil began again. Whatever she was writing, she was taking quite a long time over it. Cal seized the opportunity.

"So, what did you guys think of my toast?" he asked.

Sliske didn't acknowledge the question. Draven nodded politely. "It was very interesting," he said.

"I know. I mean, *dads*, right? Don't you just love them?"

Sliske and Draven exchanged glances, but said nothing.

"My dad, the old king, he loved that secret room of his," Cal continued, gazing off into the middle distance and smiling wistfully. "He called it his special hole. No. Wait, not that. That would've been inappropriate. He called it his, uh, his private man's area."

Cal consider this. "No. No, that's actually worse." He shrugged. "Know what? I forget what he called it. The point is, he loved that little room of his."

Feeling himself floundering, Cal struck out for the shore. "So, uh, what about your dad? Does he have a special private man's hole? I mean, a place where he hides away out of sight?"

Esera's pencil stopped. All three Nostro children fixed Cal with cold, steely stares.

"What is this?" Sliske demanded, his voice dropping into a low hiss. "Who are you?"

"What? Who, me?"

A trickle of sweat meandered down Cal's back. He dug around in his portfolio of facial expressions until he found one that conveyed surprise, confusion and absolute innocence all at the same time. At least, that's what he thought it conveyed. In reality, he looked like a badly constipated glove puppet, but luckily no-one who knew him was around to see it.

"I told you. I'm the King of Earth."

"Why are you asking about our father?" Esera demanded.

"I wasn't!" said Cal. "I mean, no, obviously I was, but it was just conversation, you know? Chit-chat." He laughed. "It wasn't like I was pumping you for information to try to find out where he is, or anything!"

The silence grew heavier. Cal softly cleared his throat. "It... it really wasn't that."

Esera went back to writing. The point of her pencil pricked the growing bubble of tension, and both Sliske and Draven relaxed. She finished with a flourish, then turned the card face down so no-one could see what she had written.

"Done," she announced.

"High time," Sliske muttered. He picked up his little mirror, breathed on it, then replaced it on the table with a *clunk*.

All eyes fell on Cal. It took him a moment to realize why.

"Oh! It's my turn. Right."

He looked down at the assortment of items in front of him, gave them all due consideration, then raised his eyebrows. "Uh... pass?"

That uncomfortable silence returned. Cal's heart bongoed inside his chest. It was Esera who spoke first.

"Oh, you clever boy," she whispered.

"It appears we have a tactician in our midst," Draven added.

Even Sliske appeared impressed. "Well, this just got interesting," he conceded.

"This could be a long game," said Esera.

"Ooh, I know!" said Cal, sitting bolt upright. "We could pass the time by talking about, I don't know, let's say our family history, for example." He caught the darkening expressions on the faces of the others, and quickly switched tracks. "Alternatively, maybe we could take it in turns to describe the layout of our houses in detail."

Cal gestured at the room around them. "I mean, this place looks interesting. Do you do tours, or...?"

"Do you *ever* stop talking?" Sliske demanded.

"No. No, he don't."

The voice came from directly behind Cal.

Cal closed his eyes and exhaled slowly.

"You said he couldn't talk," Draven intoned. "He talked."

"Yeah," Cal sighed. "Yeah, I just said that to annoy him." He raised his voice. "But you had to go and blow it, Mech. You had to go and blow it."

"Hey, fonk you, man," said Mech. "You were totally giving the game away."

"I was *not*!" Cal retorted. "They didn't suspect a thing. Did you?"

"What are you talking about?" Draven snapped.

"See? I totally nailed it. You're the one who spoiled it. You let me down, Mech. And yes, I'm going to say it, you let yourself down."

Cal crossed his arms and leaned back in his chair. "Ah well, I guess we'll just have to do it the old-fashioned way. You can beat the shizz out of these fonks and get them to tell us where their dad is." He flashed the Nostros a grin. "Sorry, guys. Kind of. Actually, no, I'm not sorry. Between you and me, I'm actually kind of looking forward to watching him pummel you." He pointed to Sliske. "Especially him. That guy's just unpleasant."

"Uh yeah," said Mech. "I mean, I would do that. Except, I can't move."

Cal's smile fell away. "Huh?" he said.

"The EMP thing. I can't move my arms or legs," Mech explained. "Sorry, man."

Cal's eyes went wide as all three Nostros slowly got to their feet.

"Oh," he mumbled. "Well, isn't that just *great*?"

THREE

True to his word, it was Sliske who made the first move. He lunged across the table, his jaw appearing to unhinge itself until his mouth looked big enough to swallow Cal's head wide.

"Splurt!" Cal yelped, shoving his chair backwards. The bag of money he'd deposited on the table became a rubbery sledgehammer that solidified as it *whanged* Sliske between the eyes. The youngest of the Nostro clan spat out a staccato, "Gu-gu," as the bridge of his nose exploded, then he crashed backwards over his chair and landed in a less than dignified heap on the floor.

Esera ducked the hammer as it turned on her, then caught it by the handle and swung it at Cal's head just as he jumped to his feet. It became a feather pillow just in the nick of time, but still packed enough of a wallop to knock Cal off balance.

"Hey, watch what you're doing with him!" Cal protested. A dozen metal spikes burst out from inside the pillow case and through Esera's hand. She screamed as they became spinning drill bits that chewed through her flesh and bone, and it took all Cal's effort not to throw up in his mouth. "Or he'll do that."

Esera tore her hand free, then tossed the pillow across the room. Cal was following its flight when Mech's voice barked at him.

"Look out!"

"Huh?"

Cal turned and saw Draven hurtling towards him. The elder Nostro hit him like a small, very localized hurricane. They stumbled toward the door, which snapped open at their approach. Cal grabbed for the door frame, missed, and suddenly found himself on the floor, pancaked beneath Draven's weight.

"You *dare* try to deceive us!" Draven spat. "Say good-bye, King of Earth."

"Wait! Wait!" Cal cried. "I have to tell you something."

Draven's jaw *kricked* open.

"Wait, don't! I'm serious! It's something you should know."

"*What*?" Draven growled, although thanks to the unhinged jaw thing it came out more like, "Wha'?"

"That game of yours totally sucks. It's literally the worst thing I've ever played. And I've played *Monopoly*. Twice," Cal said. "Also, brace yourself."

The scuffing of approaching footsteps caught Draven's attention. He looked up just in time for the sole of Loren's boot to crunch into the center of his face. Hissing in pain, he made a lunge for her leg, but the butt of a blaster pistol cracked him on the forehead above the eye, and he was suddenly much less interested in grabbing her than he had been a moment before.

"Get up. Slowly," Loren said, a blaster trained on Draven's head.

"I'd do what she says," Cal told him. "She will shoot you. Hell, I'm amazed she hasn't shot you already.

Draven did get up, but not slowly. He seemed to bound straight upwards onto it feet, yanking Cal up with him. His arm wrapped around the Earthman's throat as he pulled Cal in front of himself like a human shield.

"Let him go," Loren warned. "Now."

"You heard her," said Cal. His eyes flicked to Draven's wide mouth, with all those teeth lurking inside. "And you can shut that thing, too. It's unsightly, and flies could get in."

Draven's jaw bones ground together as he *clunked* them back into place, but he made no move to release Cal. "Who are you?" he asked. "What do you want?"

"Relax, Dravey – can I call you Dravey? Relax, Dravey, we're not here for you. We've come for your old man. That's why I was working you for information earlier. You probably didn't notice."

"We noticed," said Draven.

"Well, obviously you're going to say that *now*," said Cal.

"Let him go, or I will shoot your face off," Loren warned.

"Loren, don't. I've seen how you aim a spaceship, and it doesn't fill me with confidence," said Cal. He turned his head a little so he was addressing Draven again.

"We're here to bring your old man to justice. See, Mayor..." Cal clicked his fingers a few times. "Loren?"

"Smuna Clastres."

"Yeah, that guy, he wants rid of your dad. Something about him being a big mass-murdering monster? I don't know, I kind of glazed over for a while," Cal said. "But he wants rid. The mayor. And he's paying us to do the ridding. Handsomely, I might add."

"We had a deal," Draven seethed.

"Uh, no we didn't."

"Not you and I, you idiot. The Gorf. We had a deal with the Gorf. Clastres is unwise to try to alter it."

"Yeah, they told us about that," Cal said. "But here's the thing. The deal's over. It's off the table. It's no longer an option. It's—"

"I'm sure he gets the point," said Loren.

"Hmm? Oh. Right. Right," said Cal. "So, Dravey, what's it to be? Are you going to give us your old man, or do we have to do this the hard way?"

Draven's eyes blazed. "Let's do it the hard way."

"Fair enough," said Cal. "You totally asked for this."

He drove his elbow sharply into the midsection of the monster behind him. A spasm of pain shot through his arm. "Oh *Christ*. Totally just hit my funny bone," he grimaced. "Ow. Ow. Ow. Ugh. It's really tingling."

Draven shoved Cal against the bar and lunged at Loren, moving impossibly fast for someone of his size and age. He wrenched the blaster from Loren's grip, squeezed it until it cracked, then tossed it across the room. At the same time, he caught her by the throat, then hoisted her into the air and slammed her backwards onto the floor, pinning her down.

He looked back over his shoulder at Cal and drew his lips up, revealing all those many, many teeth. "Yes," Draven drawled. "Let's definitely do it the hard way."

"OK, let's do this," said Cal. Grabbing a bottle from the bar, he flipped it so he was holding it by the neck, then hit it against the edge of the bar top. It connected with a *thunk*, but didn't smash like he'd hoped it would.

Loren squirmed on the floor, Draven's hand still on her throat. She choked out a cry for help as Draven's jaw unhinged once again.

"Alright, alright, I'm coming," said Cal. He hit the bottle against the bar again. Again, it didn't break.

"Jesus, what is this made of?" he wondered, thudding it repeatedly against the angular wooden edge.

Down on the floor, Loren brought a knee up sharply between Draven's legs. This didn't seem to bother him all that much, unlike when she shoved her thumbs into his eyes a moment later, which left much more of an impression. Twisting sharply, she rolled the temporarily blinded space vampire over and slammed him sideways onto the floor, breaking the grip on her throat.

"Thanks for the assist," she wheezed.

Cal was studying the label of the bottle. He looked up and appeared surprised to see Loren straddling Draven, her hands tangled in his hair as she cracked his head repeatedly against the floor.

"I swear, this thing is fonking unbreakable," he said, but anything else he was about to add was knocked out of him by the impact of Sliske shoulder-barging him in the stomach. The momentum carried them both through the second door and out into the artificially lit plaza beyond.

Cal felt briefly weightless as Sliske hoisted him into the air, then felt pain as he went *crunch* against a sidewalk made of polished black glass.

He swung with the bottle, but Sliske caught it. It exploded in his tightening fist, spraying both men with purple-pink alcohol.

"Great, now it breaks," Cal groaned, then he leaned his head sideways to avoid a fist to the face. Sliske hissed as his knuckles met the sidewalk, but it was more through annoyance than pain.

A vague circle of interested bystanders was forming around them – close enough to afford the onlookers a good view of what was happening, but far enough away to give them a decent head start if it looked like things might be about to turn ugly.

The way Cal was pinned meant he couldn't get a hand to Sliske's head. He went for the nipples, instead, grabbing them through Sliske's thin silk shirt and twisting like he was searching through several radio stations at once.

Sliske reared back enough for Cal to mash a handful of broken glass into his face. This did nothing to help the monster's temperament, but succeeded in forcing him back far enough for Cal to kick his way out from beneath him.

The polished glass sidewalk was slippery with booze. Cal's attempts to get back to his feet were short-lived and disastrous. His boots squeaked. His center of balance lurched. His chin hit the ground first, filling his head with light and noise.

Through a gap in the growing audience, he could see the *Currently Untitled* docked on a landing pad just a couple of hundred feet ahead. The ship's back end was pointed directly at him, the ramp standing open in case they had found themselves in the now all-too-familiar situation of having to make a hasty escape.

A hand caught Cal by one of his feet. Yelping, he kicked and scrabbled on, pulling his foot free of the boot and this time managing to get himself all the way upright. He exploded through the crowd, hobbling and stumbling on his unbalanced footwear, only too aware of the furious figure already in hot pursuit.

The ring of Gorfs gave Sliske a wide berth. A few of them, not wishing to get on his bad side, even cheered him on as he chased Cal down.

Cal zig-zagged, dodging a grab that caught nothing but air. "Fonk off!" he cried. "We're not here for you!"

He swerved again, ran straight into the path of some kind of hovering sled, and barely staggered clear before it could hit him. He tried jumping onto the back of the thing as it passed, hoping to make his escape that way, but an electrical charge shot through him, launched him through the air, then deposited him unceremoniously onto the glass plaza.

"Fonk. That backfired," he wheezed, trying to ignore the smell of burning that now filled both his nostrils.

He'd have liked to take a moment or two to catch his breath and extinguish any small fires that might be smoldering about his person, but Sliske was still coming. Cal's muscles were taut and painful, but they got him up onto his feet and relented enough to let him lumber into something like a run.

For all the good it did him. The Nostro boy was young and fast. He also had both shoes, which didn't hurt, either. He closed quickly, until Cal could feel the brush of the vampire's elongated fingertips grabbing at his back. The *Untitled* was just twenty feet ahead now, but he wasn't close enough. He wasn't going to make it.

Time for his secret weapon.

"Miz!" he hollered. "Miz, where the fonk are you?"

A shape, large and hairy, streaked down the ramp and hurtled towards him. Cal flopped forward onto the ground and felt the *whoosh* of Mizette as she soared over his head.

Sliske barely managed a, "What the f—?" before the furry missile hit him at chest height.

For a mean and scary murderer-type, Sliske sure could scream. The space-vampire's squeals rang out across the plaza as Cal grimaced and groaned his way back into a standing position, his joints giving little creaks and pops of protest.

"Get it off! Get it off!"

Cal placed both hands on his lower back and pushed his hips forward. He let out a little moan of pleasure. "Oh. Oh yeah, that's the stuff."

"My face, *not my face*!"

With his right hand, he took hold of his left elbow and pulled the arm across his chest. Something crunched in his shoulder. It wasn't pleasant, but it wasn't unpleasant, either, and he took an odd sort of satisfaction from it.

"Help! Someone help me!"

Cal ran his hands through his tousled hair, then cupped them in front of his mouth and blew into them, testing his breath. He smiled and waved at the crowd of bloated, toad-like Gorfs that had drifted in the direction of the *Untitled*.

"Don't worry, folks. Nothing to see here."

"*It's going to kill me!*"

"Except that, obviously," Cal said, indicating the pinned and terrified Sliske. "That's pretty exciting."

He put a hand on Mizette's shoulder and squeezed lightly. Her densely-packed muscle was solid beneath the luxurious layer of fur.

"Good job, Miz. I can take it from here," he told her.

Miz snarled and snapped her jaws a few times in Sliske's face, then stood up and shrugged. "Fine. Whatever."

She eyeballed the watching Gorfs. "What are you weirdoes all staring at?" she demanded. "Take a holo, it'll last longer."

This last part she said to a circle of retreating backs, the Gorfs having hastily about-turned and scurried off in an attempt to pretend they hadn't been watching in the first place.

Cal, meanwhile, stepped closer to the scratched and shell-shocked Sliske, and flashed him one of his favorite grins. It was a particularly patronizing one he liked to use on Mech, although usually only when separated by a distance of several feet and, ideally, a number of large obstacles.

"Well hey there, you!" Cal said. "What brings a nice guy like you to...?" He frowned and turned to Miz. "What's this place called again?"

"How should I know?" Miz tutted, slouching her weight onto one hip and crossing her arms.

"That's a funny name for a town!" said Cal, beaming at her. He waited for a reaction that didn't come. "No? You're right, it was terrible. Forget I said anything."

Cal turned his attention back to Sliske. "I'm going to cut to the chase here, big guy. We're looking for your dad. We've heard he's a real shizznod, and we've been asked to, you know, slap the cuffs on him and bring him to the boys downtown. Think you could help us out with that? You'd really be doing us a solid."

Sliske turned his head and spat on Cal's feet.

"Oh, come on. There was no need," Cal protested. "That was right on my sock." He wriggled his toes and grimaced. "I can actually feel that soaking through. I hope you're happy."

He nudged Mizette. "Miz. Would you mind?"

Miz sighed and rolled her eyes. "Ugh!" she exclaimed, dropping her arms to her sides. Her claws extended with a *snikt*. "Fine."

"No, wait, no!" Sliske shrieked, his face a mask of terror, his nostrils a bubble of snot.

Cal motioned for Miz to wait. "Sorry. Were you about to tell us something?"

Sliske swallowed. His dark eyes flitted from Cal to Miz and back again.

"Just point," Cal suggested. "Just point to a window in that big building of yours and you can tell people that you didn't talk. Hell, we'll back you up. We'll say, 'Who, Sliske? Didn't say a word. Solid as a rock, that guy. Solid as a rock!' What do you say?"

Sliske's face tightened. His body went rigid as he braced himself. "Do your worst!" he spat.

"What? Fonk, no! Miz, don't do your worst!" Cal said, catching her by the arm before she could lunge. "Do, like, your ninth worst. Eighth *tops*."

Miz's tail drooped a little. "Seriously? Where's the fun in that?" she asked.

The ground shook.

It wasn't a big shake – barely a tremble, really – but there was definite movement. The Gorfs, who had been walking briskly away from Mizette, now slowed. A few of them stopped and looked down, then gasped and yelped as a second tremor shook the polished glass plaza. A few lights flickered in the windows of the buildings that lined the square. Somewhere not too far away, an alarm chirped.

Cal frowned. "What's that about?" he wondered aloud, then he looked down as he heard Sliske laugh. It was a low, hollow sort of laugh with very little actual mirth in it. It sounded desperate. Frantic, even. It was the laugh of a Kamikaze pilot who'd resigned himself to his fate. The empty, desperate guffaw of someone on the brink of losing everything, but who no longer cared.

"Now you've done it," he whispered. "*Idiots*."

The ground shook again. A crack appeared suddenly between Cal and Mizette, zig-zagging like forked lightning across the smooth, polished glass.

"Uh...?" said Miz, as another fracture appeared a dozen or more feet away. This one was shaped like a spider's web, only several hundred times larger. The whole plaza trembled when it appeared, and Sliske's laughter shot up in both volume and pitch.

"You wanted my father?" he said, the words coming out as a half-choked sob.

Another impact shook the ground. There was the sound of a lot of glass being broken at once.

Cal and Miz leaned back as a fist emerged from beneath the plaza. It rose like the head of an enormous sea serpent, twenty feet above the plaza, then thirty, then forty.

Sliske's eyes blazed. Tears rolled from them, then fell sideways down his cheeks and into his hair. "You've got him!"

FOUR

Cal whistled quietly as he watched the head appear through the hole in the plaza. It was fair to say that it was quite a large head. In fact, that would've been an understatement. It was easily the size of the *Currently Untitled*, but with none of the ship's aesthetic qualities.

A number of tusks – too many to count – sprouted like roots through its bottom jaw. It had one eye and one dry, shriveled hole where another should have gone. Its nose was sharp and crooked, and the few clumps of long gray hair it had were matted and tangled with grease.

And it was large. Stupidly large. Cal felt that couldn't really be emphasized enough.

"Uh..." said Miz, for the second time that minute. Cal slowly nodded in agreement.

"Yeah. Just what I was thinking. I mean, they said he was big, but I thought they meant, like, *beefy*, you know? Not... not..."

He gestured up at the figure. The head, both arms, and part of a naked torso were all visible now as Old Man Nostro heaved himself out of the ground.

"*That*," Cal concluded. He puffed out his cheeks and put his hands on his hips. "I knew we should've brought the bigger handcuffs."

"Father! Father, down here!" Sliske called.

The giant's eye flicked down to the fallen space vampire. His vast, scarred lips curved into a sneer, then the eye turned away again.

"Ooh, ouch. Burn," said Cal. "Guess you're not in the old man's good books."

"How can you even be that thing's kid, anyway?" Miz asked. "I mean, how did *that* happen?"

Cal took a breath. "Well, see, when a daddy space giant and a mommy space giant love each other very much..."

Miz shot him one of her more withering looks. "Size-wise, I meant." She gestured to Sliske. "He's, like, normal-sized or whatever. That thing's pretty big."

"*Pretty big*? It's like Godzilla's creepy uncle," said Cal. "But you raise a good point."

He looked down at Sliske. "Have you considered that you might be adopted? Just throwing that out there."

Miz's question was answered a few seconds later, when Papa Nostro heaved his swollen, bloated gut out of the hole. Seven or eight humanoid figures protruded from his bare flesh like blisters. Their skin was red and waxy, their features at varying degrees of smoothness. One or two seemed to have been fashioned in quite remarkable detail, while some of the others were barely more than person-proportioned lumps of fatty flesh. The eyes of the more detailed ones were open, their faces trapped in a drawn-out silent scream.

"Well that's up there with the worst things I've ever seen," Cal muttered. "I mean, it's got to be top five, right?"

Miz's mouth was hanging open. She said nothing.

"Yeah. Yeah, that's what I thought," Cal said. "Got to be top five."

The Gorfs were, sensibly, nowhere to be seen. The only remnant of their presence was the distant chorus of their screaming as they fled off into the night, and even that was drowned out by the roar of shattering glass as Papa Nostro dragged the rest of his belly bulk above ground.

"He'll kill you. He'll kill *everyone*!" Sliske bellowed.

"Huh?" said Cal, cupping a hand to his ear. "Did you say he'd *kill* everyone, or *kiss* everyone?"

"Kill," Miz clarified. "He said 'kill'."

"Oh," said Cal, a little despondently. "Yeah. That figures."

The glass fractured as the giant's hip bones pressed against it from beneath. A topiary of coarse pubic hair puff-balled through the hole from below. Cal turned his head aside, then shielded Miz's eyes. "OK, we don't want to see that," he said.

Sliske seized his chance. Springing to his feet, he hurled himself at Miz, catching her off-guard. His jaw unhinged. His long fingers tangled in her hair.

The element of surprise bought him almost three full seconds of advantage, before Miz stabbed three claws through his shoulder, and amputated one of his hands at the wrist. He tried to scream, but his flapping jaw made it tricky.

Cal winced. "Ooh. Ouch. That's gotta sting." He looked from Sliske to his enormous father, then back to Miz. "You OK here? I'm going to take down the big guy."

Miz's brow furrowed. "How?"

Cal jabbed a thumb back towards the untitled. "I'm going to blow him to bits with a spaceship."

"Oh. Oh, yeah. That should work," Miz conceded.

"Once you've finished with this guy, go check on the others, would you?"

Miz groaned. "Why do I have to do *everything*?"

"Thatta girl," Cal said. He winked at her, then he turned and hurried up the ramp into the *Currently Untitled* and shouted at the ceiling. "Kevin! Fire up the thrusters. Or the boosters, or whatever the fonk we're calling them this week."

There was no answer. Cal ran along the corridor and stopped outside the door to the bridge. "Kevin? You there, buddy?"

"Hm? Oh, sorry, sir," intoned a voice from somewhere on high. "I was miles away. Is everything alright?"

"Yes and no," said Cal. "We've found the guy we're looking for."

"That *is* good news, sir."

"Well, you'd think so," Cal said. "Except it turns out he's kind of this horrifying giant monster thing, and now he's about to kill us all."

"Are you quite sure, sir?" Kevin asked. "I'm checking the area, and I can't seem to find any trace of..."

The *Untitled* was jolted violently. A set of fingers closed across the front screen, blocking the view of the city outside.

"Ah. No. Hang on. There he is," said Kevin. "I was looking the wrong way."

Cal ran for his seat. In hindsight, he should've gone for Miz's, which was closer, or one of the 'guest chairs' that lined the bulkhead wall and no-one ever sat on. He liked his chair, though. Besides, it was the only one that had direct control over the weapon systems, and he was very keen to shoot the horrifying giant monster thing in the face.

His fingers had barely brushed against the fabric of the

chair's high back when the *Untitled*'s nose lifted. Or rather, *was* lifted. The whole ship lurched as it was jerked into the air, and everything that wasn't fastened down – a list that was made up of Cal, two coffee cups and a half-eaten *Twix* – suddenly found themselves sliding toward the corridor.

"Fonk. Ow. Shizz," Cal grunted, as he bounced off Miz's chair, then the guest chairs, then the door frame. He tried grabbing all three, failed at the first two, but managed to catch hold of the third. He hung there from the door frame, his legs dangling towards the open hatch, his shoulders, arms and fingertips already burning with the effort.

Through the hatch, he caught a glimpse of some big sweeping movements, as if the city was spiraling past him. Then he saw nothing but a sort of shiny darkness, and realized he was staring directly into the eye of Old Man Nostro.

"Kevin! Close the back door!" Cal yelped.

"I'm afraid I can't, sir," Kevin replied. "It must've been damaged when he picked us up. The mechanism is jammed."

"Well *un*jam it!"

"It's no good, sir. It's fully stuck," Kevin said. "But I have an idea. It's somewhat radical, but I think you might approve."

"What is it?" asked Cal, gritting his teeth as his grip began to slip on the smooth door frame.

"We should paint flames on the outside of the ship."

Cal blinked. "What?"

"Not all over it, obviously – that would look rather crass – but just on the wings, perhaps."

"How the fonk would that help?" Cal yelped.

There was silence for a moment.

"Help, sir?" Kevin asked. "Oh! You mean with the

current situation. Oh no, it wouldn't help with that at all, I'm afraid."

Cal sighed. "I fonking hate you sometimes, Kevin," he said, then the monster shook the ship and Cal's fingers lost their purchase. He tumbled end over end towards the open hatch, and the giant waiting just beyond it.

As he flipped, he caught a glimpse of the metal cabinet that stood just inside the hatchway. He'd either slam into it, or narrowly avoid it. Either way, it was his only chance.

"Kevin, the weapons cabinet. Open the weapons cabinet!"

"Very good, sir," Kevin replied.

The bathroom door slid open as Cal rolled past it through the air.

"Hang on, that's not it," the AI realized. "Let me try again."

"*Kevin!*" Cal roared. "Open the fonking—"

The door to the weapons cabinet snapped open. Cal hit it with a breathtaking amount of force, buckling the metal and arguably doing worse to his pelvis, hips and chest bone. The door held, acting like a shelf upon which Cal lay sprawled. It *creaked* and *groaned* beneath his weight, the hinges bending slowly outward.

Cal knew he had just a second, maybe less. He thrust his hands into the weapon cabinet and grabbed the first things he could, just as the door folded outwards and he was suddenly falling again, rolling and tumbling as he plunged through the hatch.

Fonk, he was high up! Old Man Nostro had emerged fully from the ground now. He towered above many of the buildings, at least two of which had now started to collapse under the stress of the tremors the giant had caused.

Nostro held the *Untitled* above him at close to arm's

length, meaning Cal had a fall of thirty or more feet to the monster's face. He hurriedly examined the weapons he had grabbed, and felt his gut wrench in disappointment.

In his left hand, he held a tiny blaster pistol that would lightly bruise the giant at best, and get right on his tits at worst. In his right hand, he held the ship's stupidly impractical flamethrower, which could only be activated after a set of very specific, very confusing instructions had been followed. It involved priming pumps and pulling tabs, and although he'd eventually figured it out once before, he hadn't been tumbling towards a giant, heavily-pregnant vampire monster at the time.

He decided he may as well fire the gun. The shot bounced off Papa Nostro's eyeball. The eye rippled like a ball of runny pudding, but other than a single blink, the giant didn't appear to suffer any ill-effects.

Cal hit the eye a half-second later, bounced off it, then rolled out-of-control down the monster's scarred cheek. He felt the steaming hot vapor of its breath swirling from its nostrils, then saw the jagged stumps of those fast-approaching tusks.

The larger ones, he wasn't too worried about. Sure, they were three times as big as he was, but that size brought with it a certain bluntness that was unlikely to do him much harm.

Nestled between those larger protrusions, though, was a forest of smaller spikes. They were each the size of a beach ball, but possessed zero of a beach ball's other qualities. They were hard and sharp, as opposed to soft and bouncy; pointed, not smooth. Lumps of decaying flesh were wedged in the gaps between them – something else Cal had never had cause to associate with balls, beach-based or otherwise.

He tried to read the instructions on the flamethrower's

fuel canister, but had barely made it past, 'Pull Tab A,' before he smacked into one of the larger tusks and what breath was left of him shot out of his nose in one big snort.

He made a valiant attempt at swearing – something he found helpful in most situations – but all that emerged from him was a pained squeak and, if he were being completely honest, about a cup and a half of urine.

The giant's mouth loomed beside him like a gelatinous pit. Cal saw a tongue criss-crossed with old scar tissue. He saw the cavern of a throat that could swallow men twenty times his size.

And then he saw something else. Something that, given the circumstances, very few other people in his situation might have seen.

He saw an opportunity.

A plan formed. It was not his best plan – which in itself said quite a lot about the standard of it – but it was a plan, all the same.

"OK. OK," he grimaced, maneuvering himself until his feet were wedged against the monster's rubbery top lip. He sipped some air into his tight, aching lungs, muttered something about this being fonking suicide, then he leaned over the edge and dropped the flamethrower into Papa Nostro's mouth.

It hit one of the saliva-slicked walls of the monster's mouth, then slid down to somewhere near the tonsils.

"Fonk it. That'll have to do," Cal wheezed. Closing one eye, he took aim with the blaster pistol. "Smile, you son of a bedge," he spat, then he squeezed the trigger.

The shot rebounded off one of Nostro's oversized teeth, ricocheted around inside his mouth for moment, then streaked upwards just inches from Cal's face.

"Fonk! That was close," Cal said. He took aim again.

He repeated the, "Smile, you son of a bedge," line, although with a little less emphasis and enthusiasm this time. That done, he pulled the trigger.

Nostro's head exploded, just as Cal had planned. Unfortunately, that was as far as the plan had gone, and everything that happened next came as something of a surprise to him. Although, in retrospect, it probably shouldn't have.

The eruption of flame and flesh launched Cal spinning and screaming into the air. He saw the sky, then the ground, then the burning neck stump of the giant. Then he saw them all again, several dozen times, in the space of three and a half seconds.

He blacked out, but the respite was annoyingly brief, and he was barely at the monster's nipple-height when he woke up again, still spinning, only now traveling down instead of up.

He realized, to his dismay, that he was on fire. He was also covered in brain-mush, but that was much further down his list of current priorities.

Cal passed the partially-formed offspring growing from Papa Nostro's bloated gut. They were upside-down now. Or he was.

Probably that one, actually.

He passed the forest of pubic hair, closed his eyes so he wasn't subjected to a close-up view of what would almost certainly be the largest, most unpleasant penis he'd ever seen, then decided he may as well take a quick look, since he was here anyway and was unlikely to get the chance again.

He opened his eyes and found himself surrounded by a blanket of green. It wrapped around him, drawing him into its soft, blobby folds. Cal laughed. Despite the falling and the brain mush and the fact that a good thirty per cent of him was currently on fire, he laughed.

Splurt *flobbed* out beneath him, breaking his fall like a giant cushion made of warm jello. Cal rolled around, extinguishing the flames and feeling like a five-year-old on the world's greatest bouncy castle.

He was almost disappointed when he finally reached solid ground. Splurt oozed out from beneath him, snapping back into his usual ball-shape with an elastic *twang*, and rolling to a stop next to Cal's head.

Reaching over, Cal gave the little guy a pat. "Thanks, buddy. I owe you another one."

Cal's whole body ached in protest as he propped himself up onto his elbows. Mech, Loren and Miz stood over him, gazing down. He didn't really have the energy to do much more than give them a thumbs up, then he pointed up and past them in the direction of Old Man Nostro.

They all watched in silence as the now-headless giant vampire monster toppled like a falling tree. Nostro's arms flailed out at his sides, and he crashed through three different buildings on his way to the ground.

The impact of his landing shook the whole plaza. Cal slowly craned his head and watched as several other buildings fell like dominoes. They collapsed in roars of rubble, and the air was filled with dust and noise and smoke for what felt like several minutes.

At some point during all the commotion, the *Currently Untitled* came in for a refreshingly smooth landing somewhere close by on the right, its fog lights blazing through the clouds of white dust and grime.

When the cloud had started to settle, and all was finally still, Cal got to his feet. This wasn't easy, and involved quite a lot of involuntary noises on his part.

Once upright, he brushed some of the dust off him, checked the scorch-marks on his clothing to make sure he hadn't been too badly burned, then gave a nod of satisfaction.

"Right then," he said, grinning at the others and rubbing his hands together. "I guess we should go pick up our pay check!"

CAL STARED long and hard at the number on the screen of a tablet in front of him, trying not to let his excitement show. The figure was considerably higher than the one they had initially been promised, although considering their target had turned out to be a hundred feet tall and naked, he felt it was probably only fair.

"That is very generous of you, Mr Clasters," he said, smiling and nodding his appreciation.

The short, toad-skinned Mayor's eyeballs bulged, as if someone had squeezed him around the middle. "It's *Clastres*. Mayor Smuna Clastres," he said, the words getting tangled in his long, fat tongue. "And *what*?"

"I mean, it's way more than we were expecting. Seriously, you shouldn't have," Cal said. He gave the mayor the full double finger guns and winked. "But I'm glad you did."

"This is not your payment," Mayor Clastres said, tapping the screen with a moist, squelchy finger. "This is an invoice."

"An invoice?"

"For the damages!" Clastres cried. "You destroyed half the square. Millions of credits in property damage. Not to mention the giant headless corpse that's now draped across three blocks!"

"Come on, that's hardly our fault!" Cal protested. "I mean, it's partly our fault, obviously, but it's not *exclusively* our fault. How were we supposed to know how big he was?"

"We showed you a picture," the mayor snapped back. Behind him, two anxious assistants hurriedly brought an image of Old Man Nostro up on a wall-mounted screen. Mayor Clastres tilted his head back sharply, gesturing towards it. "See?"

"Did you show us that?" Cal asked. He turned to the rest of the crew, who were gathered behind him. "Did he show us that?"

"Yes," said Loren.

"Uh-huh," Mech confirmed.

Cal raised his eyebrows in surprise, then turned back to the mayor. He gestured to the image on the wall. "Well, seems like you did. But there's nothing there to tell us the scale," he said. "For all we know, that's actual size and he's only three feet tall."

"He's standing on top of a fonking *building*!"

Cal looked closer at the image. "Is that...? Is that what that is?" He tilted his head until it was almost upside-down, as if studying an optical illusion. "Oh! Oh, yeah, now I see it. Those are windows. Gotcha. I thought they were little squares."

"Little *squares*?" Mayor Clastres sneered.

"I know, it's deceiving, right? Not clear at all. You should get a better picture," Cal said.

"Of what, his headless corpse lying half-buried in my city?"

Cal shrugged. "If that's what floats your boat, who am I to judge?"

The Mayor still held the tablet up. Cal gently nudged the Gorf's arm down and hit him with both barrels of his smile. "Now that that unfortunate business is out of the way, how about you give us our check minus, let's say, three per cent as a gesture of goodwill, and we'll say no more about it?"

Smuna Clastres was a small man in some ways, but much larger in others. His physical size was nothing to write home about – he was short and stubby, with stumpy limbs that made him look more bloated than he actually was – but he hadn't got to where he was today without a spirit and moral strength far larger than his body suggested.

Were he a younger man, he liked to think he'd have boxed this bounty hunter's ears and sent him packing. The wolf thing and the cyborg would have been more problematic, of course, but he'd have taken some satisfaction in wiping the smirk right off the human's face.

He hadn't been a young man for quite some time, though, and so he kept his hands to himself, and made a valiant attempt to cross his short arms behind his broad back.

"As you wish," he said. He proceeded slowly around to the other side of his glass desk and pulled open a drawer. The screeching of glass on glass was indescribably unpleasant, and made Miz fold down her ears in protest.

"You might want to slap some grease on there," Cal said. "That's free advice. We won't charge you extra."

"How very kind of you," said Clastres, not looking up. He fished in the drawer, before producing something a lot like a cell phone. The screen illuminated as he tapped it, then let out a series of soft chimes as he swiped his index finger in a complex pattern across it. Finally, with a nod, he gave the screen one final tap.

"Complete," the device announced, in a not unpleasant – if slightly robotic – female voice.

"It is done," said Clastres.

"Thank you, Mr Mayor," said Cal. "You won't regret it."

"I know," said the Mayor. He replaced the device in the drawer and *screeched* it closed again. "It was the right decision."

"That it was," Cal agreed. He tipped an imaginary hat and bowed slightly. "Great to meet you, sorry it had to be under such terrible circumstances, but hopefully we can do it again. Only, you know, without the giant monster next time."

Mech put a hand on Cal's back and shoved him towards the door. "Get out of here, man," he said. "And can you *please* just shut up for five minutes?"

"See what I've got to put up with?" Cal said, directing the comment to the Mayor just as Mech gave him another nudge towards the exit. It slid suddenly into the frame like the slice of a guillotine. Cal jumped in fright. "Jesus. What is with the doors on this planet? They're all in such a rush."

A final shove sent him stumbling out into the ornately-decorated hallway. He barely had time to blurt out a farewell before the rest of the crew piled out behind him and the door sliced closed again.

"What's the hurry?" asked Cal, his voice echoing around the cavernous hallway and mingling with the *clacking* of their footsteps on the glass floor. "Now you've made us all look rude."

"What's the hurry?" Mech spat. "I'll tell you what the fonking hurry is. There is a torch-wielding mob down there in the city all shouting our name."

"I know! We're superstars!" Cal said. "Are we going to swing by and say hello?"

"You do know they want to kill us, right?" Loren asked.

Cal snorted. "What? No they don't! They were cheering for us."

"They were demanding our execution," Loren corrected.

"Come on. No way. Seriously? I find that very hard to believe," said Cal.

"They were, like, throwing rocks at us," Miz reminded him.

"I thought those were gifts," Cal said.

Loren scowled. "*Gifts?*"

"They were nice rocks!" Cal said. He reached into his pocket and produced a smooth black stone the size of his palm. "See? Shiny space rocks."

He handed the stone to Loren. "You can keep that, by the way. I've got pockets full of the things. Seriously, if I fall in water right now, I'm a dead man."

They were approaching two large double doors. A pair of footmen in velvet coat snapped their heads forward in perfectly synchronized bowing gestures, then each pulled open one of the doors.

Cal was deep in thought, and barely noticed the men as he led the others out onto the walkway that led to the *Untitled*. "Although... now I think about it, all that *would* explain why those guys were burning that effigy of me."

"And why they wrote 'DIE' on the side of the ship in their own shizz," Mech added.

"Wait, so that meant die as in *die*?" Cal gasped.

"What else could it have meant?" Loren asked.

"I don't know. Some space thing, maybe? Or they could've been writing 'the' in German, I guess."

"What's German?" Mech asked.

"It's an Earth language."

"Why the *fonk* would they be writing the word 'the' in

some Earth language on the side of our motherfonking space ship?"

"In their own shizz," Miz added, just in case anyone had forgotten.

"I don't know! Maybe it's a cultural thing. I'm not an expert."

"You don't say," Loren muttered.

The Mayor's office was high on a tower above the city, but Cal could just make out the shape of Papa Nostro through the semi-transparent glass beneath the team's feet. If he squinted, he could also see a large crowd gathered in what was left of the plaza. Sure enough, even from this distance they looked agitated.

"Those ungrateful froggy bamstons!" Cal said. "I don't know, you go out of your way to help people, and how do they repay you?"

"With sixteen thousand credits," said Loren. "Minus three per cent."

Cal brightened. "Oh! Yeah. Good point." He extended the middle fingers of both hands and waggled them at the crowd far below. "Suck on that, shizznods."

Mech stopped walking. He had been tapping at the screen in his arm for the past few seconds, and now stared at it in confusion.

"What's up?" Loren asked.

"Huh?" Mech mumbled, still studying the screen.

"Come on, Mech, I thought you were in a hurry to get out of here?" Cal said, but then he noticed Mech's expression. "I know that face. That's your 'oh fonk, this is bad,' face. What's wrong?"

"They didn't pay us," Mech said.

"What do you mean they didn't pay us?" Cal demanded, stepping in closer and peering at the incomprehensible string of numbers and squiggles on Mech's arm-screen. "How could they not have paid us?"

"I mean we still got no money," Mech said. "We're still broke. They ain't paid us."

"Didn't we, like, see him pay us?" Miz asked.

"Yes! Thank you! Just what I was going to say," Cal exclaimed. "He pressed the doohickey thing."

Cal about-turned and began walking back in the direction of the Mayor's office. "Obviously, there's just been some sort of glitch or administrative error. I'm sure we'll get it sorted out in no..."

His voice tailed off as a squadron of armored guards jogged out through the double doors in a tightly-bunched formation.

"This ain't good," Mech muttered.

The whining of several ship engines rose up around them. Six one-man fighters emerged from behind the tower and came to a stop on either side of the platform, hovering in the air on shimmering cushions of dense blue light. They were sort of cloud shaped and weirdly cuddly-looking, like something from a video game aimed at six-year-olds. The guns that stuck out from the front were somewhat less adorable, particularly in the way they all swiveled in the team's direction.

Cal sighed. "Yeah, you can say that again."

"We should probably go," said Loren, then she realized that she was standing alone, the rest of the crew having already started running towards the *Untitled*. "Son of a..." she began, then she, too, broke into a run.

Cal was almost at the ship when the first blast of laser fire tore past him. It ricocheted off the *Untitled*'s hull and shot straight upwards into the dark night sky.

"They're shooting!" Cal yelped, covering his head with

his hands in the misguided belief that this would somehow protect him from a hail of concentrated blaster fire. "They're actually shooting at us."

"I noticed!" Mech spat. He spun his top half so it was turned all the way around, then raised both arms and returned fire on the troops. A wall of shielding flickered in front of them as Mech's blaster bolts struck it with a series of damp-sounding *thwumps*.

Meanwhile, the fighter ships had turned their attention on the *Untitled*, and were in the process of locking weapons. "Kevin, shields up!" Loren hollered, passing Cal and Mech with the confident strides of one of those masochists who not only ran on a regular basis, but who did it deliberately without having to be chased by anything.

"Very good, ma'am," Kevin replied, his voice rolling out through the open rear hatch and down the ramp. "Raising shields."

The *Untitled*'s three landing legs retracted suddenly, and the ship hit the glass platform with a *thack* that threatened to shatter the whole fonking thing.

"No, wait. That wasn't it," Kevin was saying as Cal raced up the ramp behind Loren.

Miz was already aboard, already strapped in, already draping one leg over her arm rest and rolling her eyes in a general sort of contempt for everyone in the universe. She didn't so much as acknowledge Loren or Cal as they jumped into their seats and grabbed for their belts.

A barrage of cannon-fire slammed into the side of the *Untitled*, and the ship gouged a deep groove in the glass as the rain of blows shoved it sideways.

"Kevin!" Cal bellowed.

"Found them," the AI announced, and the next few shots exploded harmlessly against the plasma shielding.

Loren flicked a series of controls and the *Untitled*'s thrusters ignited.

"Hey, watch what you're doing!" bellowed Mech from somewhere out back.

Loren winced. "Oops. Sorry!" she called to him. "You in?"

"*Now* I'm in, yeah," said Mech, *clanking* onto the bridge behind them. "Get going."

Loren pushed something, pulled something else, then winced as the *Untitled* carved another trench in the glass platform.

"Jesus!" Cal grimaced, clamping his hands over his ears. "Can you *not* make that noise?"

"Unfortunately, sir, Ms Loren has retracted the landing legs, hence the dreadful din we are all currently being subjected to," said Kevin.

Loren snapped her head up in the direction of the bridge's speak system. "Wait, *I* raised the legs? That was you!"

"If you say so, ma'am," said Kevin, with the air of someone who knew they were in the right, but was being the bigger person.

"You did!" Loren said. She turned in her seat. "Tell him!"

"Just get us off the fonking ground!" Cal cried. "And stop that noise!"

"It says 'missile lock', by the way," said Miz, flicking her eyes up just briefly from where she had been studying her claws.

Cal spun in his chair to face her. "Huh?"

Mizette huffed out a sigh. "There. On the screen. It says 'missile lock'."

Cal flicked his eyes to the screen. Sure enough, the

words 'missile lock' were flashing in a shade of red that seemed to have been chosen specifically for its ability to inflict the maximum amount of concern. He spun to face Mech. "What does that mean?" he asked. "Or is that a stupid—?"

A missile exploded against the shields. The lights flickered and a jet of steam hissed from a console. Splurt dropped from the ceiling and wrapped himself around Cal like a protective cocoon. Cal gave him a pat, then gripped his arm rests as the force of the impact sent the *Untitled* lurching over the edge of the platform.

The ship flipped.

Cal screamed.

And the city, the crowd, and the giant headless space vampire all came racing up to meet them.

FIVE

It was not the first time Cal had gone hurtling towards the ground completely out of control – it wasn't even the first time that hour, in fact – but all that prior experience did little to ease his growing concerns.

"For fonk's sake, Loren, pull up!" he cried, the words echoing strangely as they whipped around inside the tumbling ship.

"I'm trying! You think I'm not trying?"

"Then, like, try harder!" Mizette barked.

"Kevin, help her out," Cal ordered.

"No! I can do it," Loren protested.

"The fact we're still racing straight for the ground kind of suggests otherwise," Cal pointed out. "Kevin, do it!"

"Are you sure, sir? I wouldn't want to step on anyone's toes."

It was Mech who answered with a resounding, "Shut the fonk up and stop us falling!"

"Very good, sir," Kevin intoned.

"Wait! I've almost got it!" Loren insisted.

"She doesn't," said Kevin. "I'm not even sure what she's attempting to do, exactly."

"Shut up, Kevin!" Loren hissed.

"She's making it worse, if anything."

"Fine!" Loren wrenched her hands off the controls and held them above her head. "Let's see you do it, if you're so..."

The ship jerked, twisted, then pulled up. The view of the giant headless corpse became a vista of distant stars and a couple of much closer moons.

Kevin said nothing. It was a very deliberate saying of nothing that did not go unnoticed by Loren.

"I could've done that," she said, crossing her arms.

"Suuuure you could," said Miz. "You should totally keep telling yourself that."

Loren unclipped her belt and stood up. "Know what? I'm going to go. I'll be through the back," she said, then a staccato burst of cannon-fire slammed into the *Untitled*'s shields, lurching it violently.

"Yeah, still under attack here, Loren," Cal pointed out.

Loren stumbled, caught her chair, then flopped back into it and scrabbled for her belt. "Shizz. I forgot."

"They're short range planetary fighters," Mech said, checking the scanners. "Not built to leave the atmosphere."

"So... what does that mean?" Cal asked. "We can just blast off into space and they can't follow us?"

"Pretty much," Mech confirmed.

"Well alright!" Cal cheered. This was the best news he'd had all day. "Then let's do it. Kevin. Or Loren. One of you, anyway. Take us up!"

"Very good, sir," said Kevin. "I assume you're happy to have your lungs burst and your eyeballs explode in their sockets?"

Cal shook his head. "What? No, Kevin. No, I'm not happy to have either of those things happen. At *all*. What the fonk are you talking about?"

The last word came out as a long, drawn-out howl as Kevin spun the ship, narrowly avoiding another barrage of cannon-blasts.

"The hatch, sir. I'm afraid it's still locked in place. If we leave the atmosphere... Well, it won't be pretty for most of you, let's put it that way," Kevin said, banking the *Untitled* away from an oncoming fighter. "Although, I'm sure it will please you to know that I would be quite unharmed."

"The hatch is still broken? Why haven't you fixed it?" Cal demanded.

"I'm afraid I haven't had the time, sir," Kevin replied. "Also, it may have escaped your notice, but I don't have any arms, which doesn't exactly help matters."

"Fonk. Mech, see what you can do!" Cal said.

Mech charged out into the corridor. "On it."

The ship lurched suddenly downwards, throwing Cal a few inches out of his chair before his belt tightened and held him in place.

"Jesus. Bit of warning, Kevin. Even Loren wouldn't pull a move like that."

"I know!" Loren said, then she turned in her seat, eyes narrowed. "What do you mean '*even* Loren'?"

"What? No, I meant... I just meant..."

A fighter screamed past ahead of them. Something explosive detonated against the *Untitled*'s shields, flaring the view screen red. "Look, can we talk about this later?" asked Cal. "Now really doesn't feel like the time."

He banged his fists on his arm rests, remembered that was the old ship, then raised his eyes to the ceiling. "Kevin, give me the guns."

"Guns? You can't shoot them!" said Loren.

"I can't shoot the guns?" Cal gasped. "Are they broken, too?"

"You can't shoot those ships!" Loren corrected. "It's not right."

"What? Why?" asked Miz. "They're totally shooting us."

"Because we destroyed half their city, then ran off without paying for the damage!" Loren pointed out.

Miz stared blankly back at her. "Yeah. So?"

"I gotta go with Miz on this one, Loren," Cal said. "Yeah. So?"

"*So* we're not the good guys in this situation! They're just cops or the local military or whatever. They're not bad guys."

"They're trying to blow us to bits," Cal said. "That kind of makes them the bad guys." He turned to Miz. "Right?"

"Totally."

"See?" said Cal. "They're shooting us, we're good guys, therefore they must be the bad guys. It's just science, Loren. It's science."

The weapons targeting system unfolded from the headrest of Cal's chair until the needle-like points of the interface hovered just half an inch from his temples on either side. More cannon-fire pummeled the ship, striking a series of direct hits on its belly this time. Cal and the others were shaken like economy class airline passengers in heavy turbulence, albeit without the screaming children, sweaty aroma, or lingering aura of general disappointment.

Cal placed his hands on the weapon's interface, trying not to think too much about the needles being shoved into his brain. "They're going to tear us apart," he said. "We should at least fire some warning shots."

"Those people are just doing their jobs," Loren said.

"All those Zertex guys we've killed were just doing their jobs, too," Miz pointed out.

"That's different," Loren said. "We didn't have a choice."

Cal tilted his head left to right in a sort of weighing motion. "We sometimes had a choice."

"OK, fine, but Zertex *are* the bad guys. Or were. Or whatever," Loren said. She pointed to the view screen. "Them? They've just been told to shoot down a ship full of thieves and vandals before it gets away. That's all they know."

Cal groaned. He glanced sideways at the weapons interface hovering right by his head.

"Fine. You win. Kevin, put it away."

"Very good, sir," Kevin intoned. "I mean, it's not like I have anything better to do, what with flying the ship and trying to save you all from being blown to smithereens, and everything."

Cal ignored him. "Mech, you nearly done?" he called.

"It's stuck!" came the reply.

"We know it's fonking stuck! You're supposed to be unsticking it! That's the whole point of you being back there!"

"It says 'missile lock' again," Mizette pointed out. "Like, three times."

"Jesus!" Cal ejected. "What a day." He exhaled slowly. "What a day."

The warning messages stepped up their shade of redness to a previously unseen level of alarming. A siren blared from three different consoles at the same time. Splurt tightened around Cal like a hug made from marshmallow as three different missiles carved three different paths across the sky towards them.

"Everyone brace yourselves!" Cal warned.

Then there was a *clang* from the back of the ship, a brief but memorable moment where Cal could see the inside of his own skull, and the *Currently Untitled* rocketed out of the atmosphere and into the relative safety of outer space.

CAL GAZED down at the plate he held pinched between his thumb and the side of his forefinger, and at the slice of banoffee pie sitting dead center. It was smaller than he had been expecting. Quite a lot smaller, in fact.

He raised his eyes to the food replicator. "Uh, is there a problem?" he asked it. It didn't reply, which didn't really come as a surprise.

"Try again. Give me another one," he said.

The replicator did nothing. No burbling noises. No shuddering or shaking or *whirring*.

Silence.

Cal thumped the machine on its side.

Still nothing.

He gave it a kick.

The replicator just stood there, silent and still.

His technological know-how now exhausted, Cal shrugged and left the kitchen, still carrying the plate.

The bridge view screen showed a handful of stars and a whole lot of not much else. They were cruising along at a speed even he found manageable, and he was able to look directly at the screen without experiencing full blown vertigo and vomiting into a shoe.

Loren and Mech were hunched over Loren's console,

discussing something that might well be important, but which Cal was just going to assume was less important than what he had to say. Miz was slouched across her chair, her head back. At first, Cal thought she was asleep, but then he realized her eyes were open, and she was simply staring at the ceiling with contempt. This was not all that unusual. Miz stared at lots of things with contempt, and Cal hoped the ceiling wasn't taking it personally.

"Uh, is there a problem I don't know about?" asked Cal.

Loren and Mech both turned to look at him. Miz did, too, but only after rolling her eyes and groaning theatrically.

"What kind of problem?" Loren asked.

Cal angled his plate so they could all see it. "I ordered a banoffee pie."

"Again?" said Mech. "Fonk, man. How many of them things have you eaten today?"

"I don't know. Like... three?" said Cal. "I have no idea when the day starts and ends out here."

"Let's say from when you last woke up," said Mech.

"Oh." Cal thought for a moment. "Then more like nine. Unless... are we counting when I have it as a milkshake?"

Mech nodded.

"Then twelve," said Cal, completely without shame. "But that's not my point. Look at it."

They all looked at it. "Looks OK," said Loren.

Cal flicked his eyes down to the triangular slice of pie. Was it him? Was he seeing things?

"What do you mean? It's an inch long."

Loren shrugged. "Well, yeah. I assumed you can get it in different sizes."

"Of course you can," Cal agreed. "But I asked for banoffee pie. I didn't ask for the world's *smallest* banoffee pie. I didn't even ask for a smaller than average banoffee pie.

I placed the same order in the same way I've done, like, a thousand times before."

Miz exhaled in a way designed to indicate that she was done with this conversation and would be playing no further part in it, then went back to glaring at the ceiling.

"Maybe the replicator's concerned about you, man," Mech suggested. "Maybe it's watching your waistline."

Loren looked Cal over. "You are getting kind of bulky around the hips."

"I still have sixteen space rocks in my pockets," Cal pointed out. He waved the plate around in front of them, trying to steer the conversation away from his hips and back to the matter at hand. "So nobody knows anything about this?"

Mech and Loren both shook their heads. Miz ignored everything and everyone.

"Kevin!" Cal called. He held the plate a little higher. "Do you know anything about this?"

"Yes, sir," Kevin replied.

Cal waited for more.

"OK. Well... care to explain?"

"It's some kind of dessert, sir. I seem to recall you having it before. I think you rather enjoyed it."

Cal sighed. "No, I mean why is it like this?"

"Presumably, sir, so the firmness of the biscuit base can offset the smoothness of the—"

"No. Jesus. Why is it small, I mean?"

"Oh, that," Kevin intoned. "I believe we're out of Mush."

Cal frowned. "Huh?"

"Mush, sir. We've depleted our stocks."

"What the fonk is...?" Cal began, then he decided to

aim the question at the others, instead. "What the fonk is Mush?"

Mech and Loren were just as clueless as he was. "Don't ask me, man," said Mech.

"No idea," Loren admitted.

Cal raised his eyes in the direction of Kevin's voice again. "What's Mush?"

"Mush is the raw material used by the replicator," he explained. "It's sort of a tasteless pink sludge, the molecular structure of which the replicator rearranges to produce... well, those pies, for the most part, but whatever else is requested of it, too."

"Wait, so this is really just pink sludge?" Cal asked, pointing to the tiny triangle on his plate.

"*Was* pink sludge, sir. Now it isn't," Kevin corrected.

Cal looked to the others again. "Did you guys know this?"

"No. I didn't," said Mech. "But it makes sense. I mean, I never really thought about how the thing can just produce food out of thin air. I just... I guess I just never seen one run out before."

"It's most unusual, sir," Kevin told him. "A container of Mush should last anywhere up to twenty years."

"So how come we've run out?" Loren asked.

"I, uh, I fear some of Master Carver's more... calorie dense dishes may have depleted supplies somewhat prematurely."

Miz, who had been doing her best not to listen, couldn't help but sit up. "Wait. So... what? We're, like, out of food?"

"I'm afraid so, ma'am."

"What, *none*?" asked Loren.

"Oh yes, there's *some*, ma'am," said Kevin, and Loren relaxed a little.

"OK. Good."

Cal popped the little slice of banoffee pie into his mouth, chewed briefly, then swallowed with visible difficulty.

That done, he proceeded to lick the plate.

"*Now* there's none," Kevin announced.

"Oh, great! Thanks, Cal!" Loren snapped.

Cal waved a hand dismissively. "Relax. It's fine. We'll just get some more. We can buy another pack, right?"

"Yes, sir," said Kevin.

"See? Nothing to worry about."

"They're two-hundred-thousand credits each."

Cal coughed so hard the partially masticated banoffee pie was fired back up into his throat. He pounded his chest for several panicky seconds, turning gradually more and more purple until, with a cry that was bordering on primal, he forced it back down.

"*How much*?!"

"Two-hundred-thou—"

"I know! I heard you the first time!" Cal yelped. He looked around for somewhere to sit his plate, but nowhere presented itself, and he was fonked if he was walking all the way back to the kitchen. "Splurt!"

Splurt dropped down from the ceiling like a long strand of snot with eyeballs. He enveloped Cal's hand, then retreated upwards, taking the plate with him. Cal gave him a thumbs up. "Thanks, buddy."

He sat in his chair and turned it so he could see everyone at the same time. "OK. So how much money do we have?"

"None," Mech replied.

"By 'none' do you mean 'not a lot' or do you mean actually none?"

"I mean we got nothing. Not a single credit. Not since your Earth friend hacked us and stole it all."

Cal stared wistfully ahead into space. "Aah, Dave," he said, then he shrugged. "Still, we blew him up and stopped his evil plan, so I guess we're kind of even."

He drummed his fingers on his arm rests. "So... what do we do? We need to make money fast, right?"

Loren indicated her control panel. "Mech and I were just scanning for work. There isn't much, but we found something. Pays pretty well."

"Is it another bounty hunter thing?" Cal asked. "Because, I don't know if you noticed, but those aren't going well for us."

"It's a humanitarian run," Loren explained. "Delivering medicine and aid to Mokolai."

"Who's Mokolai?" Cal asked.

"No-one. It's a planet," said Mech. "There's a disease – the Gorax Blight, they call it. Anyone suffering from it gets sent to Mokolai."

"Oh. So it's like a leper colony?" said Cal. He swiveled his chair from side to side. "What does it involve, this Gorax thing? Is it nasty?"

"Isn't that the one where people, like, shizz themselves through their eyes?" asked Miz.

Cal's jaw dropped. "Through their *eyes*? How is that...? I mean..." He spent a few quite harrowing moments trying to imagine this. "Through their *eyes*?"

"That's one of the early symptoms, yeah," Mech confirmed.

The pitch of Cal's voice raised a full octave. "One of the *early* symptoms? Jesus, how does it end? How can your condition deteriorate from shizzing yourself through your fonking eyes?"

"Well, see, there's this rectal parasite that—" Mech began, but Cal drowned him out.

"No! Stop. Don't want to know. We're not doing that one."

Loren piped up. "It pays almost—"

"Don't care. Not interested," said Cal. He gestured to her console. "Find us something else. Something that doesn't involve butt-worms, or people, you know, soiling themselves through their face."

"There is nothing else," said Loren.

"What? That's it? A whole fonking galaxy and that's the only job on the notice board? Come on, there's got to be something."

"There ain't, man," said Mech. "I mean, maybe we could go visit a couple of planets, see if there's anything going on locally."

"Or we could just, like, rob someone," Miz suggested.

"We can't do that," said Loren.

Miz shrugged. "Why not? I mean, we're all criminals."

"She has a point," Cal conceded.

Loren shook her head. "No, you three may have been thieves or... whatever, but I wasn't. I'm not."

Cal raised an eyebrow. "Oh, really?" he said. "Whose ship is this? Or the last ship we had. Did you buy that one? Did you buy this one?"

"You know what I mean," Loren said.

"Sure, maybe you were all Zertexy and upstanding member of society before we were all thrown together, but now you're one of us."

"Yeah, well maybe..." Loren began, then she bit her tongue and turned back to her console.

"Maybe what?" Cal asked.

Loren shook her head. "Nothing. Forget it," she said. "I

just don't think we should go robbing anyone. We're not pirates."

Cal watched the back of her head for a moment, like he was trying to see inside it. Finally, he shrugged. "Last resort then." He sighed and leaned back in his chair. "How contagious is this eye-shizzing thing?"

Mech shrugged. "I dunno. Like a six."

Cal nodded slowly. "Out of ten?"

Mech shook his head. "Huh? No, out of eight."

Cal frowned. "Out of *eight*? Who the fonk ranks things out of eight?" he asked.

"I do."

"But... I mean, it makes no sense. You rank things out of five, out of ten, or out of a hundred."

"Why?"

"Because that's what normal people do, Mech," Cal told him. "That's just what normal people do. It's the rules."

Mech grunted. "Fine. Out of five, then."

"It's *six out of five* contagious?" Cal spluttered. "Jesus. Sorry, Loren, we're becoming pirates."

"No, it ain't six out of five. It's three-point-seven-nine out of five," Mech said.

Cal blinked. "Are you fonking with me, Mech? Is that what this is? *Three-point-seven-nine out of five*. Are you messing with me?"

"No! You asked me how contagious it was. It's a little over six out of eight, but since you want me to adjust my whole motherfonking scale all of a sudden, it's three-point-seven—"

Kevin, mercifully, interrupted.

"Sorry to intrude, everyone, but I thought you'd want to know about the distress signal."

Everyone, even Miz, looked up.

"Distress signal?" Loren asked. She turned her attention back to her console and tapped a few buttons. "Where is it coming from?"

"Over that way, ma'am," Kevin said.

Several seconds of slightly uncomfortable silence passed.

"You know we can't see where you're pointing, right, Kevin?" said Cal.

"Ah. Yes. Quite, sir," said Kevin. The right-hand third of the screen became a star map, with a flashing red beacon positioned just above center. A small green icon down at the bottom right corner showed the position of the *Untitled.*

"It appears to be a cruise liner," Kevin explained. "One of those big ones filled with tourists."

"Rich tourists?" Cal wondered.

"Very possibly, sir."

"Alright!" Cal punched the air. "Looks like our luck's changing, boys and girls. A whole load of rich folks just called for help, and we're the cavalry."

He spun in his chair, then slapped his hands on his knees. "Loren, plot a course. Kevin, try to scan that ship and find out what's going on. Mech, try phoning them, or whatever it is we do. Miz..."

He looked over to find her scowling back at him. He winked. "What you're doing now is just perfect."

Cal rubbed his hands together and grinned with excitement. "I've got a good feeling about this one, guys," he said. "I think this cruise liner could set us up for a very, *very* long time!"

SIX

The cruise liner was the biggest ship Cal had ever seen. Even from this distance – which might have been anything from ten to a thousand miles away, what with Cal having zero comprehension of space distances – it was enormous. Size was pretty much the only thing it had going for it, in fact. It was unlikely to win any prizes for style unless it somehow found itself transported to the early 1970s, and even then only if half the judges had been bribed or blinded.

It was shaped like an old tin bathtub, the back end flat and boxy, the front sloping upwards to form a rounded sort of point. Thousands of pinpricks of light and almost as many pinpricks of darkness lined the side that the crew could currently see, and presumably there was just as many on the other side, too. Windows, he assumed. The windows of thousands of cabins, filled with lots of frightened rich people, all of whom would soon owe him a great debt.

Quite what that debt would be, Cal didn't yet know.

"Still nothing?" he asked.

Mech shook his head. "Nope. Either their comm-systems are all down, or they deliberately ain't responding."

"Keep trying," Cal instructed.

"Well, it's on automatic redial, so I was going to keep trying, anyway," Mech said. "I ain't doing it just because you told me to. I want you to know that."

"Fair enough," said Cal. "Kevin, what do we know?"

"Rather a lot, sir," Kevin replied.

Cal held up a hand. "Specifically, about this ship."

"Oh. Oh, then nothing, sir," said Kevin. "Would you like me to look into it?"

"I would, yes. I mean, I'd have thought that was obvious, but apparently—"

"Done, sir," Kevin said. "The *Binto Odyssey* is a luxury cruise liner operated out of Trexus VII by the Binto-Rojaxx Corporation. It was the sixteenth vessel built by the company, and is a Trooloo Class Cruiser with accommodation for up to twenty-thousand passengers."

"OK..." Cal said, but Kevin wasn't finished.

"Its hull is primarily made up of a Carillium alloy designed to repel light to moderate cannon-fire. Its shields are quantum phase-based, and powered by several large, if now somewhat outdated, warp spheres located deep within the lower structure. Its top speed—"

"Are they rich?" Cal asked.

"Is who rich?"

"The people. The twenty-thousand passengers."

"Oh. Them. Yes, sir. Obscenely," the AI replied. "It's really rather disgusting, actually."

"Disgustingly rich," Cal said. He leaned forward in his chair, as if getting those few inches closer might somehow make him wealthier by osmosis. "You hear that, Mech? They're *disgustingly* rich."

"I heard," said Mech. "Best news I've heard all day."

"Like that's saying much," Miz muttered. She had a point. It hadn't been a great day so far, but things were definitely looking up.

"Life signs?" asked Loren.

"Yes, ma'am."

Loren waited, then sighed. "How many?"

Kevin began, very quietly, to count. "One. Two. Three. Four. Five. Six," he said, the words becoming a whisper than drifted into a long, pregnant silence.

A minute passed.

"Wait," said Kevin, then: "One. *Two*. Three. Four."

"Just roughly will be fine," Cal told him.

"Are you sure, sir?"

"God, yes."

"As you wish. In that case, I'd estimate there are... lots," Kevin said. "Likely the full complement of passengers, although without a manifest to cross-reference, that's merely a projection on my part."

"Right," said Cal.

"By which I mean, it's a complete guess."

"Gotcha. Now shut up," Cal drummed his hands on his arm rests. "Mech?"

"Still nothing back," Mech said.

Cal stared ahead at the *Binto Odyssey*, and all those blazing lights along its side. "Is there any way we can get aboard?"

Loren tapped her console and a schematic of the rear of the cruiser appeared on screen. "Looks like the landing bays are energy shielded, but this tech is two decades old. We can hack it."

"Well, then it's decided!" Cal announced. "We get aboard, find out what the problem is, and save the day."

He grinned broadly, the prospect of full-sized banoffee pies spurring him on. "What could possibly go wrong?"

THE *CURRENTLY UNTITLED* shuddered gently as it descended gracefully through one of the *Odyssey*'s inner shields and alighted in a landing bay.

That done, it bounced twice, screeched thirty feet along the deck, and came to a stop with its nose resting against the ground.

There was silence, like a moment of calm before a particularly nasty storm, then the *Untitled*'s back end came down and its rear legs slammed into the deck with a *ka-klang* that rolled off across the landing bay area in all available directions.

Had someone standing outside the ship been blessed with exceptionally good hearing – and had they not just been deafened by the crashing metallic din – they might have heard a single female voice emerge from inside.

"Smooth, Loren. Like, real smooth," it said. "Seriously, that was *totally* your best one yet."

"HELLOOOOOO!"

Cal's voice reverberated along another corridor, and was met with another lengthy silence. They were on one of the accommodation decks – the fourth they'd investigated – and this one was as empty as all the rest.

The inside of the *Binto Odyssey* was fussily opulent, with lots of wooden paneling, patterned wallpapers, and ornate trims of precious metals and luxurious fabrics. There was too much of all of it, and it was all arranged in a way that was jarringly overblown and unpleasant. Had the Queen of England handed over palace interior design duties to the Kardashian family, this would almost certainly have been the result.

"I don't get it," said Cal. "Where is everyone?"

Mech sighed. "That is the eighth fonking time you've asked me that question."

"I wasn't asking you," said Cal. "I was asking Loren."

Loren blinked in surprise, like she hadn't been paying attention. "What?"

"Nothing. Doesn't matter," said Cal.

He knocked on a cabin door. "Room service. Anyone home? I have space burritos."

They waited for a response, like they'd done at a dozen other doors. As before, none came.

"It don't make no sense," said Mech, tapping a series of controls on his arm. "Sensors say this place is full of life. I got life signs showing up all around us. All different species."

"Could they be invisible?" Cal wondered. He lunged at a couple of empty spots, flailed his arms around in a couple of half-circles, then shrugged. "Doesn't look like it. Miz, you getting anything?"

Mizette's nostrils were flared wide. "It's, like, hard to explain. I'm getting a scent, but it's not like anything I've ever... It's like, like, a million smells all mixed together."

She pointed to her ears, both of which were pricked up. "And what's that noise?"

Everyone listened.

"What noise?" Cal eventually asked.

"That buzzing. Or squeaking. Or, like, humming, or whatever."

"Not getting it," Cal said. "Loren? Mech?"

Loren shook her head. "No."

"Nothing here," said Mech.

Cal shifted his gaze to Splurt, who was perching on his shoulder. "Buddy? You hear anything?"

Splurt made a gesture that was not unlike a shrug.

"Looks like it's just you," Cal told Miz. "If it changes, let me know."

Loren, who had been walking a few paces ahead, had reached the end of the corridor, where it met another one that ran at ninety degrees to it and branched off in both directions. She stopped and stepped back, smoothly drawing her blaster from her holster.

"What you got?" Mech asked.

Loren pointed to her eyes, then held up three fingers.

"Is this Charades?" Cal whispered. "I love this game! Uh, eye three. Eye trio. Wait! Face triplets! Is it face triplets?"

Loren glared at him. "I mean there are three people around the corner," she hissed.

"I hadn't finished guessing. I'd totally have figured..." Cal's eyes widened. "Oh. Let me see."

Creeping to where the wall ended, Cal quickly ducked out, then even more quickly ducked back in again. It was a strategy he had employed several times in the past when trying to check out a situation without being spotted. As with every other instance, it hadn't really worked.

"I moved way too fast. Didn't see anything," he whispered. "I'll look again."

With some effort, he managed to position himself to

only a tiny sliver of his face would be visible to anyone looking along the second corridor in the direction of this one. Sure enough, three figures stood around thirty feet away. They looked like exactly the sort of passengers he'd expect to see on a ship like this – old, overweight, and with an air of wealth rising off them like heat ripples from hot tarmac.

"What they doing?" Mech asked, his voice a low murmur.

"Nothing," said Cal.

Some time passed.

"What about now?"

"Still nothing. They're just standing there."

The others all joined him in peering around the wall. The three figures hadn't moved. *Literally* hadn't moved. They stood still as statues, the one face Cal could see frozen with its mouth half-open.

"What the fonk?" Mech muttered.

"Only one way to find out, I guess," Cal said. He stepped out into the corridor. The three figures continued doing nothing.

"Hey, there!" Cal said. He waved. No-one turned or waved back. "Uh... Everything OK?"

The three statues continued to be the very definition of statuesque. Cal shrugged and strode towards them.

"Be careful," Loren warned.

"What, in case I trip up and poke my eye out on them?" Cal said. He stopped beside the closest figure. He was mostly human-looking, but with reddish skin and flecks of dull yellow and orange in his eyes. A white... moustache, Cal decided, although that wasn't quite the right word, grew from his sunken cheeks and across the bridge of his nose. The trailing ends hung down below his weak chin, stopping just above the collar of what was probably a very expensive suit.

Cal waved a hand in front of the man's face. "Helloooo?"

He rapped his knuckles on the guy's forehead. It made a *thonk* sound.

"Solid," Cal said. He tapped a finger against the point of the drooping 'tache, then hissed and drew back as its point pierced his skin. "Ow! Son of a..."

A spot of blood appeared on his fingertip. He put the finger in his mouth and sucked on it, buying the others a rare few seconds of relative peace and quiet.

"Are they statues?" Loren wondered.

"Sensors don't think so," said Mech, indicating the display on his arm. "Says they're alive."

Miz stopped beside one of the other figures – a sour-faced woman wearing a coat that was almost as furry as Miz herself. "They don't smell alive," Miz said. "I mean, they do, but... I don't know. It's weird."

"Well, that's useful. Thanks," said Loren. "Really informative."

"Yeah, I know," said Miz, either missing the sarcasm or choosing to completely ignore it. "Unlike your contribution of, you know, like, standing around looking dumb."

"What's going on there?" asked Cal through a mouthful of finger. He was studying a section of the wall where a six-feet-wide zig-zag stretch of wallpaper was peeling off, revealing a wall black with decay.

Three full carpet tiles on the floor below it were thread-bare and filthy, while the tiles on either side looked as if a distinct line had been drawn through them, with everything close to the rotten area appearing dirty and worn, and everything on the other side of the invisible line looking good as new.

The ceiling was much the same. An angular shape had been stamped on the white paintwork, marking it with damp and decay.

"That's too localized to be natural," Loren said. "Unless, I don't know, there was some kind of leak in the wall behind it? But even then, it wouldn't just stop abruptly like that."

Cal took his finger from his mouth and prodded the wall. He expected to poke a hole right through it, but instead he felt a vibration that seemed to cover the whole area like water flowing over the surface of a rock, and his finger stopped a fraction of an inch from the black swirls of mildew.

"Any of you ever seen anything like this before?" Cal asked.

"What, rot? Yeah, man," said Mech. "Ain't you?"

"No, I mean like this," said Cal, indicating the definite lines where the decay met the pristine wallpaper on either side. "Why would it stop like this?"

"There's more over there," Miz pointed out. Sure enough, a little further along the corridor, several feet of wall had decayed in the same way as this section. Someone had written something on it, too, sprayed in red in foot-high letters.

At least, Cal assumed they were letters, but as his visual translation chip was doing nothing to decipher them, he began to have his doubts.

"Can any of you guys read that?" he asked.

The others all shook their heads. "No," said Loren.

Cal nodded. "So... what does that mean?"

"It means it ain't written in any known language," Mech said.

Cal gasped. "You mean... this could have been written by *aliens*?"

The others watched him, waiting for the penny to drop.

"Oh. No, I mean, like proper aliens. You know?"

"Not really," Loren said.

"No, I don't really know what I meant either," Cal confessed. "Forget I said anything."

"Done," Mech replied.

Miz shrugged. "And I wasn't even really listening, so..."

"All good then," Cal said. He gestured along the corridor in both directions. "So, what now?"

Mech spent a few seconds tapping on his arm. "There's a big communal area six flights up. A restaurant, maybe."

"Great idea!" said Cal. "We should grab lunch. I don't know about anyone else, but I am starving."

"I meant we could go check it out," Mech snapped. "See if there are survivors up there."

"If we can even see them," said Loren.

"Well we sure as fonk can't see them from down here," Mech pointed out, and it was hard to disagree with.

"Oh yeah, we should absolutely do that, too," Cal said. "I just meant that while we're continuing to investigate the spooky abandoned ghost ship, we may as well have a bite to eat."

He put an arm around one of the passenger statues. "I'm sure it's what these guys would have wanted!"

THE COMMUNAL AREA Mech had detected did indeed turn out to be the ship's enormous food court. As they'd set foot in the place, though, even Cal's hunger had all-but evaporated.

Whatever had happened downstairs had happened here, too, only it had happened more forcefully, and over a much larger area.

Fifty or sixty guests seemed to be running from something in panic, but just like those down below, they were now frozen in place, their faces trapped in a rictus of fear. Most incredibly, a few of them seemed to have stopped mid-bound, so they were suspended a few inches above the ground, one foot pointing ahead, the other trailing behind.

Around sixty per cent of the food court was in a perfectly respectable condition, although it probably could have done with some modernizing twenty years previously. The other forty per cent, though, was harder to explain.

Pockets of the place looked... older, somehow. It wasn't just rot at work here. The tables in these areas were broken, the metal bent and rusted. In one area, a fire seemed to have broken out, reducing the floor to a dark sea of embers which had been criss-crossed by footprints that stopped abruptly at the invisible line delineating the area's edge, and never appeared anywhere else in the room.

Cal whistled quietly through his teeth. "I have seen some weird shizz lately. Big orange space clouds, giant spider-dragons. Clowns. Jesus, those fonking clowns. Parallel dimensions. A little dwarf guy with a metal head." He smiled at the others. "Remember him? Remember little dwarf Cal with the metal head? No-one could understand what he was saying? I wonder what happened to that guy."

Mech sighed. "Were you making some kind of point?"

"Hmm? Oh. Yeah," Cal said. He shrugged, making Splurt wobble on his shoulder. "Probably. I'll be honest, I've forgotten."

Miz wandered over to a table where an overweight orange-skinned old man with a neck like a bag full of cream was leaning back in his chair. By the looks of him, he had leaned too far, and was now technically falling backwards in his chair, but he was frozen in place, his face fixed in a grimace of terror, all his weight supported at an impossible angle by the chair's two back legs.

There was a glass in the air in front of him, suspended at an angle so the peach-colored liquid it contained was spilling over the sides. Miz sniffed it up close, then gave the glass a prod. It didn't move.

Loren, meanwhile, had joined her at the table. She picked up one of the other glasses with no problem, stuck a finger in, then touched it against her tongue. "Darrumian Slush Brandy," she said. "Except it isn't slush, so it must have been here a while."

Cal shoved his hands into the pockets of his cargo pants and strolled on into the cavernous food court. "So, what are we looking at here?" he asked. "Anyone got any theories?"

"I got one," said Mech. "We should get the fonk out of here and never look back."

"We can't do that," said Loren. "Someone needs to figure out what's going on."

"Oh, I agree," said Mech. "But does that 'someone' need to be us? No. No, it don't." He looked around them and shuddered noisily. "There is something really fonking weird going on here. *Really* fonking weird."

Cal spotted a bank of food replicator standing back to back over on his right. There were six of them, with stacks of plastic trays piled neatly around them, ready for use. Cal immediately changed direction and headed for the closest one.

This – this one sudden deviation in his route – would come to be one of his life's great regret. Years later, when he thought back about what he could have done differently, he'd keep coming back to that abrupt shifting of weight from his left foot to his right, the swinging of his arms as he changed direction, and those few strides that would change Cal Carver's life forever.

"Hey, they might have some of that Mush stuff," he said. "If we're going to go, we may as well..."

He glanced back at the others. Mech and Loren were both staring at the spot he'd been standing in a few seconds before. Miz was still examining the mid-air glass, her tongue extending towards the spilling liquid she went in for a lick.

Loren had dropped the glass. Or was in the process of dropping it, at least. Her fingers had opened just enough for the tumbler to live up to its name. It had made it half an inch towards the ground before it, along with Loren, Mech and Miz, had all frozen solid.

Cal's feet scuffed to a stop. "Uh, guys?"

No-one responded. No-one moved. Splurt wriggled anxiously on Cal's shoulder.

"It's OK, buddy," Cal assured him, but the churning dread in his gut told him otherwise. "They're just... having a joke, that's all. Right, guys? Haha. You got us!"

No-one responded. No-one moved.

"Guys?" Cal said again, and this time his voice was reassuring no-one.

A sound reverberated around the dining area. It was something a bit like a scream and a bit like a howl. Cal spun in the direction it had come from, but saw no-one and nothing that hadn't been there a moment ago.

Another screech answered the first, this time from somewhere closer. Cal couldn't pinpoint it. Above him, maybe? Below?

Shizz. Was it him? Had *he* made the noise? He didn't

think so, but the body reacted strangely under stress, and this – right now – was pretty fonking stressful.

A throaty roar boomed through one of the dining area's many doorways. It was long and deep, and resonated with fury, like the song of a whale that had just had its beer spilled. The other noises – the scream-howls – became higher and more frantic, before fading off into the distance.

The low, guttural growl came again, and Cal felt the floor beneath him vibrate. He turned back to Mech, Loren and Miz. They hadn't moved. They were frozen. Solid.

And something mean and scary was coming.

"OK, guys, I'm going to need to you to wait there until we figure this out," Cal whispered. He could hear more noises out beyond the doors now – fast scuttling sounds, which were worrying, and the slow, steady *slap-slap-slap* of approaching footsteps, which was even more so. "I'm pretty sure you'll be fine if you just stay, you know, frozen or whatever, so don't go doing anything stupid like moving or blinking or whatever, got it?"

He waited for a response that he knew wouldn't come.

"Great job," he said. "Keep up the good work."

Then, with Splurt on his shoulder and the growling of some unknown monster echoing all around him, Cal Carver turned on his heels and ran.

SEVEN

CAL SWUNG WITH HIS AXE. It wasn't a great axe – it barely even qualified as an axe at all, in fact, being little more than a chair leg inexpertly welded to a broken piece of bulkhead – but it could be relied on to do the job when it mattered. Assuming the job was one that involved either chopping or bludgeoning something to within an inch of its life, or possibly to several inches beyond.

The sharpened piece of bulkhead cleaved through one of the Mongrel's multitude of legs, amputating it below the knee. It wouldn't bring the thing down, of course – it never did – but it would keep it distracted long enough for Cal to do what he'd come to do.

Cal ducked the swipe of an armored tail and rolled clear. He swung out with the axe again, hacking off a chunk of grisly gray flesh that landed with a *shlock* on the floor. The tail whipped back towards him again, but Cal had been anticipating that. He vaulted over it, then spun and buried the axe into the spot where tail met butt.

The Mongrel squealed and spat and thundered its feet

against the floor. It spun sharply, wrenching the weapon from Cal's grip. He almost moved to retrieve it, but knew that was suicide. Besides, it would keep the thing busy while he made his move.

Darting around the forest of feet, Cal skidded to a stop in front of the only working food replicator for six levels and barked out his order. "Vitamin and protein capsules. Month's supply. Hurry."

The machine's inner working emitted a worrying series of *clanks* and groans, then it began to rumble and shake.

"Come on, come on," Cal muttered, shifting his weight from foot to foot and shooting anxious glances back at the Mongrel. It was still pre-occupied by the axe in its ass, but its shaking and twisting was already working the weapon free. He didn't have long left.

The little door in the front of the replicator opened half way. Cal forced it the rest of the way, then held a little floral-patterned wash bag under the dispenser. Multi-colored capsules rained down into the bag, almost filling it. Cal waited until the downpour had stopped, then hurriedly zipped the bag closed and shoved it into the satchel he had slung across his chest.

He turned to leave, then hesitated.

"Banoffee pie," he instructed, but before the machine could fire up again, the Mongrel's tail slammed into it, tearing it from its housing and spraying globules of gloopy pink Mush in all directions.

"Son of a bedge!" Cal grunted.

Grabbing for his axe handle, he yanked the weapon free. A fountain of black blood hit him in the face, making him cough and splutter.

It took him just a second or so to pull himself together,

but by then the Mongrel was looming over him, its mandibles snapping, its horrifyingly human eyes glowering hatred.

"This is for my pie, you fonk!" Cal spat, then he swung the axe over his head and buried it right between the mandibles. The outer shell of the pincers cracked under the impact, and the Mongrel twisted in pain and shock, tearing the axe from Cal's hands again.

Spying his chance, Cal dived beneath its chin and charged through the forest of its legs. Not looking back, he raced for the door that led out of the staff kitchen and into the corridor beyond. The door was one of a handful on the whole ship that weren't all frozen shut, and it juddered open at his approach.

Hurtling out into the corridor, Cal wasted a moment smearing a big X on the wall beside the door in the Mongrel's blood, then he hurried around the corner and into the waiting arms of Splurt, who dangled down from a hole in the ceiling.

"Go, go, go!" Cal instructed, and Splurt wrapped around him like a cocoon. There was a jerk, a *boing* and a sudden upwards sensation, and Cal was hoisted back into the relative safety of the maintenance tunnels.

It had been six months since he first ran from the food court, and it was safe to say that things had not been going well.

The first few days had passed in a blur of monsters and hunger and fear. Had it not been for Splurt, Cal knew he would've died well over ten times in the first forty to forty-five minutes alone.

Most of the ship was off-limits, as many of the doors had frozen shut. Nothing Cal or Splurt did could make the doors open, so they had been forced to find an alternative means of getting away from the creatures Cal had eventually dubbed 'Mongrels'.

Fortunately, Splurt had discovered the maintenance tunnels that ran through most of the *Binto Odyssey*. They were narrow, dark and uncomfortable, and Cal had spent much of those early days convinced he was about to recreate one of the more memorable chase-and-death sequences from the movie, 'Alien', but none of the Mongrels ever tried to come in.

Well, no. That wasn't strictly true. A couple of them had *tried* to come in, but they were too large to fit through the hatches. Those who tried to force their way through were met by some pretty stubborn resistance in the form of Splurt, and quickly came to realize their mistake.

Splurt oozed along the darkened tunnel now, carrying Cal along with him. The warm air of the ship's fonk-knew-what exhaled towards them like the breath of a sleeping giant, and Cal felt himself relax. Those welcoming gusts meant they were almost home. Or what now passed for it, at least.

With a quick upwards scamper, Splurt brought them into a taller circular space from which eighteen different tunnels ran off. It was the Section 8 (Lower) Maintenance Network Hub, Cal reckoned – mostly because this was printed on the walls in large blue letters – and unlike the tunnels themselves, its ceiling was high enough that Cal could fully stand.

"Thanks, buddy," Cal said, giving Splurt a pat as the large green slug became a small green blob. "Great job, as always."

Cal reached for the axe on his back, before remembering he'd left it behind. He felt a pang of loss and grief, like he'd just been told an old friend had died, then he unhooked his bag, dropped it on the floor, and took a seat next to the makeshift stove. He enjoyed the sensation of warmth that crept through his fingers and toes, but did nothing to outwardly show it.

It wasn't a real stove, of course. He didn't really know what it was. Part of the engine, he assumed. It was big, metal and hot, which was all the information he had any real desire to know about it. He'd developed a nagging superstition that, should he ever find out what the thing was or why it was hot, it would immediately cool down, stealing away his only heat source and means of cooking or boiling water.

Not that he cooked much these days. It wasn't like he had anything *to* cook.

Cal fished in his satchel until he found the wash bag. Unzipping it, he took out two red pills and two blue-and-yellow capsules. He'd found a packet of each of them on the floor of one of the few cabins he was able to get access to, and then had been relying on the food replicator to produce more ever since. It was quicker than ordering a balanced meal, and since the only replicators he knew of were all guarded by big scary things that wanted to eat him, speed was usually of the essence.

He tossed the pills into his mouth and snapped his head back, swallowing them down with some difficulty. His stomach rumbled with disappointment. Cal prodded at it. "Yeah, yeah, shut up," he told it. "Next time, OK?"

He rolled up his sleeve. There was a gash on his arm just above his wrist. It wasn't deep – just a raw, bloody scrape, really – but it was enough to make Splurt wobble in distress.

"Hey, relax," Cal soothed. "It's fine. I'm fine. Just a scratch."

Splurt rippled again.

"No, OK, I'll give you that, but I mean it this time," Cal said. "Besides, you can barely even see that scar these days."

Splurt shuddered.

"No, you cannot look, you little weirdo," Cal said. He laughed drily. He had no idea what Splurt was saying. Not really. He had no idea if the little guy was really saying anything at all, but it was comforting to imagine he was. "Just take my word for it, OK, buddy? I'm fine. I'm not going anywhere."

Cal bent forward. Splurt raised up until he was pressing against Cal's forehead. Their eyes locked.

"We're in this together. Right?"

Splurt made a gesture that could have been construed as a nod.

"Attaboy," said Cal. "You and me against the world."

He straightened, then reclined until his back rested against the stove. He held himself there for as long as he could stand the heat, then flopped sideways onto the mattress they'd found on a supply run a few weeks back, and which Splurt had painstakingly dragged all the way up here through six levels, three Mongrels, and a gang of Jumped-Ups.

It was a good mattress, Cal reckoned, although he suspected it was built for a much heavier species, and he found it a little on the firm side as a result. Still, it was better than the floor, and meant Splurt no longer felt obliged to turn himself into a four-poster vibrating waterbed whenever Cal so much as yawned.

"Tomorrow, we'll figure out what's going on," Cal said, his voice becoming slurred as sleep sidled up to him. He'd said those same words, or slight variations of them, every night since that first night, and Splurt could only ripple encouragingly in reply.

Splurt watched Cal's eyes close. He listened for the soft rattling of his breathing that signaled he had fallen asleep.

Then, when he was certain Cal was no longer awake, Splurt stretched out until he formed a thick woolen blanket, spread himself over the sleeping human, and then tucked himself in around him.

CAL HAD SPENT the first few weeks etching little notches in the wall of the maintenance hub to help him keep track of time. Unfortunately, he had no idea what time it actually was at any given point, since all the ship's clocks displayed different numbers or, in the case of those on the lower spa deck, a series of question marks and a face with a squiggly mouth.

Some of the walls couldn't be written on. Throughout the whole ship, there were things he could physically interact with, but many more things that he couldn't. Those doors that wouldn't open. The food replicators that seemed to be undamaged but refused to acknowledge his requests.

The big-eared guy kneeling in the theatre aisle up on deck sixty-seven, who Cal had spent an enjoyable afternoon sitting astride and pretending he was a motorbike several months back.

No matter what he did to those things, no matter how hard he tried, he couldn't move them or mark them in any way. They were locked in place. Frozen. Completely immobile, and utterly impervious to damage.

The walls in the maintenance hub were plagued by the

same problem. Some of it he could scratch into – and, later, draw on – just fine, but other areas repelled any attempts to make a mark on them, as if they'd been coated with a molecule-thin invisible forcefield.

Still, he'd found a spot he could interact with, and he'd started counting off the approximately-day-length periods of time on it. He made it his personal mission. His quest. Every approximately-day-length period of time, he'd make another line. This would be his life's work, he decided. This would be his reason to be.

He etched six lines before he got bored. He'd coasted through the first couple on auto-pilot, become utterly fed-up by the third, but then been excited at the prospect of drawing the fifth line diagonally through the other four, which had helped to keep his enthusiasm up.

Once he'd crested that dizzy high, though, it all sort of felt a bit flat. While he managed to stick it out until the seventh approximately-day-length period of time, after that things became substantially less regular.

He switched to marking off weeks, because he felt like that was less of a commitment. It was tricky to estimate how long a week was with any degree of accuracy, though, so he based it on how often he slept.

He slept a lot, although never for long periods of time. Sometimes he'd deliberately settle down on his Splurt-bed. Other times, he'd grab some shuteye while barricaded inside a room, or propped up in a wardrobe somewhere, waiting for a wandering Mongrel to pass.

Back at the start, he spent several nights sleeping near Loren, Mech and Miz, with Splurt keeping watch to make sure nothing snatched him away. But, as the days had passed, he'd taken less comfort in being near them, and had begun to feel guilt at being unable to free them from whatever weird space shizz held them trapped.

He'd retreated to the maintenance tunnels after that, and had never slept down in the dining area since.

As a result of his irregular sleeping pattern, Cal completely lost track of days, which meant he completely lost track of weeks, which meant his whole time-recording strategy went right out the window. Nowadays, if he remembered, he'd carve thirty or forty notches in the wall at once, with no idea what sort of relation any of it bore on reality.

Still, it passed the time.

Somewhere between two and eight months after Cal's fight in the staff kitchen, he and Splurt were back in the *Odyssey's* main food court, watching Mech, Miz and Loren do absolutely nothing at all.

Or *almost* nothing at all. If someone had a lot of time on their hands and was paying *very* close attention, they'd notice some slight differences. Miz's tongue was now practically touching the liquid she'd been attempting to lick for over half a year now, and the glass Loren had dropped was almost a full inch and a half closer to the floor. It wasn't much – it was barely anything, in fact – but it gave Cal hope that they were still in there somewhere, and if they were still in there, then maybe they could hear him.

"Splurt, watch the doors," he instructed.

Splurt *flobbed* his eyes in opposite directions. When it was clear he couldn't watch all the exits from there, he grew six more eyes and raised them up on gooey stalks.

"That's... neat," said Cal. He shuddered slightly, but said no more about it. Instead, he turned to Loren and the others and scraped together the broadest smile he could muster, given the circumstances.

"Hey, guys! How you doing?" he asked. "Good? That's great. Mech, what you been up to, buddy?"

Cal listened, nodding. "Nothing whatsoever. Well, good for you. We all need a little R&R once in a while, am I right? Granted, you've done sweet fonk all for months now, and some might argue that it's time you got moving but hey, who am I to...?"

His voice lost all energy and stumbled into silence. He looked from Mech to Miz, then lingered a little longer on Loren. Finally, he sighed. "Come on, guys. Where are you?"

CAL SAT on the one table he could interact with, and which he'd dragged over in front of the rest of the crew some weeks – or maybe months - previously. He tossed one of his few remaining vitamin pills towards his mouth, missed, then spent a full minute trying to find the thing in his beard.

Once he had, he placed it carefully on his tongue, and grimaced as he swallowed it down. His throat had been swollen and sore ever since one of the smaller Mongrels had spat in his face some time back. How much time, he couldn't say, but no longer than a week, he reckoned.

Coming here to the food court had become a comforting routine. Seeing Mech, Miz and Loren helped remind him of who he was. During those times when he awoke in a cold sweat, panicking that he'd gone crazy and all this was just some detailed delusion, he'd return here and just sit watching them for a while. He didn't feel the need to speak to them much these days – just being near them was enough. Today, though, he had something important to tell them.

"I think I've figured it out."

Part of him – the part that still clung onto such childishness – had hoped he might see a glimmer of something in Loren's eye at that, or some flickering of lights on Mech's arm. Miz was now fully licking the mid-air liquid, so she was unlikely to give much of a response, but all the way here he had fantasized about... something. Some suggestion that he was talking to his friends, and not just three statues.

But no. There was nothing.

The glass was another inch closer to the ground now. Oddly, though, the other occupants of the dining hall hadn't moved in the slightest. The guy toppling back in his chair was no nearer the ground, for example, and his glass – unlike the one Loren had dropped – was still exactly where it had always been.

Cal had wondered about that for a few weeks, but as it was just one of a number of things on his 'Things I Don't Understand' list, he eventually just shrugged and stopped thinking about it.

"It came to me last night," Cal said, jumping down from the table. One of Splurt's many eyes turned to check he was OK, then went back to guard duty. "I couldn't sleep, so thought I'd do something useful. I decided I'd try to figure out what the problem is here. You know, with you guys not moving, and everything?"

He twitched. It was something he was doing quite regularly these days. He'd noticed it almost as an outside observer would, and seemed to have just as much control over it.

"OK, cards on the table, I actually spent about twenty minutes trying to remember the names of all the Fraggles, but *then* I decided I'd try to figure out this situation. And, well, I think I did it."

Cal glanced back at Splurt for a moment, then drew in a deep breath. "Space magic," he announced. He grinned. "I know, right? Makes sense."

He began to pace back and forth in front of them. "See, thinking about it, this sort of shizz used to happen all the time in old fairy tales. People would get frozen, or I don't know, pushed into an oven made of baked goods. Or whatever."

Another twitch.

"My point is..."

And another.

"My point is..."

He stopped talking. Stopped walking. Just stopped.

"I guess I don't know what my point is," he admitted, his voice dropping into a monotone as the realization of that fact crept up on him. "That doesn't really help at all, does it? I mean, how do you fight Space Magic?"

Cal clicked his fingers, his eyes widening. "With a *Space Wizard*!"

His face fell.

He twitched again.

He didn't know any Space Wizards. He didn't know any normal wizards either, for that matter. Even if he did, none of the landing bays were accessible, so he couldn't go out and pick them up.

A screech echoed through one of the doorways somewhere over on the left. Splurt rippled in warning, and grew several appendages, each of which ended in something heavy and blunt, or pointy and sharp.

Cal raised a hand, indicating he'd heard, then beckoned for the little guy to follow him. "I gotta split, guys, OK?" he whispered. "You all just hang out here. Make yourselves at home, or whatever. I'll be back soon, and we'll get this figured out."

Pausing only to briefly cup Loren's rock-solid face in one hand, Cal ducked low and headed for one of the room's many exits.

It would be three years before he returned.

EIGHT

Cal found the wedding cake in a mini kitchen near the ballroom on the eighty-fifth floor. It didn't look much like a traditional Earth wedding cake – it was a near perfect pyramid with the point removed to leave a flat area at the top – but the little plastic figures of two people with their arms hooked together that were buried up to their knees in the light pink frosting gave it a certain weddingy vibe.

He had approached it cautiously, like a hunter might approach a flighty prey. He'd existed on vitamin pills and unprocessed Mush for months by this point, and the mere sight of the cake had first made him cheer, then made him dance, then made him weep hot salty tears of joy for forty-eight solid minutes.

In hindsight, he knew why he'd done this. It was a delaying tactic. He wanted to cling to that taste a little longer. Not the taste of the cake – he knew that wasn't going to happen – but the taste of hope. The feeling that maybe, just maybe, this was going to be his first lucky day in... how long? Years? He couldn't remember.

Still, maybe today. Maybe today.

He touched the cake. Solid.

Completely, wholly, totally solid.

He licked it, anyway. He licked it quite a lot, in fact. Splurt watched him, impassively, while Cal tongued and slobbered over ever nook and cranny of the frosting. Even the bride and groom didn't escape his tongue's attentions.

Eventually, Cal sunk back onto his haunches and smacked his lips together a few times.

"Nothing," he grunted, and he said no more.

Three months later, while Cal was being chased from one of the engine rooms by a gang of Jumped-Ups all chittering in their strange alien language, he was almost knocked off his feet by the taste of... not strawberries, but close enough. Space Strawberries.

No, Space Strawberry *frosting*.

He laughed. He kept laughing, in fact, right up to the point where one of the Jumped-Ups' spears tore through his calf muscle. He stopped seeing the funny side at that point, although even as he fell his tongue was working the roof of his mouth, trying to eke every last drop of flavor that had exploded in there from nowhere.

The Jumped-Ups weren't like the Mongrels. They roamed in gangs sometimes dozens strong, scavenging through the ship, claiming any food and resources they came across. They reminded Cal of cavemen – primitive and brutal, but still significantly smarter than anything else roaming the decks, himself arguably excluded.

They'd eat him, he knew. He'd hidden in the maintenance tunnels and watched from above as they'd turned on members of their groups and devoured them. Often, there didn't seem to be any real motivation for it. One would simply lunge at another, then the rest of the gang would pile on and tuck in.

Cal lay on the floor, the end of the spear sticking cleanly through his flesh, his blood pouring through the gaps in the walkway beneath him and onto one of the big sticky-up engine parts thirty feet below.

This was how he'd die, he reckoned. Eaten alive by a pack of savages. Still, there were worse ways to go.

Granted, he couldn't think of any, but surely there *had* to be worse. It would be pretty unfair if, after everything he'd already been put through, he was then subjected to the single worst death in the whole of the fonking galaxy.

Mind you, the way his luck had been going of late...

He'd made himself another axe. This one was better than the first, with a longer handle and a much sharper blade. It was weighted perfectly so he could swing it with ease, and even throw it should the need arise. It had become almost an extension of himself in the past year or so.

Unfortunately, he'd left it back at one of the hubs which, in hindsight, had probably been a mistake.

He was defenseless, then. Defenseless, injured, about to be eaten and alone.

Not a great combination.

The Jumped-Ups were almost on him. Cal turned his head away, having absolutely no desire to see them closing in on him, their eyes blazing with hunger and glee.

"Totally should've helped out the eye-shizzers," he muttered, voicing out loud one of the biggest regrets of his life thus far.

And that was when he saw *her*. She bounded along the walkway with a gracefulness that her tight leather pants should have made impossible. Her blaster was at her hip, but she made no attempt to reach for it. Instead, she just winked at Cal as she leaped over him, wrenched the spear from his leg in one smooth and miraculously painless jerk, then twirled it above her head like a ninja with a Bo staff.

Cal didn't realize he was crying until he felt the tears on his arm. He watched, eyes blurred, as Loren smashed the butt of the spear into a Jumped-Up's nose, shattering it. He marveled as she dodged blows, deflected weapons, and used the spear's tip to hack through throats and stomachs and – in the case of at least one poor bamston – groins.

She'd always been a fighter, but she was more than that now. She was a warrior. She was a vengeful goddess, laying her wrath down upon the unjust.

She was back. That was all that mattered. She was back.

It took Loren less than a minute to dispose of the Jumped-Ups. She turned then, face slick with their blood, and she smiled. Oh, God. She smiled. Cal felt his heart soar. She was back. She was alive, and everything was going to be OK.

Loren's smile, then her face, collapsed like melting rubber.

"N-no," Cal whispered, his guts twisting as he watched everything that had been Loren collapse into a pulsating ball of green goo. "Splurt, what did you do? You *idiot*!"

Splurt rolled backwards a little and rippled uncertainly. He grew an arm and stretched it out as Cal struggled to his feet, but Cal batted it away. "Get off me! I can do it! Don't touch me!"

Pain exploded through his leg and Cal collapsed in an undignified heap of blood, snot and tears. This time, he didn't resist when Splurt wrapped a supportive arm around him. Splurt didn't know what he'd done wrong, but he assumed a form he knew to be acceptable, and Cal found himself gazing deep into the eyes of Dorothy out of *The Golden Girls*.

"Not her, OK, buddy? Not Loren," Cal whispered. "Not... not them."

Dorothy out of *The Golden Girls* gazed loving at him through sad old eyes, nodded her understanding, then kissed him lightly on the forehead.

"Thanks, pal," Cal said. He caught the walkway's handrail and began to pull himself up. "Now let's go home."

CAL STEPPED BACK to admire Mech's hat. It had fallen out of a closet while Cal had been exploring one of the lower decks, and he'd spent a frantic few seconds punching the shizz out of it, fearing he was under attack.

It had come as a source of some relief, then, when he discovered it was just a hat, and then a source of great joy when he realized that it wasn't merely a hat at all. It was a ridiculous hat. And he knew just where to put it.

"Oh man, all that purple and orange totally sets off your eyes," Cal said, placing a finger on his chin and nodding like an art critic at a gallery opening. "And the way those fake pigtails hang down over your shoulders... It's breathtaking, Mech, breathtaking."

He limped over to the falling glass. His leg had long-since healed up, but despite his and Splurt's best efforts, the muscle hadn't knitted together neatly, and he still got the occasional shooting pain if he put his weight on it the wrong way. Limping helped. Hopping helped even more, but simultaneously stripped him of anything resembling dignity, so he stuck to limping.

Besides, his hips were giving him problems these days, and he wasn't sure if hopping was in their best interests.

"I give it six months," Cal announced, sizing up the distance between the glass and the floor. "Splurt? You think? Six months?"

Splurt rippled.

"A year? You think?" Cal straightened up. Doing so involved him making a sort of, "*Ung*," noise and pressing both hands against his lower spine. He ran his fingers through his beard, then up over the thinning hair on his head. "Well, we'll see, I guess."

He hobbled over to the table he always sat on and leaned against it, catching his breath. "We should have a party. When it smashes, I mean. We should make a big deal of it, you know? We'll call it Smashdown Day. Or maybe just Smashdown. Yeah, that sounds better. *Smashdown*."

Splurt wobbled.

"No, we can't have little sausages on sticks."

Splurt trembled.

"Yes, I know you like them, but we've got no replicators, have we? Where are we supposed to find little sausages?"

Splurt did nothing but stare up with his wide, perfectly-round eyes.

"Don't look at me like that," Cal said. He sighed, then a thought occurred to him. "I could do us little carrots on sticks. Well, I probably can't do the 'on sticks' part, but we could do the little carrots part. We should have another crop coming right around Smashdown. How would that be, huh?"

Splurt vibrated.

"There's my little guy!" Cal cheered. "Little carrots not on sticks it is!"

The garden had been a gamechanger. They had discovered it on the third-from-topmost deck, a vast expanse of soil basking in the rays of an artificial sunlight generator.

That entire deck had been accessible to him. This meant it was also accessible to the Mongrels and the Jumped-Ups, and the whole floor had been teeming with them. Realizing that this deck was the difference between life and death, Cal had proceeded to systematically clear out the monsters, aided only by his wits, his axe and a certain adorable green ball of violent psychotic tendencies.

Everything useful in the garden was long-dead, and several thousand weeds had risen to dominance. Even with Splurt's help, it took Cal a week to clear an area about half the size of a basketball court. Once he had, he'd haphazardly scattered a few of the seed tubes Splurt had found stashed in an overhead locker, and hoped for the best.

That was four harvests ago. He'd learned a thing or two since then, and while the majority of it had been about how to eat space vegetables without immediately throwing them back up, some of it had been about the actual process of farming.

Cal spent another few moments admiring Mech's new hat, then turned to Splurt. "Uh, could you give me a moment here, buddy? There's something I need to say."

Splurt formed himself into a perfect sphere and rolled off across the food court. Now that they'd wiped out most of the Mongrels, he didn't have to be on high-alert all the time, and spent most of their visits here weaving in and out of the table legs, playing a game whose rules Cal could never quite figure out.

Cal walked around the rest of the crew, looking them up and down. He stopped beside Miz. Her tongue was no longer touching the solid liquid, and her head had turned just a fraction to look in the same direction as the others. He estimated she'd be facing front in... what? Fifty years? A hundred? Long after his time had passed, anyway.

"Fonking Space Magic," he mumbled, then he continued past Miz, banked around Mech, and stopped in front of Loren. "Hey, you," he said, tapping her lightly on the end of her nose. "Fancy seeing you here."

He twitched. It was something he did less often now, but something about being here with them brought it out in him. He didn't know why, but assumed it was for the same reason that he never thought about his advancing years or physical appearance when he was anywhere else on the ship, but always felt self-conscious when around Loren and the others.

"You're looking good," he told her. He smiled, showing the gap he'd been awarded for getting too close to a Mongrel's tail. "Holding up better than me, anyway. Though that's not exactly saying much."

He tried to brush a strand of hair from her face, but it was as unmovable as it always ways. "Anyway, listen, I've been thinking. Space Magic. You know what I said before, about fairy tales and curses and all that stuff? Well, here's the thing. There's a way to break the spell. From what I can remember, it's pretty reliable – a prince comes swooping in, spots the sleeping princess and... well."

Cal looked down, his face flushing red with embarrassment for reasons he couldn't quite put his finger on. He looked up again, and his gaze met Loren's distant not-quite-there stare that was focused on a spot several feet behind him.

"They kiss," he said, the words choking him. "He kisses her, I mean. And the spell is broken. She wakes up."

Cal twitched. He was wringing his hands together, and only now noticed how weathered and calloused they looked. After studying them for a while, he raised his eyes again. "I'm going to kiss you now, Loren. I hope that's OK."

He leaned in, but the angle of her head made things difficult. In the end, he had to sort of squat down a little and lean back, then shuffle forwards until he was within lip-locking range.

It was unlikely to go down as one of the great kisses of history.

"Please work," Cal whispered, then he craned his neck, clenched his buttocks to raise him half an inch higher, and he kissed her.

Her lips were warm, but solid, and he felt like he was kissing a radiator.

Cal held the kiss until his back ached and his hips threatened to go on strike, then extracted himself. He watched her face for much longer than was necessary to know it hadn't worked. His grand plan – the culmination of a decade or more of applied thinking – had failed.

He smiled sadly, showing his gap again. "Still," he whispered. "Totally worth it."

AS THE DAY of the Smashdown drew nearer, Cal found himself becoming more and more excited. Other than the harvests; Charades Night, which Splurt always made far too easy; and the promise of the occasional satisfying bowel movement, there wasn't much left for him to look forward to.

Smashdown, then, became the highlight of his immediate future, and Cal became like a kid counting down the days until Christmas. He checked in at the food court regularly, using Splurt to measure how far the glass still had to fall.

Between the time he brought in the Space Onion crop and the time he sowed some of those purple potato-things he'd recently discovered a packet of, the glass had plunged almost a full inch.

By the time the potato-things were ready to dig up, Cal could just barely fit a hand between the container's base and the floor.

After he'd eaten the potato-things, and dealt with the days of terrifying hallucinations about being made entirely out of bubbles that followed, there was less than a pinkie finger width remaining.

One full lifecycle of little Space Carrots later, Cal could barely slide a sheet of paper into that same gap. This meant just one thing. The day was upon them. Smashdown was finally here.

CAL HAD MADE T-SHIRTS. Technically, they weren't t-shirts, and technically he hadn't made them, either. He'd really just written "SMASHDOWN" on an old maintenance boiler suit and cut the arms and legs off it, but it was close enough.

He'd spent a few hours making Splurt a shirt from the scraps, but then Splurt had simply grown one out of his own blobby body, which had kind of put Cal's efforts to shame.

Cal could barely contain his excitement. That glass had been falling for a *stupidly* long time, and now – at last – it was going to smash. The smash wouldn't happen all at once, of course, but gradually over a period of months. Still, today would be the initial impact that would kick-start the chain of events that followed. Today would be a day long remembered.

"There. Perfect!" said Cal, after he'd finished adding another hat to the growing collection on Mech's head. This one was a wide-brimmed floppy thing with a band of luminous sequins. It was up there with the most hideous hats Cal had ever seen. "And yet, somehow you carry it off," he told Mech. He turned to Splurt and, in an exaggerated stage whisper, said, "He totally doesn't."

Cal took his seat by the table. Not *on* the table this time, because it had been turned over to several bowls of little carrots and a pile of home-made confetti. Splurt, on the other hand, did sit atop it, pulsating gently as he eyed up the vegetables and presumably tried to convince himself they were sausages.

"I can't believe it's finally here," Cal said, gesturing to the glass. From here, it looked like it was sitting on the ground, but there was still the tiniest of tiny gaps beneath it. Smashdown could be just moments away. "You excited, buddy?"

Splurt rippled in a way that suggested he was quite excited, but possibly not to the same extent that Cal was.

"You have no idea how long I've been looking forward to this," Cal said.

Splurt had a pretty good idea, actually. Cal hadn't stopped talking about it for the past eight-to-twelve months, and had spent eight weeks making all the little flags that now decorated the food court.

Still, if it kept him happy.

Cal sat up suddenly and licked his lips. "Yes! It worked. *Perfect timing*." He pointed to his mouth. "The cake. I can taste the cake. I started licking it every day a few weeks back so I could taste it."

He let his head sink back so it lolled around on his shoulders. His mouth fell open. "Aw, man, that tastes good. That tastes *great*."

With a bit of effort and some creaking bones, Cal slid himself off the chair and onto the floor. He lay down, affording himself the best possible view of the glass at the precise moment of impact. The smash itself should be instantaneous, he thought, taking place over only a few hours or a couple of days, at most. The first crack, though, should be visible more or less as soon as the glass touched down.

"Any minute now," Cal whispered.

He waited. There was no gap between the base of the glass and the floor now.

"Any minute... *now*. Wait... *now*."

He held his breath for as long as he could.

"*Nnnnow*."

EIGHT HOURS LATER, Splurt helped Cal up from the floor. He'd fallen asleep after five or six hours, but Splurt had decided to leave him there. He needed more rest these days, and while he was asleep Splurt wasn't being bombarded by the psychic waves of disappointment and grief that had started to come rolling off him when it became clear the glass was going to remain in one piece.

"It didn't break," Cal wheezed. The glass was now standing upright on the floor, still completely intact. "Fonking thing didn't break."

Shaking his head, Cal turned to leave, then he stopped beside the chair he'd been sitting on earlier. Grabbing it, he swung it above his head, then brought it down hard on the glass. The chair shattered. The glass did not.

Cal glared hatred down at it, his eyes blurred by tears. "Fonking thing didn't break."

POST-SMASHDOWN, Cal became increasingly subdued. He was less chatty than usual in the weeks that followed, then barely spoke much at all over the next few months. By the time a year had gone by, his vocabulary consisted of little more than tuts, sighs and the occasional dissatisfied grunt.

Time passed in a sort of slow, lingering silence. The Mongrels and the Jumped-Ups were long gone, even the memories of them now decades old, and there were no more threats or dangers to break up the days.

Cal had been back to the food court just once in the years since Smashdown, after he'd lost his way and found himself there quite by chance. He lost his way more and more often these days, and had come to rely on Splurt to act as his guide.

Splurt tended the garden, too. Cal had guarded this role fiercely for as long as he was able, but his back was too buckled now, and his arms no longer had the strength. Splurt had taken to it as if he had green fingers – which, admittedly, he often did – and was soon producing food far faster and more effectively than Cal had ever been able to.

Too much food, in fact, especially now that Cal had stopped eating. It hurt too much to swallow and, well, he didn't really see the point. Eating kept him alive, and the million and one aches and pains in his muscles and bones told him that time should've long-since passed.

It took some effort to raise his head from the pillow. He watched Splurt enter, and saw the panic in the little guy's eyes. Cal rippled his fingers in a calming gesture, then beckoned his oldest friend closer.

Time had taken its toll on Splurt, too. The once-gelatinous blob was now dark and crusty in spots. He could still shapeshift, but it seemed to be proving more difficult of late, the shapes becoming vaguer and less convincing.

Cal's hand shook as he held it out to Splurt, and the ache in his arm made him flop it down onto the bed. Splurt's crusty exterior bulged as he extended a stumpy, child-sized hand of his own. It slipped into Cal's and their fingers interlocked.

The breath rattled in Cal's chest now. It came in shallow sips, his lungs unable to handle any more. He'd like to say it had been a good life, but that would've been a stretch. Bits of it had been good. Great even. The past forty years or so had been pretty fonking tedious, though, and there had been enough bad stuff even before this damn ship to make him consider himself pretty hard done by.

Still, it was over now. Or would be, soon enough.

Cal closed his eyes. Or rather, his eyes closed all on their own. He felt the bed slide away beneath him, and he was carried along as if on a rolling ocean. This was it, then. This was what dying felt like. This peaceful transition between—

His head *thonked* against a door frame.

"Ow! Jesus!"

Cal opened his eyes and saw the ceiling passing above him. Beneath him, Splurt had become something not unlike a hospital bed, and wheeled him along through the *Binto Odyssey's* network of corridors.

He wanted to ask where they were going, but his

strength had all but left him. Instead, he surrendered himself to his old friend, knowing Splurt would never knowingly do anything to hurt him.

His head hit off another door frame. He grunted. Splurt rippled apologetically, then swept him on through the ship.

Cal slept fitfully, balanced on the jagged ridge between life and death. It would not be the death he had imagined for himself. That death had been a good one, facing down some giant alien menace, or sacrificing himself to save the galaxy, or calling Mech a robot one too many times. This – a decaying husk on a ship full of ghosts – was not the death he had hoped for.

When he next opened his eyes, he saw them, and a gasp or a sob or something in between burst from his lips.

They were all facing front now, Mizette having turned to see what the fuss was about many years previously. Splurt propped Cal up so he could get a clearer look.

He saw Mech with his assorted hats, and felt a chuckle like dry leaves fluttering somewhere in his chest. He saw Miz, her eyes wide and inquisitive, her tail frozen mid-wag.

He saw that fonking glass, still perfectly intact and upright on the floor. Seriously, what were the chances?

And he saw her. Most of all, he saw *her*. Loren. Her eyes wide with worry, her mouth turned down in concern. Concern for him. For where he had gone. For what could be happening to him.

If only she knew.

Cal lay there, with Splurt wrapped around him, just looking up at them all. His crew. His friends.

His family.

"Oh, Splurt," he said, and he realized that he had been wrong. All this time, he had been wrong. This *would* be a good death.

Good enough.

And there, surrounded by his Space Team, Cal Carver of the planet Earth closed his eyes and surrendered into the open, waiting arms of former Hollywood actor, Tobey Maguire.

Forever.

NINE

Or not.

Cal's eyes opened and he sat bolt upright, bending at the waist like he was spring-loaded. Mech, Loren and Miz were still staring back at him, just as they had been a moment before. Still motionless, still frozen, still...

"Ew. Like, who's the creepy old guy?" asked Miz.

"Holy shizz!" Loren yelped, drawing back in fright. Her eyes narrowed as she studied him more closely. "Cal? Cal, is that you?"

Cal's jaw dropped. "What?" he mumbled. "Who? How the... I mean... That's not..."

"Where the fonk did all these hats come from?" Mech demanded. His neck *whirred* as he looked around at the dozens of home-made flags that hung on strings from the ceiling. "And what the fonk is 'Smashdown'?"

The word triggered something inside Cal. He sprang up from his Splurt-bed, rediscovering an energy he hadn't known in years. Roaring, he raced towards Loren, then toe-punted the glass that had been on the floor in front of her.

He watched with an immense sense of satisfaction as the tumbler arched through the air and hit the far wall.

Thunk.

It slid down and landed on the floor, completely intact and the right way up.

"Son of a..." Cal wheezed, then he spun around, squinted, and stabbed an accusatory finger at Loren and the others.

He began to scream. It wasn't clear why, exactly – Cal, himself, didn't really know – but he screamed for almost a full thirty seconds, then ran in a circle a few times and blacked out.

He woke up again before he even hit the ground, managing to eject another short, sharp scream before his old bones clattered against the hard floor, taking the wind out of him.

Cal decided it was best if he lay there for a while. Just lay there, doing nothing, gazing up at the all those little Smashdown flags which looked almost as new as they had done when he'd made them all those years before.

The others were staring at them. Fonk it. Let them stare. He'd stopped giving a shizz about what anyone thought of him decades ago. Granted, he'd been surrounded almost exclusively by monsters at the time, but the point was... The point still...

His wrinkled brow furrowed. What was the point? He'd forgotten.

He smiled gummily when Loren appeared beside him. Just like the flags, she, too, looked good as new. She gently slid her arms beneath Cal's shoulders, and he surrendered to her grip as he realized just how frail he'd become. "Cal? Are you OK?" she whispered.

Cal managed a slow nod.

"What happened?"

"About fifty years happened," Cal managed, then he was wrenched out of her arms and yanked suddenly onto his feet by some invisible force, like a puppet being dragged upright on its strings.

There was an odd sensation radiating out from the center of his chest. It wasn't a heart attack – he'd had those. This was something different. It felt... not good, exactly, but not bad, either.

He spasmed violently. OK, that was less good.

What happened next, none of them could really explain. From Cal's point of view, he felt like the universe was both collapsing in on him and exploding out of him at the same time. If he'd had to liken it to a noise, it would have been: "Krak-ump," which wouldn't really have made it any clearer for anyone.

Mech, Loren and Miz also got the impression he was doing two things at once, although not the same things as Cal was experiencing directly. His whole body seemed to become utterly, impossibly still, and yet it simultaneously began to shudder and shake, vibrating faster and faster until it was simultaneously both a blur of speed and a rigid, unmoving statue.

"Think it's too late to take the eye-shizzing gig?" Mech wondered.

"Shh," Loren urged, although she didn't know why. Cal was making no sound as he stood there both moving and not moving, so Mech talking didn't really affect anything in the slightest.

Miz leaned over and nudged the cyborg with her elbow. "You know you're wearing make-up, right?"

"Huh?" Mech brought his forearm up to his face and checked out his reflection in the screen. Sure enough, his cheeks, eyes and lips had all been painted, dusted and smeared with a selection of vibrant colors. "What the fonk is this?" he demanded, earning himself another curt reprimand from Loren.

Finally, whatever was affecting Cal stopped. It stopped abruptly, and with enough force to launch him across the room, where he skidded over a table, fell off the other side, and landed on the floor with a *crunch*.

"Well, there go his hips," Miz muttered.

Loren approached slowly, holding a hand out and gesturing for the others to stay back. As she neared the table, she could make out the crumpled heap of his shape on the other side, folded up on himself in a way that couldn't possibly be comfortable.

"Cal?" she asked, stopping a foot or two from the table. "Cal, are you OK?"

Cal sprang upwards, screaming, his eyes wide with terror, his beard...

He grabbed at his face.

His beard. Where was his beard?

"Where's my beard?" he asked, and his voice came out stronger and more piercing than it had done in decades.

Cal felt his hair. Last time he'd checked it had been long and wispy, but now it was short and thick, and almost certainly in need of a wash.

He saw the relief on Loren's face, but it paled into comparison with the relief he knew must be written all over his own.

"I'm alive. I'm alive and... And I'm *young*!" He laughed. "I'm young! I can do anything!"

He tried to touch his toes, but failed.

"Fonk. No. Can't do that. But still... I'm young, Loren. I'm fonking young!"

"Young-*ish*," Miz corrected, and Cal laughed again. He threw his arms around Loren and hugged her, savoring the softness of her against him. She was alive. *He* was alive.

And he was young.

Ish.

"So, I gotta ask," said Mech. "What the fonk is going on?"

"Oh, it was horrible," Cal said, reluctantly pulling himself away from Loren. They both held on a little longer than either of them intended, before detangling their limbs and stepping apart. "I aged. I, like, I aged."

"We saw that," said Loren. "How?"

"Same way as everyone else," Cal explained. "One day at a time. See, while you three were standing there doing nothing for half a century, I lived out my whole life. Here. On this fonking ship."

Cal, Loren and Miz all exchanged looks. "Sorry, not getting it," Loren said.

Cal darted past her to where Splurt was still in a sort of half-trolley, half-blob shape. "Buddy! It's me. I'm here. You OK?"

Splurt *boinged* back into ball shape. His crusty exterior was glossy and smooth once more.

"Alright! We're back!" Cal cheered, then he spun back to face the others. "Look, it's pretty simple. You guys were standing there, I walked over there, and then suddenly... *whoosh*. You know?"

"No, man. We don't know. What the fonk is 'whoosh'?"

"I mean... *whoosh*," said Cal, adding an arm gesture as if that somehow helped clarify. "You guys slowed down. Or I sped up. Or... I don't know. Space Magic. I lived out my whole life while you just stood there. And then I died, and then... Then... Well, then I came back. Here and now. And you're moving again."

He grabbed Miz by the shoulders and tangled his fingers in her fur. "You're moving again!"

Mech scowled. "Nope."

"Nope? What do you mean, 'nope'?" Cal asked.

"Ain't buying it."

"How do you think you got those hats on your head, Mech? Hmm? Or that make-up on your face?" Cal asked. "Or that note on your back that says 'Kick me'."

Miz leaned over so she could see Mech's back. "Oh. Heh. Nice," she said, then she kicked Mech on the back of the leg and tried to pretend it hadn't hurt.

"Cut that shizz out!" Mech snapped. He looked down at the hats he was holding in his hands, then pulled the others off his head and studied those, too. Finally, he met Cal's eye. "You serious?"

"Totally," said Cal, then he let out a sharp, sudden gasp. "Oh fonk. Oh God, I just thought of something."

"What?" asked Loren. "What is it? What's wrong?"

She said it to Cal's back. He was already off and running, sprinting out of the food court, giddy with his refound strength and vigor.

"Ball room! Meet me at the Ball Room! Splurt will show you where it is!"

"Ball room?" Miz asked. "Like, why?"

But the answer didn't come. Cal was already gone.

THEY FOUND him sprawled in the middle of the dance floor, face down in a strawberry-frosted wedding cake and groaning with pleasure. As they entered, he pulled his head free with a *schlop,* and grinned up at them through a mask of pink frosting. He looked, at that moment, like the happiest person Loren had ever seen. Even though he also appeared to be crying.

"This is so good," he said, the words mumbled and indistinct through the mouthful of cake. "You have no idea how long this fonking thing has been taunting me. Seriously, we're talking *decades.*"

Miz's nostrils flared as she picked up the smell of the frosting, and she took a step closer. Cal wrapped his arms around the cake, completely destroying it as he pulled it to his chest. "Mizette, I love you honey, but if you touch this cake I will scratch your God damn eyes out." He smiled sweetly. "OK? Same goes for the rest of you. This baby is all mine."

"I don't get it," said Mech.

"It's a cake, Mech," Cal replied, shoving a fistful of the thing in his mouth as if to demonstrate. "See? It's just a cake."

"No, I mean the rest of it."

Cal looked down at the cake. "The little plastic guys?"

"No! The rest of *it.* The time thing. You growing old."

"I already explained that," Cal said. "Space Magic. Got to be."

"See, what the fonk is 'Space Magic'?" Mech grunted.

"It's like regular magic," said Cal, spraying crumbs all down his front. "Only in space."

Mech muttered darkly. Loren jumped in before violence could break out.

"Even if it did happen like you say – even if you and Splurt somehow, I don't know, sped up, then how come you came back? How are you... normal, I mean."

"He ain't normal," Mech said. "He's a long fonking way

from normal."

Cal opened his mouth to offer an explanation, then realized he didn't have one. "More Space Magic?" he guessed. "*Anti* Space Magic? Fonk knows. The point is, I'm back, I'm young, and *oh my God, there is a giant face at the window.*"

Loren glanced at the others, then back to Cal. "Huh?'

"Face," said Cal, pointing past them. "Giant face. At the window."

The others turned in the direction he'd pointed, not quite sure what, if anything, they expected to see. Loren wasn't quite buying the rapid aging thing, but Cal had clearly gone through some kind of trauma. There was no saying what sort of hallucinations he might be...

There was a giant face at the window.

More specifically, there was an enormous eye and part of a colossal nose at the window. It was a dark, glassy eye, and not especially friendly-looking. It watched, unblinking, as Cal slowly got to his feet, crossed to the window, and quietly closed the blinds.

"OK, everyone else saw that, right?" Cal asked. "That wasn't some mental breakdown or psychological cry for help?"

"Not unless you were crying real fonking loud," Mech muttered.

"Was that an eye?" Miz asked. "Because, like, it looked like an eye."

"Aye! *I* would say that's an *eye*," Cal replied. He shook his head and grinned. "I have absolutely no idea why I said that. Totally not the time." He threw his arms around Mech. "Man, I missed you guys."

"Get off me," Mech grunted, shrugging him away.

Cal jabbed a thumb back in the direction of the covered

window. "This is *so* us, don't you think? Minding our own business, then – *bam* – giant face at the window. This is so totally us."

No-one else seemed as entertained by the situation as Cal was. Loren tried to peer through the narrow gap in the blinds, but to no avail. "Is it still there?"

Cal pulled the cord that raised the blinds.

It was still there.

"Yup."

He tried pulling a different cord, but only one half of the blinds lowered, while the other end raised. "Shizz. Hang on," he said, tugging another cord. This time, both ends of the blinds raised, completely revealing them to the giant eye outside.

"It's totally staring at us," Miz pointed out.

"I know, I know. Hang on. I've got this," Cal said. He pulled two of the cords at once. The end that was currently raised lowered, while the end that was lowered raised. "Jesus. So many strings," Cal said, his voice taking on a slightly hysterical edge. "Why are there so many strings?"

"Hurry the fonk up," Mech said.

"It's unnecessarily complicated," Cal protested. He pulled all three cords and the blind dropped suddenly.

"Ta-daa!" he announced, turning and holding his hands out at his sides.

There was a *crash* from behind him. Cal's smile faltered, just slightly.

"It just fell off the wall, didn't it?"

Loren nodded. "Yup."

"Is the big face gone?"

Loren shook her head. "Nope."

Cal chewed his lip. "OK. Maybe if we stay *really quiet...*"

A voice boomed around the ship, shaking the floor beneath them, making Splurt ripple anxiously, and turning the remains of Cal's cake into tiny nuggets of cakey rubble.

"You have been tried and found to be in breach of temporal law," it announced. It was an odd voice – neither male nor female, and Cal was pretty sure he felt it in his bones rather than heard it in his ears.

"Is it talking to us?" he whispered.

"Well it's looking right at us, so..." Mech reasoned.

"Sure, *that* eye's looking right at us," Cal conceded. "But I'm assuming he has two. Maybe the other one is looking at whoever he's actually talking to, and this one just happens to be—"

"SILENCE, CAL CARVER!"

Cal shook his head. "Nope. He's totally talking to us," he whispered.

"You mean he's talking to *you*," Mech pointed out.

"SILENCE, GLUK DISSELPOOF!"

Cal resisted the urge to respond to Mech, and just fixed him with an infuriatingly smug smirk, instead.

"The punishment for your misdeeds is total chronal disassociation," the voice continued.

Cal raised his eyebrows. "That doesn't sound so bad."

"You shall all be forcibly removed from the time stream and cast into a void of endless suffering, while any and all actions committed by you during your lifetimes shall be wiped from the annals of history. Thus speaks the Time Titan."

"Actually, that does sound kind of bad," Cal admitted. He looked at the others. "Right? That's bad?"

"I fonking hate you, man," Mech grunted. "How do you always get me into this shizz?"

"I have no idea," Cal admitted. "But come on, don't I

always get you out of it?"

"No. No, you don't."

Cal frowned. "Don't I? Huh. I should really work on that." He turned to the window. "Hold on. Whoa there, big face," he said. "What are we supposed to have done, exactly?"

Miz's nostrils twitched. She raised her head, her fur prickling.

"You illegally meddled in the causality of all things," the Time Titan announced.

"Right," Cal replied, drawing the word out. "Meaning what, exactly?"

"Meaning you shall be punished by—"

"Removal from... whatever. No, I get that bit. I mean can you be more specific about what we actually did?"

"You interfered with the machinations of the time stream."

Cal looked at the others and lowered his voice. "That's more vague, right?" He turned back to the window before anyone could answer. "We think that's more vague. Can you be more *specific*?"

"You—"

"Also, can you back away from the window a little? Talking to a big eye is kind of freaking me out."

"No. I shall—"

"Hey, come on, pal," Cal said, offering one of his most well-rehearsed smiles. "I've had a hell of a day. Do me a favor here."

The Time Titan hesitated. Finally, it tutted. "Fine," it agreed. "But everyone shut your eyes."

"Say what?" asked Mech.

"I'll move back a bit, but first you've got to shut your eyes."

Cal wagged a finger at the big eye. “Hold on. You’re not going to cast us into that void of eternal suffering when we’re not looking, are you?”

“No.”

“Be honest!”

“Look, do you want me to move back or not?”

Cal called Mech and Loren into a huddle. Miz was too busy sniffing the air to join in. She had padded away a little, moving vaguely in the direction of a little DJ booth at the corner of the dance floor.

After a few seconds of whispering, the huddle broke apart. Cal addressed the window with an offer. “What if we kept our eyes open, but turned around?”

The Time Titan considered this. “That is acceptable,” he intoned. “But no peeking.”

“Deal,” said Cal.

“I mean it.”

“Jesus, OK. We won’t look. You have my word,” Cal said.

He, Loren and Mech all turned their backs on the window.

“So, what do we think?” Cal whispered.

“About what?” Mech grunted. “I don’t even know what’s going on anymore.”

“About the time guy. What do we think?”

“He’s big,” said Loren.

Cal raised his eyebrows. “Is he big? I hadn’t noticed,” he said, then his voice dropped to a hiss. “We know he’s fonking big! I mean what do we do?”

“You may turn around,” announced the Time Titan.

As they did, a low involuntary whistle escaped Cal’s lips. “Is he... I mean, just so I know, Loren. Is he still big?”

The Time Titan was most definitely still big, even now

that he was substantially further away. If anything, the distance somehow made him look bigger, despite the shift in perspective.

He was totally hairless, from the top of his giant domed head to the tips of his house-sized toes. His skin was a shimmering gray, or possibly a dull silver, and his eyes were two black pools that shone with the light of a billion reflected stars.

Around his neck was the chunkiest gold chain Cal had ever seen. Hanging from it was a clock face. Or, more accurately, an infinite number of different clock faces all existing in the same place at the same time, most of them ornately decorated with precious metals and shiny stones.

Aside from this one piece of bling, the Time Titan was completely naked. Fortunately, he had no giant space genitalia to speak of, which came as a relief to all present.

His arms were down by his sides, and the whole figure seemed quite rigid, almost like it were standing to attention.

"There," boomed the Time Titan. He didn't move his lips, and despite his increased distance there was no decrease in his volume. "It is done."

There was an awkward moment of silence, as if the Time Titan couldn't quite pick up the thread of the previous conversation.

"So *there*," he said, mustering quite an impressive amount of gravitas given the statement's less than dazzling content.

Cal puffed out his cheeks. "Well, that told us," he said. "Now, you were going to be more specific about what we're supposed to have done wrong. Shoot."

Miz stopped outside the DJ booth. It was the size of a very small shed, or maybe a bus shelter made to hold two people who knew each other very well. It had been painted a really quite eye-watering shade of orange, then inexpertly adorned with an overabundance of fake gemstones and flashing lights.

There was text emblazoned across the front of it in luminous green. Miz had never seen the Comic Sans typeface before. If she had, she'd have thought it remarkably similar to the font used here.

Her visual translation chip was having some difficulty with the writing, and it fluctuated between a couple of alternatives. The text on the booth either said: *MC Jokemeister General – The Cheesiest Beat's & Wackiest Laugh's* (stray apostrophes included), or: *I'm so very, very alone.* Miz wasn't sure which of the two was correct, but she had her suspicions.

She sniffed the door. Her ears pricked up.

The Time Titan's voice reverberated through the ship.

"You have caused a localized time fracture aboard this vessel. You have detonated an illegal chronal weapon, resulting in the deaths of several hundred future generations."

"Aha!" said Cal. "Now we're getting somewhere." He shook his head. "We didn't do that."

The Time Titan seemed to falter in his stride. "Sorry?"

"We didn't do that. That wasn't us."

There was a pause.

"Wasn't it?"

"No. I mean... I don't think so," Cal replied. He turned to the others. "Guys? Did we detonate an illegal whosamajig?"

Loren and Mech both shook their heads.

"Not that I know of," Loren said.

Cal turned further. "Splurt?"

Splurt, who had been quietly passing the time by

turning into some of Cal's favorite childhood cartoon characters and was currently the fat one out of *The Gummi Bears*, also shook his head.

Cal looked around for Miz, then spotted her over by the DJ booth. She had one hand on the handle, the other held above her, claws extended. "Miz, did you...? Hey, what's up?"

"DON'T OPEN THAT DOOR!" cried the Time Titan.

But it was too late. Miz tore the door from its frame, revealing an elderly man in a long red smock that came all the way down to the floor. Miz was as unfamiliar with Santa Claus as she was with inexplicably popular computer typefaces, otherwise she'd have noted another quite remarkable similarity in the way the old man looked.

He wore the same chunky chain around his neck as the giant figure outside, although his was partly covered by his long white beard. His eyes darted left and right beneath snow-colored eyebrows, and his hands wrung together as he shifted uncomfortably on the spot.

"Oh... bugger. Uh, I can explain!" said the man, and the Time Titan's voice echoed through the ship. With a *click*, he deactivated a little electronic device attached to his throat. When he next spoke, it was in a voice that was substantially more subdued. "Might as well turn that off, I suppose. The game's up."

"Like... who the fonk are you?" Miz demanded. Cal, Mech and Loren appeared behind her, which made the old man shrink back a little.

"I am the Time Titan," he said, with far less authority than he had just moments before. Outside, the enormous silver figure fizzled out of existence. The old man smiled anxiously. "Please... Don't hurt me."

TEN

The Time Titan shuffled out of the DJ booth and immediately found himself surrounded by Mech, Loren, Cal, Miz and Gargamel out of *The Smurfs*.

"You've got five seconds to tell us what's going on, old man, or Loren here will shoot you in the face," Cal warned.

"What? I will not!"

Cal sighed. "Jesus. I'm trying to intimidate the guy, Loren. Can you just go along with it?"

Loren ignored him. "Look, no-one's going to hurt you," she said, bending forward a little to bring her face down closer to the old man's. "We just want to know what's going on."

"I told you. I'm the Time Titan. You've broken chronal law, so... Well, you know. All that other stuff." He looked around at them all reproachfully. "You've really made a terrible mess."

"We didn't break shizz," Mech told him. "We just got here."

"Speak for yourself," Cal muttered. "Right, buddy?" He and Gargamel bumped fists.

"Exactly my point," said the Time Titan. He jabbed a bony finger in Cal's direction. "He and... the green thing, they altered their time lines!"

The Time Titan regarded his accusatory finger, as if just noticing it for the first time, then quickly tucked it behind his back. "I mean... That sort of thing... Well, it's not on. It's lucky I rewound you when I did. Had you died, who knows what sort of disequilibrium that might have created? Who knows what the repercussions could have been?"

Cal's eyes widened. "Wait! So *you* brought me back? You made me young again?"

"Indeed. I restored you to your prime. And not a moment too soon."

"Hear that, Loren?" Cal said, firing off a lop-sided grin he considered particularly good. "To my *prime*."

"I heard," said Loren. "Congratulations."

Cal winked, then turned back to the old man. "And so, I guess it was you who fixed Splurt, too?"

The Time Titan's bushy eyebrows furrowed. "Pardon? Oh, him. No, there was nothing wrong with him. Or it. Or whatever it may be. His time line is like nothing I've ever seen." He stared at Gargamel out of *The Smurfs* for a while, then shook his head. "I suspect he was just making himself look old in order to make you feel better."

Cal looked round just as Splurt collapsed back into ball-shape and started to roll off. "You wait right there, mister," he said, and Splurt squelched to a stop. "You're telling me you made me look at all that horrible crusty shizz for nothing?"

Splurt shuddered, making him ripple like jello. Cal squatted beside him and rubbed what passed for his head. "Thanks. You little weirdo."

With a rubbery *boing*, Splurt hopped up onto Cal's

shoulder just as Cal turned back to the old man. "Look, uh..."

"The Time Titan," said the Time Titan.

"I can't call you 'the Time Titan'," Cal told him.

"Why not? It's my name."

Miz tutted. "It's a dumb name."

"Well now, Miz, I wouldn't say..." Cal began, but then he shrugged. "No, she's right, it's a dumb name. Besides, there's no way that's your actual name. You totally made that up."

"I didn't."

"How about...?"

Cal looked the old man up and down, his eyes moving slowly from his curly crop of white hair, down past his rosy cheeks and wispy beard, and all the way to the bottom of his red smock.

"I think—" said the Time Titan, but Cal silenced him with a gesture.

"Hold on. I'm getting there," said Cal.

Mech sighed and squeezed the bridge of his nose. "The man's got a name. He told us his fonking name."

"Tim," Cal announced. "We'll call you *Tim*. Tim the Time Titan. Time Titan Tim. Like it?"

The Time Titan shifted his weight on his feet. "Well, I mean..."

"Great!" Cal cheered. "That's the spirit! Now sorry, Tim, what were you telling us?"

The newly-Christened Tim opened his mouth to say something, realized he had absolutely no idea what it was going to be, and so closed it again.

"He rewound you," Loren said. "That's what he said."

"Right! Yes!" said Cal. He stepped forward and grabbed

Tim's hand, which made the old man flinch. Cal pumped the hand enthusiastically, like he was trying to draw water from a well. "I want to thank you for that, Tim. You're a real lifesaver. And I mean that literally."

Cal shrugged. "Would it have been nice if you'd showed up fifty years previously? You bet it would! But you got there in the end, and that's what counts, right?"

"Uh... yes. Yes, I suppose it is," said Tim. He looked down at his hand when Cal pulled his away, flexed the fingers a few times, then let it drop down by his side again. He regarded the rest of the group. "So you're saying you *didn't* detonate a chronal weapon on board this ship?"

"That's exactly what we're saying, Tim. I'm glad you picked up on that," said Cal. "We don't even know what a chronal weapon is. Do we?"

There was a general murmuring of agreement from the others that no, they didn't know what it was.

"See?"

"Oh dear. Oh... *buggeration*," Tim said, wincing behind his beard. "That means that whoever *did* set it off, well, they're still out there. If they can do that today, there's no saying what they could do tomorrow. Or yesterday, for that matter."

"Exactly what I was thinking," said Cal. He slipped a hand around Tim's shoulders. "As soon as I saw you I thought, 'Now here's a guy with a problem. Here's a guy who could use our help. Our fast, efficient, *surprisingly affordable* help."

"What? Oh. I'm not sure..."

"You want to find out who used the... what was it?"

"Chronal weapon," said Tim. "Essentially, a time bomb."

"Like one of those ones you see in cartoons?" asked Cal. "With the clock and the dynamite and all that jazz?"

Tim shook his head. "No. Like one of those ones that can fracture time itself."

"Oh, *that* sort of time bomb. Gotcha," said Cal.

Loren looked around the dance floor at all the people frozen, mid-step. "Is that what happened here?" she wondered. "Did time fracture?"

"I'm afraid so," Tim confirmed. "The detonation was powerful, but extremely localized. It took me almost a full thirty minutes to detect it and trace its point of origin, then almost three whole seconds to travel here from across the galaxy."

"Slacker," said Cal, but no-one really paid him any attention.

"Three *seconds*?" Loren gasped.

Tim blushed, just a little. "I know. I took a wrong turning at the Homax belt. It'll be a long time before I can live that one down."

"So... what are you saying?" asked Mech. "Someone built a bomb that can break time? How the fonk can you break time? Time ain't a thing."

"Oh, it's very much a thing," said Tim. "In many ways, it's the only thing. And it can be stretched and manipulated, or it can be broken completely."

"And what happens then?" Loren asked.

"Everything. And nothing," said Tim.

"Going to have to ask you to be a little more specific again there, pal," said Cal. "Also, supplementary question – what happened to the big space guy outside?"

Tim looked mildly embarrassed, and shuffled awkwardly beneath his smock. "That was a projection. I brought matter forward from right after the formation of the universe, and shaped it into the figure you saw. I thought it would be... more impressive."

"Are you kidding me?" said Cal, just a little accusingly. "Don't you ever let me hear that kind of talk again, Timbo. You're *way* more impressive than some enormous space baby."

"Uh, he totally isn't," said Miz.

Cal titled his head left to right in a way that suggested he conceded the point. "I mean, she's right. That's crazy talk. The giant space guy was *way* more impressive. But still." He gave Tim a playful punch on the shoulder. "You *Wizard of Oz-ed* us. Great job. We totally fell for that."

"I didn't," Miz pointed out.

"No, *she* didn't. And the rest of us had our suspicions, but still." He winked. "Great job."

Mech's fingers *whirred* as they balled into fists. "Look, can we just get this shizz all explained away so we can get the fonk out of here? Tell us about the time bomb. What *exactly* does it do?"

"I'm not sure I can accurately explain," said Tim.

Mech shrugged. "Fine. Then I'm out. If anyone needs me, I'll be back at the ship not giving a fonk about any of this."

"Wait," said Tim.

Mech stopped. He wasn't sure if it was his decision or if Tim had somehow forced him to, but he stopped.

Worry darted across the Time Titan's face for a moment, before something firmer and more resolute moved in to replace it. "I can't explain," he said. "But perhaps I can show you."

TIME PASSED. Lots of time, all at different speeds, and not necessarily in the right direction. It flowed like a rainbow of liquids, with all the colors following the same path, but all going at their own pace.

The red line trundled along at what Cal decided was 'normal' speed. If he looked at it directly, he got the sense of the seasons blending gradually into each other, and of years passing at exactly the rate he thought they should.

The strand next to it was orange. It whooshed by in a blur, moving so quickly it generated ripples of heat in the air around it and emitted a high-pitched buzzing like a wasp on Helium.

Where the yellow should have been was nothing but an empty gap. Tim explained the color was there, but it was moving too fast for Cal or the others to see. Personally, Cal thought this was bullshizz and the old man had forgotten to add it in, but he decided to give him the benefit of the doubt.

The green moved much more slowly than the red, and slower still than the orange. Beside it, the blue was completely motionless, frozen like an icy river. Next to that, two different shades of purple were flowing backwards, one much more quickly than the other.

The rainbow pattern twisted around the ballroom, weaving between the motionless dancers and banking up over the heads of Cal and the others. Tim stood in the center of a colorful hoop, gesturing around him.

"This is the timestream," he explained. "Or a very simplified version of it, at least. See that red line? That's time flowing at its regular speed. Tick. Tick. Tick. Exactly as you'd expect."

"Knew it," Cal announced, looking pleased with himself. "I totally guessed that."

Tim made a gesture with his hands and the rainbow grew larger. Splurt developed a hand and tried to touch the colors, then trembled with delight when his fingers passed straight through them.

"Notice the other strands? How they're all physically beside one another, but flowing at different rates?" Tim continued. "Now imagine a billion of those. A billion billion. Shift from one strand to another and suddenly you're moving faster, or slower, or backwards, even. It's a highway. A highway through time."

"Gotcha," said Cal. "By which I mean I'm sure one of us follows and can explain it to the rest of us later. What's it got to do with this place?"

"This is the time stream out there," said Tim, gesturing to the window. "And *this*... This is the time stream in here."

The colors fragmented and whizzed off across the walls, floor and ceiling. At first, Cal thought someone must've turned on the DJ booth's lights, but then he realized he was still looking at the rainbow, except now it was in thousands of little pieces all scattered throughout the ballroom. Some of the pieces intersected, creating new bands of color that flowed at several different speeds at once, and pulsed angrily as if they weren't best pleased about it.

Whenever Cal looked at any of those new colors, his skin crawled. They were... not right. That was all he knew for sure. Looking at them dredged up some ancient and primal uneasiness from deep down in his gut.

There were things in there. Things from long ago, and still to come. Things that would never exist – *should* never exist – and yet at the same time, *would*. Somehow, they would.

A pressure began to build in Cal's head, like a knot of pain behind his eyes. He looked away from those wrong colors, but he could still see, hear them, feel them pulsating and twisting and howling and—

"Turn it off," said Loren. From her voice, and the way her blue skin was turning faintly green, Cal knew she'd felt the same thing he had.

Tim made a tickling gesture with the fingers of both hands. The colors blinked out, one by one, leaving the room much darker than it had felt before. For a long time, nobody spoke. Although Splurt did briefly become Mighty Mouse.

"So that's what a time bomb does, huh?" said Cal.

"It, like, what? Puts colors everywhere?" asked Miz. "What's the problem?"

Loren rolled her eyes. "I think you missed the point."

"Yeah? Well I think *you* missed the point!" Miz retorted.

"How does that even make sense?"

"How do *you* even make sense?" said Miz, then she nodded her satisfaction and crossed her arms, the argument apparently won.

"It's fortunate the explosion was confined to this vessel," Tim explained. "Had it been larger – had the time stream beyond the ship's shielding been affected – then the damage could have been insurmountable."

Cal frowned. "Meaning?"

"Meaning all of time could have shattered."

"Meaning?"

"Meaning everything would stop happening. And yet, paradoxically, everything would happen at the same time."

Cal nodded and whistled quietly.

"Uh-huh," he said. Then: "*Meaning...?*"

"Meaning it'd be bad motherfonking news," Mech snapped. He turned to Tim. "Right?"

"Yes. It would be 'bad motherfonking news', as you so

rightly say." He waved a hand in Cal's direction. "It was unfortunate you stumbled upon a fragment like you did."

"*Unfortunate*? I spent my whole life living on... Wait. There were monsters. Or monster-aliens. Or alien... I don't know. There were these big scary things. Where did they come from?"

"From here. On the ship," said Tim. "When the bomb detonated, you see, all those passengers were affected differently. Those you see here, unmoving, are frozen. They're the blue line you saw."

He rapped his knuckles on the head of a wedding guest.

"Trapped in a billionth of a second. Unmoving. Unaware." A frown troubled his brow. "I mean, I hope they're unaware."

He shook his head, chasing the thought away, then gestured around him at the empty air. "Meanwhile, some of the others took that orange line you saw. The one that flowed much faster. That was the line you found yourself on," he said, nodding in Cal's direction. "On that timeline, hundreds of generations were born and died in a matter of seconds. The things you saw – the monsters – were the results of cross-breeding, in-breeding, and ten and a half minutes of *vastly* accelerated evolution."

"So what are you saying? They were the passengers?" asked Cal, feeling a twinge of guilt over having killed them all.

"No. They were the distant descendants of the passengers. The passengers themselves have been dead for millennia. On their time line, anyway. Just under quarter of an hour in this one."

"Oh," said Cal. He brightened. "Oh, well that's *fine*, then. Fonk 'em."

"What about the other lines?" asked Mech. "The

purples, or whatever? Those were going backwards. Did anyone wind up in one of those?"

Tim nodded tactfully. "They did. Yes," he said.

"Then where are they?" asked Mech. "How come we don't see them?"

"The, uh, physical form is not designed to go backward in time. It's not natural, you see? It's designed to go forward in time, usually – but not always – at a steady, regular pace. It's what we expect, and what we have evolved to do. Going backwards presents tremendous dangers, even to me."

"So, what happened to them?" asked Loren.

"They all blew up."

"They *blew up*?"

"Exploded into tiny bits," Tim explained. "Then those bits exploded into tinier bits, then those bits into even tinier bits... And so on and so forth. You get the idea."

"Why didn't I blow up?" Cal asked. "When you rewound me, or whatever? Not that I'm complaining."

"Luck," Tim admitted. "There was a very good chance you would, but since you were already a third of a second away from death, I thought it worth the risk."

He smoothed down his beard and darted his eyes around the group. "I wouldn't really have done that stuff I said earlier," he admitted. "You know, erase your history, cast you into a void of endless suffering, etcetera. I wouldn't know where to start."

Miz had wandered over to another of the frozen figures. It was a young girl dressed proudly in a shiny sequined silver dress. She wore matching shoes, and the outfit really set off the purple of her skin. She was smiling and had clearly been bouncing with excitement when her time line had stopped.

The girl's face was turned upwards. Miz followed her gaze and saw hundreds of colorful spheres up near the ceiling, all of them paused, mid-fall.

"Like, what'll happen to all these guys?" Miz asked. "I mean, not that I care, but can you, like, restart them, or whatever?"

Tim's expression answered before his voice did. "I'm afraid not. The damage is too great. Everything is too far gone."

"Then how come you could save this shizznod?" asked Mech, indicating Cal.

"Well no need to sound so ungrateful about it!" Cal protested.

"He was not here when the chronal weapon detonated. He was not affected directly. These people, this ship... They took the full brunt. I'm afraid they're lost. Everyone's lost," Tim said. To his credit, he seemed genuinely upset by what he was saying. "All that remains is to collapse the ship's time line, so as to prevent the risk of it contaminating others."

"Meaning...?" Cal asked again.

"Meaning I will collapse its past, its present and its future in on one another. It will be erased from existence. Erased from time. It's already unstable, even I should be able to manage that."

Cal, Loren and Mech all nodded slowly, despite none of them having any idea what the old coot was talking about. Miz slouched her weight on one leg, deliberately not looking at the excited little girl in the silver dress and matching shoes.

"So... hold on," said Cal. "If the ship is erased from time, won't that mean that we didn't come to it? That none of this stuff happened?"

"It doesn't work like that," said Tim, looking almost amused at the suggestion. "You came here. Your experiences are indelibly imprinted on your mind. Erasing the ship from time will not wipe the memories from your head. It will merely prevent anyone else traveling back to interact with it from the future, or anyone traveling forward to interact with it from further in the past."

"Oh. Well... great. That's much clearer. That's pretty much what I expected," said Cal, then he shot Loren a sideways look and gave a little shrug.

"You have a ship, yes?" said Tim.

"We do," Loren confirmed.

"Then you should probably get to it," Tim told them. "I have already begun the process of chronal collapse. Soon, this ship won't ever have existed."

"Right," said Cal.

"Unless you've been here, in which case it will have."

"Uh-huh," said Cal.

"But only while you were aboard it."

"Got it. Makes sense," Cal lied.

He reached forward, caught Tim's hand, and pumped it vigorously. "So, this has been great. Really informative, and I want to thank you for stopping me dying of old age."

Tim smiled behind his beard. "Think nothing of it. Happy to help."

"No, but I mean seriously. I feel great! I owe you one."

"I restored you to your physical prime," Tim said. "Let's call it compensation for the inconvenience you experienced."

"Sounds like a deal!" said Cal. "Oh, but one thing – are there likely to be any, you know, ill effects of spending fifty or so years trapped on the same ship with just Splurt for company? Mentally, or whatever? Asking for a friend."

Tim's smile became a little less convincing. "Well... it's hard to say. Rewinding you restored your brain – reformatted it, if you will – so while you may remember many of the things you experienced here, there shouldn't be any strong negative or positive feelings connected to those events. All the experience, with none of the emotional baggage."

"Great!" Cal said. "I think this means I'm officially the wisest and most experienced member of the team! You know, not counting Splurt, because fonk knows how old he is."

Loren jabbed a thumb in Mech's direction. "What about him? He's hundreds of years old."

"Oh. Shizz, yeah. I forgot about that," said Cal. He tapped his finger against his chin. "Although, he's had his memory wiped, so I'm pretty sure it doesn't count. Fonk it. Let's just all agree that *I'm* the wisest and most experienced, then reassess if any other evidence presents itself." He flashed a grin at the others. "Sound good?"

"I ain't agreeing to that," said Mech.

Cal gave an apologetic sort of shrug. "Well, like I just said, I'm the wisest and most experienced, so... overruled. Sorry, Mech. Tough break."

He about-turned before Mech could say any more and swept towards the door. "Now, let's get back to the ship. Believe it or not, I kind of want to say hello to Kevin. I actually kind of missed the sound of his voice."

CAL STOOD ON THE BRIDGE, his mouth hanging open, his gaze locked firmly on the ceiling above.

"What do you mean *I could have spoken to you at any time*?" he demanded.

"Well... just that, sir," Kevin intoned. "I was hooked into the *Odyssey's* communications systems and, as you may recall, I and this vessel are both rather experimental in nature. By accelerating my processing power up to maximum, I was able to perceive you and Master Splurt's accelerated time lines. It was quite fun to watch, actually."

"Quite fun to..." Cal shook his head. "Why didn't you say something?!"

"I seem to recall that shortly before you disembarked you told me to 'shut up' sir," Kevin replied.

Cal almost choked. "Not for *fifty fonking years*!"

"You didn't specify, sir," Kevin said. "Perhaps that's something to keep in mind for the future. Not that I'm blaming you, you understand. I'm sure there are lessons we can both take away from the experience."

"But—"

"Especially you."

The *Untitled* rumbled as Loren fired up the thrusters. Cal wanted to say more to Kevin – a lot fonking more – but he settled for just glaring angrily for a few seconds, then he hurried to take his seat before Loren crashed them into a wall.

The chair felt familiar but slightly awkward when Cal lowered himself into it, like a chance meeting with an old fiancée. It squeaked as he wriggled from side to side, trying to find a comfortable position.

"You OK?" asked Loren, looking back over her shoulder.

"Fine. Just... It's weird, you know? Being back. It's like—"

Draped across her chair, Miz yawned theatrically. "I

mean, like, no offence, but how long are you going to keep going on about this stuff?"

"I've barely mentioned it!" Cal protested.

Miz snorted. "Tsh. Sure. You keep telling yourself that. You got old. You died. You're back. We get it. Move on."

Up front, Mech raised his eyebrows. "Hell, girl, even I think that's cold. The man's been through a lot."

"A *lot*," Cal agreed.

"Yeah, yeah, don't milk it," Mech told him.

Miz tutted. "Whatever. I just think—"

She swallowed the rest of the sentence as the *Untitled* shot backwards, clipped the edge of the landing bay floor, and backflipped out into space.

"Jesus!" Cal yelped, his knuckles turning white on his arm rests as the ship spiraled away from the *Odyssey*. "What was that?! What the fonk just happened?"

Loren didn't turn around.

"Loren? Was that... Tell me that wasn't you."

"I thought the landing brake was on," Loren admitted.

"God, I did not miss that," Cal wheezed. On screen, he caught a glimpse of the *Odyssey*, before it rolled away again as the *Untitled* flipped.

When the cruiser next appeared, something had happened to it. It was almost formless, like it was caught between a number of different shapes at the same time.

By the time the *Untitled* had completed another spin, the *Binto Odyssey* had never existed.

Kind of.

"Well, that's that, I guess," said Cal in the silence that followed.

"Wait. What's that?" said Mech, pointing ahead. The ship rolled backwards away from whatever it was, and they had to wait until it had done another full revolution before they saw what he'd spotted.

It was a glass. A glass that looked *very* similar to the one Loren had dropped in the food court.

"Smashdown," Cal whispered. Draped over his shoulders, Splurt shuddered at the mention of the word. "Jesus, can *nothing* destroy that fonking thing?" Cal wondered.

There was a *clunk* as the glass collided with the front of the ship. Cal watched in silence as it rolled all the way up the view screen, then floated off into space, completely undamaged.

"Son of a..." he mumbled. He briefly contemplated having Kevin shoot the damn thing with the cannons, but there was a more pressing issue to deal with first. "Hey, Loren, not sure if you've noticed, but we're currently somersaulting through space. Maybe you could do something about that when you get a chance. No rush."

"Yeah, yeah," said Loren.

"Although, ideally, before I throw up."

"Just give me a—"

"Too late!" Cal announced. Clamping a hand over his mouth he jumped up from his chair. The seatbelt had something to say about that, though, and quickly slammed him back down.

"Nng!"

Splurt grew a tendril and stabbed it at the belt release. Cal mumbled some sort of thanks then sprinted out into the main corridor, bouncing and staggering despite the artificial gravity.

The bathroom door flew open at his approach, but it was too late. As the door slid open, Cal's guts unleashed their full fury. A thick soup of half-digested space vegetable was forcibly ejected from his mouth in a concentrated spray of vomit.

To Cal's surprise, there was someone else in the bathroom. To their surprise, they suddenly found themselves plastered with a torrent of warm puke.

"Well," said the Time Titan, scooping Cal's stomach contents from his eyes and flicking a semi-digested piece of space carrot off his beard. "I suppose I really should've seen that coming."

ELEVEN

The Time Titan explained that Cal shouldn't worry, as he could simply rewind his personal time line to a point where he *hadn't* just been projectile vomited on, and everything would be fine.

He *could* do that, but he wouldn't, because mucking around with the time stream – *any* time stream – usually brought with it some quite cataclysmic repercussions. Instead, he had a shower, borrowed a pair of pants and a Philadelphia Eagles shirt from Cal – both of which were several sizes too large – and then joined the crew on the bridge.

The *Untitled* had stopped spinning and was now hanging more or less completely stationary in space, since no-one had any real idea where to go or what to do next. Everyone – even Miz – turned as Tim shuffled onto the bridge in his oversized clothes, his hair and beard all puffed out and frizzy from being dried.

"Hello again," Tim said. "That's better. Nice shower you have. Very powerful. Gets into all the nooks and crannies. Right up there."

Miz turned her chair to the front again, went back to picking her fingernails, and pretended she hadn't just heard any of that.

"Uh, yeah. Well that's a horrifyingly visual image," said Cal. "Now, uh... You're on our ship."

Tim nodded and smiled. "Yes."

Cal nodded and smiled back. "Aaaand you're on our ship because...?"

"You said you could help me," Tim reminded him. A shadow of anxiety passed across his face. "You *can* help me. Yes?"

"Help you? Well, I mean... Yeah. Yeah, I'm sure we can help you. Right, guys?" said Cal.

"Help him do what?" Mech asked.

"Help you do what?" asked Cal, feeling the need to pass on the message.

"Well... you know."

Cal turned to Mech. "You know."

"Why are you repeating what we say? I can hear the man just fine," Mech said. He addressed Tim directly. "No, we don't know."

"We don't know," Cal confirmed.

"What do you want us to do?" Mech finished.

Cal opened his mouth, but Mech jabbed a finger at him. "Don't. I mean it. Just don't."

"I wasn't going to," Cal said.

"Yes. Yes, you were."

"Guys!" snapped Loren. She glared at them both, then focused on Tim again. "Sorry about them. You were saying?"

"The bomb," said Tim.

Loren blinked. "Sorry?"

"I believe he said, 'the bomb,' ma'am," said Kevin.

"What about the bomb?" asked Cal. "We told you, it wasn't us."

"No. And I believe you. I trust you completely," said Tim.

"Well *thank you*, Timbo. That means a lot," said Cal.

"Also, I scanned through your time lines and checked," Tim continued. "Can't be too careful."

"Oh. OK," said Cal. "That means a little less, but... go on."

"I want you to help me find out who made the bomb, then assist me in bringing them to justice."

Mech's eyes narrowed. "What's in it for us?"

"Hey, come on, Mech!" said Cal. "The guy's here pouring his heart out and asking us for help. What are you, a monster?"

Mech shifted awkwardly, but said nothing. Cal shook his head reproachfully, then turned back to the Time Titan. "I mean, I assume there *is* something in it for us, yes?"

"Oh yes!" said Tim.

"Great!" He stood and extended a hand. "Then you, my friend, have got a—"

"The satisfaction of knowing that you've helped ensure the continued stability of the time stream."

"*—fonking nerve* sneaking onto our ship and laying this shizz at our door," Cal concluded, turning his would-be handshake into an reproachful point. "Satisfaction doesn't pay the bills, Timbo. So, much as we'd love to help..."

"You don't understand," said Tim. Even without the gizmo he'd worn on his neck earlier, his voice reverberated around the *Untitled*. Cal stepped back and lowered himself into his seat again. Tim took a breath, composing himself, before continuing in his normal voice.

"The kind of technology required to do what was done

aboard that cruiser – the kind of *power* it must have taken... I've never known anything like it."

Cal swiveled his hips, making his chair swing from left to right. "Well, that's very interesting, Tim, but I don't see what it has to do with us."

"What if it happens in a city next time? A school?" Tim asked. "What if someone detonates such a device in the heart of a sun? Whole systems could be wiped out. Billions could die. Or worse, might never have lived. Would you want that on your conscience?"

Cal shrugged. "It's not our problem, so it wouldn't be on our conscience."

"I can see back along your time line, Cal. I can see what makes you who you are," said Tim. "We both know full well that it would. It would be on all of your consciences."

Miz flicked her eyes up from her fingernails. Tim didn't look at her, but pointed, just briefly. "Less so her."

Splurt rippled around Cal's neck. "And I have no idea about that thing," Tim admitted.

Cal drummed his fingers on his arm rests. He rubbed his tongue across the front of his teeth. It was nice having all of them back. He'd missed those little guys.

Swinging his chair, he turned to face the others. "What do you say, guys? Want to help save the Universe?"

Tim gave a half-chuckle. "Well, I'm not sure it's quite—"

"At-at-at!" went Cal, holding up a finger. "Timbo, I'm trying to help you sell this shizz here. Best if you don't interfere."

"Right. Yes. Sorry," said Tim.

"Can you just stand there for the new couple of minutes and maybe not listen?" Cal asked him.

Tim blinked. "Not listen?"

"Put your fingers in your ears or something," said Cal. "It'll just take a minute."

The Time Titan looked down at his unfamiliar clothes for a moment. "But—"

"Just cover your ears, already!" Miz snapped.

Tim jumped in fright, then clamped his hands over the sides of his head.

His pants, which he had been holding up, fell down. Everyone on the bridge – including Splurt, and very possibly Kevin, although it was hard to know for sure – stared.

"I tried to warn you that would happen," Tim said, his voice a little louder than normal.

Nobody replied for a while, then Cal closed his hanging-open mouth. "Jesus. OK. My fault. Uh, maybe just go out into the corridor?"

"What?"

"*Go into the corridor*!" Cal shouted.

"Right-o," said Tim. He turned, hands still clamped over his ears, pants still around his ankles, and shuffled off the bridge, his butt cheeks only half-hidden by his too-long football shirt.

Once the door had closed, Cal turned back to the others. "Holy fonk!" he exclaimed. "Did you see the size of that guy's wang? It was *huge*."

Loren shook her head curtly. "Can't say I noticed."

"How could you not notice?" Cal asked. "I thought he had three legs at first! Jesus." Leaning back in his chair, he jabbed a thumb in the direction of the door. "No wonder that guy can bend time and space. His penis probably does it all on its own."

Loren shook her head again. Her blueish skin had taken on a purple tinge around the cheeks. "Can we talk about the bigger issue here?"

"Trust me, 'issues' – if that's what you kids are calling it these days – they don't get much bigger than that one." Cal puffed out his cheeks. "I mean, where does he keep it? No wonder he wears a dress."

"Can we please stop talking about—"

"I'm amazed he doesn't need a fonking wheelbarrow."

"OK! He has a big... member," said Loren. "Good for him. Let's move on. Are we going to help him or not?"

"I'm starting to think we should," said Cal. "If we hang around with him, maybe his enormous wang will rub off on me."

He replayed that sentence in his head.

"That didn't come out the way it was intended."

Loren rolled her eyes and turned to Mech. "What do you think?"

Mech nodded. "Yeah. It was pretty big."

"Not about that! Forget his penis."

Kevin's voice piped up. "Oh, I think it will be rather a long time before any of us can do that, ma'am," he said. "It's taking up a full trillionth of a per cent of my databanks."

Loren threw up her arms. "I give up."

"Which doesn't sound like much, now that I say it out loud, but it is," Kevin concluded.

"Want to know what I think?" asked Miz.

This took everyone by surprise. Miz rarely voiced her opinion willingly, unless it was in the form of withering comments about Loren's flying ability, landing techniques, or general personality.

"Are you thinking, 'If that's what it looks like when it's limp, then what the Hell does it look like...?'" Cal began, then he caught Loren's glare and swallowed the rest of the sentence before it could reach the end. He cleared his throat. "Because I'm definitely not thinking that."

"I'm thinking we should do it," said Miz. "We should, like, you know, help or whatever."

"*You do*?" said Cal, trying to hide the surprise in his voice, but failing completely. "I mean, you do, huh?"

"There were, like, kids on that ship," said Miz. She sounded distant, remembering something that had technically now never happened. Her voice became softer. Softer, Cal thought, than he'd ever heard it. "She had this dress on. She looked all, like, proud, or whatever."

Miz wriggled in her chair, suddenly uncomfortable as she realized the others were all staring at her. She shrugged, and her shields were suddenly up again. "But do what you want. I don't care," she said. "And yes, for the record, that thing was *huge*."

Cal dipped his head towards her in a nod of gratitude. "OK. Good contribution. Gold star for Miz. Mech? What do you think?"

"About the bomb thing. Not his penis," Loren made clear.

Cal sighed. "Loren, can we stop talking about the man's genitalia for a minute? We're having an important discussion here."

Loren's eyes widened for a moment, then became narrow slits of annoyance. She glared daggers at Cal, but he just smirked and kept his eyes on Mech.

"Sorry, Mech, you were saying?"

"You wanna know what I think? I think this whole thing is crazy," said Mech. "But I don't see how we got much choice. Like the man says... Weapon like that? Could rack up one nasty big body count."

"And he did restore you back to normal," Loren pointed out.

"To my *prime*," Cal corrected. He flexed his muscles to demonstrate, but it didn't really do much to prove whatever point he was trying to make.

"Either way," said Loren. "You kind of owe him one."

"I let him borrow my pants," said Cal.

"But not a belt, sir," Kevin pointed out.

"No. In hindsight, that was a bad call," Cal admitted. He shrugged. "Well, I guess this is happening. Space Team is saving the galaxy! Again." He thrust a hand up in the air. "Group high-five!" he cried, but there were no immediate takers. "Anyone? No?"

"I'm doing it, sir," Kevin informed him.

"Thanks, Kevin. Much appreciated," said Cal. "Anyone else?"

Splurt became an unsettlingly human-looking detached arm and held himself up in the air just as Cal had done.

"That's not *quite* what you're meant to... Know what? Forget it. Good job, you guys." He shot pointed looks at Mech, Loren and Miz. "Not *you* guys, who all let me down badly, but Splurt and Kevin, who did their best. And that's all I ask for."

He considered this. "Well, that and for Miz to stop opening the bathroom door when I'm in the shower, but that's it. Those two things are all I ask for."

He considered this, too.

"And your undying loyalty and respect. But other than that..."

"Just shut the fonk up and get the man back in here," Mech barked.

"Uh, before we do," Loren began. Her chair creaked

beneath her as she shifted her weight. "There's something... I mean..."

She felt the weight of everyone's gaze on her, tensed for a few seconds, then exhaled and relaxed. "It's fine." She caught Cal's eye. "We'll talk about it later."

"Is it about the toilet seat?" Cal asked.

"We'll talk about it later," she said again, then she turned back to the front and took a renewed interest in the controls.

Cal watched the back of her head for a while. "Uh. OK," he eventually said, then he turned to the door. "Kevin, open up so we can get Tim back in here."

"Very good, sir."

The door swished open. Cal and Mech – who were the only two currently looking in that direction – both hissed and grimaced simultaneously as they were met by the sight of Tim bending over and trying to retrieve his fallen pants. He still had his hands over his ears, so was having to do so using just his elbows, which was proving exactly as difficult as it probably sounds.

"Oh God! Oh God, no," Cal blurted.

Loren and Miz both turned to the door, then recoiled as if they'd been physically struck.

"Ew!" was all Miz had to say on the matter.

"Man, I did not need to see that," grunted Mech, turning away.

"How do you think I feel?" Cal asked. "At least you can have your brain reformatted!"

"I ain't a fonking robot," said Mech. He glanced back over his shoulder. "And why are you still looking?"

"Jesus, why *am* I still looking?" Cal wondered, quickly spinning his chair back to the front. "Kevin, get his attention and tell him he can take his hands away from his ears now."

"As you wish, sir."

"Also, were you recording any of what just happened?"

"All of it, sir."

"Then burn the footage and eject it into space," Cal ordered. "We do *not* want to stumble upon that again."

It took a minute or two for Kevin to convey the message to the Time Titan. Cal spent it with his eyes closed, trying to think of beaches or flowers or puppies or anything else that wasn't a half-naked elderly man's gently splayed buttocks.

When Tim finally returned to the bridge, hands gripping the waistband of his borrowed pants, everyone made a very deliberate effort not to meet his eye.

"So, uh, we had a chat, and we decided we'll help you out," Cal informed him. He was struck by an overwhelming urge to giggle, but bit his lip and managed to hold it in.

"That's tremendous news!" said Tim. "If you hadn't agreed, I'd have been in rather a tight spot."

"Right," Cal cheeped.

"Really in a hole."

Cal bit his lip harder. He heard Mech's shoulders rattle as the big cyborg tried to stop them shaking, and saw that Miz had a hand clamped over her mouth, holding it shut.

Cal nodded. "Mm-hmm."

"Shafted right up the—"

Cal was the first to go. He exploded in a fit of the giggles, which opened the floodgates for Mech, Miz and even Loren. The bridge echoed with the sound of their hysterics.

Tim watched them, bemused, as they all laughed until they cried.

"Did I miss something?" he asked.

It took Cal several seconds to pull himself together

enough to reply. "No. No, it's... *Oh, God,*" he wheezed. "Phew. No. No, it's nothing. We were just remembering a joke we were told once by..."

He was off again. He clutched his sides, his face turning purple as the harrowing hilarity of it all overcame him once more.

Four minutes later, when he and the others had finally laughed themselves out, Cal patted both sides of his face, stretched his jaw a few times, wiped away his tears, then risked meeting the Time Titan's gaze once again.

More laughter fluttered in his chest somewhere, but he managed to stamp it back down. "As I was saying, we've decided to help you out." He quickly held up a finger. "Please, don't say anything there."

"I wasn't going to."

"OK. Good. So, we've decided to help you out," Cal reiterated. "What do you need us to do?"

"Well, I suppose we should start by finding out who built the chronal weapon," Tim said. "As I say, I've never known of such technology. Whoever built it must be a genius."

Cal nodded. "So you thought you'd use a genius to catch a genius. I like your thinking, Timbo."

"You ain't no genius," Mech replied.

"Maybe not in the *traditional* sense of the word," Cal admitted. "But if we open up the criteria a little..."

"To include people who aren't geniuses?" asked Loren.

"Exactly!" said Cal. He frowned. "What were we talking about?"

"Using a genius to catch a genius," said Tim.

"Right! So we were."

"And we were also establishing that you ain't no genius," Mech added.

"You're right. I'm not," Cal conceded. He spun his chair to the front, a grin lighting up his face. "But we know a man who is!"

There was a long moment of silence.

"So, like, are you going to tell us who it is?" asked Miz.

Cal sighed. "That was supposed to be a big dramatic moment," he said. "Jesus. It's like you people have never even seen *Star Trek*..."

TWELVE

"ARE you sure you're hailing him?" Cal asked.

Mech muttered something quietly, then raised his voice. "Yes. Like I said eight times already, I'm sure I'm hailing him."

Cal tapped a fingernail on his arm rest and gazed down at the planet below. "Are you hailing on all frequencies?"

Mech turned from the screen. "Say what? What the fonk does that mean?"

"You know. Like, don't just hail him on one frequency, hail him on *all* frequencies."

"I'm hailing him on the motherfonking comms frequency. It's the only frequency we have."

Cal blinked in surprise. "We only have one frequency? That can't be right." He looked up to the ceiling. Splurt had disappeared up there somewhere an hour or so earlier, shortly after they'd entered warp, but that wasn't who Cal was looking to talk to. "Kevin?"

"Yes, sir?"

"Quick question. How many frequencies do we have?"

"I'm not sure. Would you like me to check?"

"Please."

"Very good, sir."

Cal clicked his tongue against the roof of his mouth while he waited.

"I'm telling you, man," said Mech, but Cal held up a hand for silence.

"Hold on. We'll get to the bottom of this."

They waited some more.

"Sixteen thousand, eight hundred and twenty-seven, sir," Kevin announced.

Cal leaned forward in his chair. "Ha!"

"No. Hang on."

There was another moment of silence.

"One, sir. Sorry, I was looking at the wrong column."

"God. Seriously?" asked Cal, sinking back in his seat. "Well... can we get more?"

"I told you, man. I told you I knew what I was doing, but you had to keep sticking your damn nose in. You couldn't just leave it in my hands."

"Quick question for *you* this time, Master Mech," said Kevin. "Did you mean to press the 'mute' button?"

Mech's smug expression froze on his face. His eyes darted to the console in front of him. "What? Uh. Yeah. Yeah, I meant to press the..."

He saw Cal. The grin he wore was almost slicing his whole face in two.

"Fonk you, shizznod!" Mech muttered, then he jabbed the button and went back to hailing on their one and only available frequency.

"You sure this is a good idea?" Loren asked, looking back over her shoulder at Cal. "This guy's pretty creepy."

"He's not creepy. He's just... eccentric."

"He made, like, a gajillion clones of himself," said Miz, not looking up from her fingernails. "That's pretty creepy."

"OK, yes, he's creepy. But he's also a genius. A creepy weirdo genius with a gajillion clones is still a genius, right? And we need a genius."

Cal spun in his chair until he faced Tim. The Time Titan was back in his own clothes now, his smock only lightly stained and very faintly smelling of vomit.

"This guy we're taking you to see, he's an inventor. He made this ship, actually. He also made Kevin, but don't let that put you off. He knows his stuff."

"He also had a whole big room full of weird monster versions of himself," Mech added.

"But again," said Cal, smiling. "Don't let that put you off. If anyone knows how to build a Time Bomb, it's..."

"Dorid Tarkula," said a voice from the screen. A younger version of the man they knew – another clone, unquestionably – stared out at them. "Who's calling, please?"

CAL and the others stood outside the tall doors of Castle Tarkula, listening to the sound of approaching footsteps on the other side. Splurt was sitting on Cal's shoulder, trembling almost imperceptibly.

"I know, buddy. I'm excited to see her, too," Cal said. "But we don't know if she's even still..."

The door opened, revealing a slight-framed young girl with red hair, pastel green skin and an array of raised white bumps that were dotted across her nose like freckles. Excitement shimmered in the piercing blue irises of her wide oval eyes, and despite what appeared to be a piece of industrial machinery clamped across her mouth, Cal could tell she was smiling.

"Soonsho!" he cried, then he was almost knocked off his feet when she slammed into him and wrapped her arms around his back. Splurt grew several arms of his own so he could get in on that action, and Cal's eyes bulged slightly as he was sandwiched between both their bodies.

After dragging herself away from Cal, Soonsho worked her way down the line, hugging Loren, Mech and – a little more warily – Mizette.

She stopped before Tim, her long red lashes blinking as she gazed up at him.

"Hello!" Tim said, a little uncomfortably. Soonsho stared at him in absolute silence. "Um... Interesting mouth thing."

"She's a Cantaloupe," Cal explained.

Mech tutted. "She's a Cantatorian."

"You sure?" asked Cal. "Then what's a Cantaloupe?"

"How the fonk should I know?"

Cal shot Mech a slightly patronizing half-smile. It was an expression he had spent a lot of time perfecting, and which was intended to suggest that Cal knew the person he was smiling at was wrong, but he was far too magnanimous to press the issue. It was one of his favorite expressions, because he knew how much it wound Mech up.

"She's a fonking Cantatorian!" the cyborg grunted.

"Sure she is, Mech. Whatever you say," said Cal.

He contemplated raising both eyebrows and chuckling wryly, but wondered if that was perhaps a step too far.

He did it, anyway. The way Mech's expression darkened told him he'd made the right decision.

"Anyway, she has a stupidly powerful voice."

"You mean like a singing voice?" Tim asked. "That's

what Cantatorians are famed for, isn't it? Their hypnotic song."

"I mean like a *one word will destroy mountains* voice. You know that planetary shield we almost hit? That was made using her voice. Or something. I didn't really listen to the details, but I'm pretty sure she was involved."

"We didn't almost hit it," Loren objected.

Miz sneered. "Then why were you screaming, 'Oh shizz, oh shizz, we're going to hit it!' over and over?"

Loren shifted her weight uncomfortably. "I was... being overly cautious. We weren't anywhere near it."

"We definitely were," called Kevin's voice from inside the *Untitled*. It was parked a few feet behind them, just inside the castle's courtyard walls, and a full fifth of a mile away from the clearly designated landing pad Loren had been aiming for.

"And... what?" asked Tim. He pointed to the gadget on Soonsho's face. "Is that to stop her talking?"

"No."

The word emerged from the mouth device as an oddly inhuman sounding synthesized voice, taking everyone by surprise.

"It's so I *can* talk."

Cal beamed at her. "Well, listen to you. A whole sentence, and our skeletons are still intact! Way to go, Soonsho! I guess this is working out pretty well for you, huh?"

"For both of us."

Dorid Tarkula – the original Dorid Tarkula, with his wrinkled-but-rosy cheeks and slightly stooped frame – stepped from the doorway with an almost imperceptible electronic whine. He wore a pair of what Cal could only describe as 'robot pants'.

Actually, there were lots of other ways he could've

described them, but of them all, 'robot pants' was by far his favorite.

"Dorid!" said Cal. This time there were no hugs – the guy had tried to kill them all with deformed clone-things, after all – but the old man didn't seem too disappointed.

"Greetings to you all," Dorid said, nodding at the group in general. He was a little out of breath, and a little more red-faced than usual. "What brings you back to Castle Tarkula? Problems with the ship?"

"Hmm? Oh, no," said Cal. "Well, I mean, there's Kevin... But no. The ship's great. We just need to ask you something."

"Oh. I see. Well, it's not the best time..."

"It'll only take a minute," Cal assured him.

Dorid glanced back into the castle, then pulled the doors closed. "Go on," he said.

"What do you know about Time Bombs?"

Dorid ran his tongue across the back of his teeth, considering the question. "Like with the clock on the front?"

"No, but great minds think alike," said Cal. He shot Mech a look that claimed victory for some imagined argument. "I mean like a bomb that... In fact, know what? I'm going to let Tim explain."

Cal beckoned Tim forward and made the introductions. "Dorid, this is Tim the Time Titan."

"It's just The Time Titan."

"Tim the Time Titan, this is Dorid Tarkula. And not just *a* Dorid Tarkula, *the* Dorid Tarkula. The original and – to my mind, at least – still the best."

While Cal had been speaking, Dorid had taken to looking Tim up and down. "Time Titan, you say?" He placed a thumb on Tim's cheek and pulled down, revealing the gooey red bit beneath his eyeball. "What does that involve, exactly?"

He pulled his hand away, as if only just realizing what it was up to. "Sorry. Force of habit. Used to being around clones all day."

"Think nothing of it," said Tim. "I quite enjoyed it, actually!"

An awkward silence fell.

Tim softly cleared his throat.

"I don't know why I said that," he muttered. "Nerves, probably. I'm not great with new people."

Cal clapped his hands together. "OK. Moving on. Yes, Dorid, Tim is a Time Titan. He has command over time and space."

"Just time," Tim corrected. "And I don't have 'command'. I just have a certain... influence."

"Whatever," said Cal. "The point is, he's asked for our help – it's another save the galaxy sort of a deal – and we thought you might be able to point us in the right direction."

There was a muffled *thud* from somewhere inside the castle. Soonsho's eyes darted anxiously to Dorid's, but he either didn't notice or deliberately didn't meet her gaze.

"What was that?" asked Miz.

"Nothing," said Dorid. "Continue."

Another *thud* came. This time, it was followed by a crash.

"It don't sound like nothing," said Mech.

"We're moving some equipment around. That's all," Dorid explained. "Quanturum."

Cal, who had been staring at the door like he was trying to see through it, shifted his attention back to Dorid. "Huh?"

"Quanturum. This 'Time Bomb' you speak of, I'm

assuming it is something built to catastrophically disrupt the time stream, yes?"

"That is correct," Tim confirmed.

"Then, if I were building such a device, I'd use Quanturum."

"What is that?" asked Cal. "Like a fabric softener?"

"Of course. Yes," said Tim, patting his beard like it was a much-loved pet. "Quanturum is a metal – an ore – with unique time-altering properties."

"In what way?" asked Loren.

"Think of it like a magnet," Dorid explained. "Only instead of attracting and repelling metal, it attracts and repels time."

"Obviously," said Cal, shooting Loren a withering look.

"Depending on its polarity, it can speed time up or slow it down," Dorid continued. "Although its effects are so infinitesimal as to be barely noticed." He nodded with the satisfaction that came from solving a puzzle. "Yes, if I were building a Time Bomb, I'd use Quanturum."

"OK. So where do we find this stuff?" Cal asked.

"Nowhere," said Tim. "It's dangerously unstable. It tore itself apart eons ago."

"Not *all* of it," said Dorid. "I'm aware of one remaining source. If someone did build a Quanturum bomb, then that had to be where they got it from."

"Well, that's convenient!" said Cal. "So, give us the address and we'll go check it out. We'll have this whole thing wrapped up by lunch time."

"I'm afraid it won't be that simple," Dorid began, then the doors behind him shook as something hit them from the other side.

"OK, that doesn't sound like someone moving equipment," said Loren, her hand slipping to her blaster.

Miz's ears had pricked all the way up now. "It isn't," she said. "Get back!"

The warning came just a fraction too late. The castle doors flew outwards, sending Dorid sprawling onto the rough, stony ground. Dozens of other Dorids – some just a little younger than the original, others barely out of their twenties – poured out of the exit, their faces fixed in masks of terror, their voices raised in alarm.

Grabbing the fallen Dorid by his feet, Soonsho heaved him out of the path of the stampeding clones. The old man coughed out his gratitude through a mouthful of gravel, then leaned on the girl as he got back to his feet.

"You got five seconds to explain what the fonk is going on!" Mech barked. "One."

"It wasn't my fault!" Dorid sobbed. "It should have worked. It made perfect sense."

"Two!" Mech continued. "Don't make me say 'three'."

"We thought it would protect them. Make them more resilient!"

"Three. Shizz, man, you went and made me do it!"

Soonsho put her hand on Mech's chest. "It was my idea," she said through her voice synthesizer. "I wanted to help."

"Four!"

"Help do what?" asked Cal.

A sound shuddered through the castle wall, shattering the brickwork and ejecting rubble several dozen feet through the air. The falling rocks *clanked* down on the *Untitled*, pitting the hull with dents and making a terrible mess of the paintwork.

"My ship!" Cal yelped.

"My house!" Dorid cried.

"Four-and-a-half!" Mech bellowed.

"Jesus, will you stop counting? No one is listening," said Cal. He spun and caught Dorid by the shoulders. "What is it? What did you make?"

A fist erupted from inside the castle, sending more of the brickwork crashing down on top of the *Untitled.*

"Ow," said Kevin from somewhere inside.

On the side of the fist, two misshapen eyes glared down, and a horribly stretched mouth pulled into a furious snarl.

"Th-that," Dorid whispered. "I'm afraid I made *that.*"

Mech's metal bottom jaw dropped open with a *clank.* Like the others, he gazed up at the huge face-fist, quietly wondering if this day could get *any* worse.

"Five," he muttered, then the fist hammered down on him, driving him three feet into the ground.

"Told you to stop counting," Cal said. He recoiled in horror as the thing's actual face appeared through the hole in the castle wall. It looked like someone had made a giant wax sculpture of Dorid's face, then accidentally left it on a radiator for forty minutes. The features all bled into one another, so it was impossible to tell where an eye ended and a nose began.

Loren groaned. "I'd say 'well there's something you don't see every day,' but we literally just fought a giant monster a few hours ago."

"Meh. Fifty odd years ago," said Cal. "Depends on your time line. Also, what do you mean 'we'? If memory serves, I totally fought that guy on my—"

Splurt yanked him to the ground as the fist became an open backhand that swept towards them. Loren dived clear, shoving Dorid and Tim ahead of her, while Miz and Soonsho scattered.

Cal let out an *oof* as he hit the dirt. The bottom of the

hand passed just inches above Cal's face. As it did, something wet and slimy slobbered across his skin.

"Did that... Did that thing fonking *lick* me?"

Splurt stretched towards the *Untitled* like a giant green slinky, pulling Cal along by the feet and introducing his head to a number of large rocks.

"Ow! Fonk! Hey, buddy, I thought – Jesus, that's going to leave a mark – you were supposed to be on my side?"

Closer to the castle, Mech heaved himself out of the hole and primed his arm blasters. "So, that's how you want to play it, huh? You want to bring the rough stuff, you ugly fonk? I can bring it right back."

He raised both arms. The face-fist crunched into him, sending him somersaulting across the courtyard. There was a screech of bending metal as he hit a gun turret that had been in the process of rising up out of the ground.

"Castle defenses initiated," it announced. "Commencing fire."

The turret spat laser blasts up at the monster, making it thrash furiously. This did the castle wall no favors, and Cal was just able to hear Kevin's despondent *sigh* as yet more rubble collapsed on top of the *Untitled*.

"It's not working," cried Loren, drawing her own blaster and opening fire on the monster. "We're just getting on its nerves."

"It's sonically shielded," Dorid explained. "I incorporated some of Soonsho's DNA into the clone formula. I thought if my clones could be provided with organic sound-based attack and defensive capabilities, it might help if we ever found ourselves under assault by invaders."

"And how did that work out for you?" asked Cal. "Because from where I'm standing, it... Wait." He frowned as he replayed Dorid's sentence in his head. "Attack?"

The mouth on the thing's fist opened and a blast of concentrated sound obliterated the top half of the gun turret. Mech had taken only a glancing blow, but it was enough to drive him back into the turret's wreckage and scramble several of his less heavily-shielded systems.

His legs spun so they faced backwards. One of the rocket boosters in his left foot briefly ignited. He said the word, "Prong!" loudly, and for reasons he didn't understand.

"OK, I was going easy," Mech grunted. "But now we're gonna do things the hard way."

Grabbing the dial on his chest, Mech gave it a three-quarters twist. His limbs hummed with the additional power, as his eyes became duller and more distant. "Now Mech fight!"

The giant hand caught him by the head. With a sudden flick, he found himself hurtling upwards at speeds that would have killed anything not principally made of a semi-indestructible metal alloy.

With his brainpower muted, Mech's first thought was that he was going to fly all the way up into space and keep on going. His second thought was, 'Ooyah!' as he smashed against the roof of an invisible dome shield. This was quickly followed by his third thought – 'Waaaaaargh!' – as he plummeted back in the direction of the ground.

"Splurt, break his fall!" Cal cried.

The little green ball became a much larger green limb.

"My word," gasped Tim. "That's... that's impossible."

"You think this is impressive? You should see his Dorothy out of—"

A screech from the Dorid monster's fist shook the ground beneath them. For a moment, the soundwave was practically visible as it emerged from the twisted aperture and vibrated through the air.

Another sound followed, just barely audible over the piercing squeal of the monster. It was the fast, sudden *squelch* of Splurt exploding.

The shockwave of sound tore through his still-gelatinous form, scattering him into a thousand individual blobs that splattered across the ground, and across the faces of Cal, Tim and the others.

For a moment, the world stopped turning.

Cal stared. Not at anything in particular. He just stared.

Loren looked from Cal to all the little green smears that had been Splurt.

Had been.

Past tense.

Several feet away, Mech hit the ground with a *crunch* and quite a lot of swearing.

Miz grimaced. "Ew. Like, he's in my fur."

"Splurt?" whispered Cal, scooping a blob of green mush off his cheek and addressing it directly. "Buddy?"

He had hoped for a tiny pair of eyes to appear in the goo, but the Splurt chunk didn't respond. All around them, all over the ground, the Splurt chunks didn't respond.

"No, no, no, no!" Cal spat, dropping to his knees with a soggy *thunk*. Bits of Splurt were all around him, like blobs of congealing grease. He frantically pulled them towards himself, smooshing them together on the ground between his knees. "No, no, come on, buddy. Come on!"

"Cal," said Loren. She put a hand on his back, but he shrugged it away. "Cal," she said again. "It's no good."

Cal stopped scooping. The pile of goo he had assembled between his knees oozed outwards until it was nothing but a shallow puddle.

"It killed Splurt," Cal whispered. He deposited a single

lifeless handful of slime on his shoulder, then slowly got to his feet, his fingers curving into fists. "That thing just killed Splurt!"

Miz looked up from where she was picking bits of the little guy out of her fur. "Wait, what?"

"The shield," yelped Dorid. "We must lower the shield."

"What?" asked Loren, finally tearing her eyes away from the green smears on the ground around them. "What shield?"

"Castle defenses," Dorid explained. "In an emergency such as this, a dome shield seals in the whole castle, preventing anything getting in or out of the grounds. We must lower it. We must get away."

He gasped as Cal's hand caught him by the front of his apron and yanked him closer. "Drop that shield, and I'll kill you," Cal warned. There was no polished charm in his voice now, no well-rehearsed smile on his face. "That son-of-a-bedge is staying in here with me."

THIRTEEN

The Dorid clones had all fled around to the back of the castle, away from the imminent dangers of being stepped on, crushed by rubble, or screamed into a gelatinous paste. The dial-shifted Mech had finally figured out where his feet were and was now in the process of remembering how they worked.

The *Untitled* was half-buried, the monster was mostly free, and Splurt... Well, Splurt was still a number of gloopy stains on the landscape.

And Cal was out for blood.

"Soonsho, scream this melty-faced motherfonker down," he barked, jabbing a finger up at the Dorid-Beast.

Soonsho reached for the device strapped across her face, but Dorid caught her wrist, stopping her. "No! It's sonically shielded. If Soonsho hits it, the resultant sound explosion will be cataclysmic."

"Then what do we do?" Cal demanded. "How do I kill it?"

"I don't... I'm not sure you can," Dorid said.

"Challenge accepted," said Cal. He pointed with both

hands. "Miz. Mech. Keep it busy. Loren, with me. Everyone else get the fonk out of the way."

Miz hesitated. The Dorid-monster was *huge*. Stupidly huge.

"Like, what are we supposed to do?" she asked.

Cal stopped, mid-turn. "That thing killed Splurt," was all he said. It was all he had to.

"We'll think of something," Miz replied. "Go."

She turned in time to see Mech launch himself through one of the few intact parts of the castle wall, his body punching a hole through it like a wrecking ball. He brought both fists smashing down on one of the creature's feet, and the air crackled as if in the throes of an electrical storm.

Miz shrugged. "OK, let's try that," she said, then she snapped out her claws, bounded towards the castle on all fours, and pounced through a gap in the rubble.

Meanwhile, Cal dragged Loren up the ramp and into the *Untitled*.

"What are we doing?" Loren asked.

"We're going to blow that giant piece of shizz to Kingdom Come," Cal said. He was oddly matter-of-fact about it. It didn't sound like a threat, merely a statement that this thing was about to happen, and that was that.

Loren stopped at the gun cabinet, but Cal pulled her on. "Not with those," he said, then he raced ahead onto the bridge and dropped into his seat. "Kevin. Guns."

"Which guns, sir?"

"All of them."

"If we're shooting something, sir, perhaps it would be best if I did the—"

"No. This one's mine," Cal said. "Guns. Now."

He sat back and straightened, then watched from the corner of his eye as his headrest unfolded around him and the two spiked prongs of the weapons interface *boinged* free.

Loren joined him on the bridge. The *Untitled* was facing away from Castle Tarkula, so there was no sign of the monster. Instead, all she could see was the rolling black landscape stretching off into the distance, the faint shimmer of the shield dome, and a not-insubstantial amount of rubble.

"We're using the ship? How can we use the ship?" Loren asked. "We can't take off with the dome there, and we're facing the wrong way."

"No, we're not," Cal told her. "You're going to toast that fonking thing with the thrusters, while I kill it with torpedoes."

"Missiles, sir," Kevin corrected.

"Whatever they're called!" Cal snapped.

"Missiles," Kevin repeated. "It's definitely missiles."

"Kevin, will you just shut the fonk—?"

The needles pierced Cal's temples and poured silky blackness into his brain. One moment, he was sitting in chair, the next he was hovering in mid-air, gazing out at that rolling landscape of black.

Looking back over his shoulder, he saw the Dorid-thing. It hopped on the spot, hissing and snarling as it slapped at the hairy figure currently clinging to his inner thigh with her razor-sharp claws.

"Tell them to get clear!" Cal instructed.

The sentence was repeated a second later, amplified by the *Untitled*'s external speaker system. Miz glanced back then dropped out of sight behind a pile of rubble. It exploded outwards and Mech crashed through, with Mizette bounding along behind him.

"They're out of the way. Loren, light it up!"

The *Currently Untitled*'s rear thrusters ignited, filling Cal's view with a haze of brilliant blue. The Dorid-monster stumbled back, its already melted flesh becoming even more so.

Cal raised his hands. They weren't his real hands, he knew, just some digital representation of his digits through which he could manipulate the ship's weapons. Assuming, of course, he could remember how. It had been a long time, after all. An entire lifetime, in fact.

"Just like riding a bike," he said, then he thrust his hands forward and roared in triumph.

Nothing happened.

"Shizz. Wait. Hang on. I got this," he said. He drew both hands back to his hips, then shoved them forward again. The movement closely mirrored one of the signature attacks from the *Street Fighter II* video game. Any other time, Cal would have been unable to resist the urge to shout, "Hadoken!" at the top of his voice, but not today. Not now. There were no jokes to be made, no laughs to be had. Splurt was dead, and this fonk was going to pay.

Nothing happened. Even when Cal threw a series of open-palmed jabs at the monster in front of him, nothing happened.

"Should I switch them on now, sir?" Kevin asked.

"What? They're not on?"

"Not yet, sir, no. It would have been a most peculiar question for me to ask if they were already—"

"Yes! Switch them on!"

Cal felt his hands hum with power. He flexed his fingers and tendrils of purple energy crackled between them.

This was more like it.

Before he could fire, a scream from the monster flipped

the *Untitled* over, slamming it against the shield and making all the rubble slide off it like snow from a thawing rooftop. A beam of cannon-fire erupted from the palm of Cal's hand, struck the top of the dome, then punched through what was left of the castle roof.

"Shizz. Loren, straighten us out!"

"Trying!" Loren called back. She twisted the controls and the ship's nose woodpeckered against the ground. "I am *not* going to miss shizz like this," she muttered.

"You can say that again," said Cal, then he frowned. "Wait, what?"

Another scream pounded them. Metal groaned as the ship was squashed between the shield and the sound waves. Cal tried to take aim at the creature, but their current angle made it impossible for him to turn far enough.

He could only watch as the thing kicked free of the now mostly collapsed castle. Could only watch as it *squelched* through the slick green sheen on the ground that had, until recently, been the best friend he'd ever had. Could only watch as its mouth opened wide and its vocal chords constricted and...

There was a sound.

No, not a sound, an *emotion* that poured in through Cal's ears, turning his anger and grief into something purer. Something better.

Cal went from confusion to fear in a heartbeat. Confusion about where the sound was coming from, and fear that it would end – that it would just suddenly stop – and he wouldn't be able to hear it or feel it or experience it ever again.

Overriding them both, though, was joy. Joy that he *was* experiencing this sound now. Joy that he was alive enough, even if only for this one moment, to hear what he now heard, feel what he now felt, know what he now knew.

Peace. Utter, absolute peace.

From his partially upside-down viewpoint, Cal saw Soonsho standing before the monster, the metal mouthpiece still fixed to her face. The sound was emerging from within the mask, beautiful despite the electronic edge to it. Or perhaps even more so because of it.

"Miss Sooss appears to be singing, sir," said Kevin.

"Yuh," said Cal, the word dribbling half-formed from his lips.

"It's not bad, I suppose," Kevin continued. "You know, if you like that sort of thing."

"Yuh."

The Dorid monster had stopped thrashing around now. It stood perfectly still, gazing in rapt wonder at the teenage girl standing before it, singing her heart out.

Without the pressure of the beast's sound waves holding it in place, the *Untitled* dropped back onto its legs. The impact shuddered through the ship, the *clang* drowning out Soonsho's song long enough for Cal to snap out of his trance.

He felt an ache where the song had been, and realized Soonsho had stopped singing. He watched as Miz dragged her clear, then saw Mech give him a thumbs up.

"Kill that motherfonker!"

Cal didn't need to be told twice. Raising a hand in the monster's direction he poured all his anger and hurt and hatred into a single powerful blast.

He wasn't sure what he'd fired, exactly, but it had precisely the effect he'd hope for. A teardrop-shaped bolt of energy punched straight through the Dorid-thing's chest, slap bang where it's heart should be.

Its twisted horror-show of a face went slack. The face-hand poked gingerly at the almost perfectly circular hole through its torso.

And then, like a great oak before a woodcutter's axe, the monster toppled backwards and crashed through what was left of Castle Tarkula.

"Excellent shooting, sir!"

"Thanks, Kevin," said Cal. He watched with a sense of grim satisfaction as the monster hit the ground.

"I mean, you have just crushed to death all the clones who were hiding back there, obviously."

"What?" Cal gasped and clamped a hand to his mouth. "Oh, *shizz*. Did I?"

"I'm afraid so, sir."

"What is it with you and killing those guys?" Loren asked.

"I don't do it on purpose!" Cal protested.

"You shot the first two we met in the face," said Loren, reminding him of their original visit to the castle.

"No, I happened to shoot and their faces got in the way. That's a very different thing," Cal explained. He winced. "Seriously, Kevin? All of them?"

"Actually, no, sir. One of them might well pull through," said Kevin.

There was a moment of silence.

"Ah. No. No, he didn't."

"Fonk. OK, my bad!" said Cal, raising his voice in the hope that Dorid and the others heard him.

"It appears death is rather upon this place today, sir," Kevin intoned. "You know what with Master Sp—"

"Kevin!" Loren snapped. "Stop talking."

Cal, who was still a digital projection floating in the air outside the ruins of Castle Tarkula, picked a random puddle of green goo to stare at. He wasn't sure what he hoped to achieve by this, short of full reanimation, but he felt like there was *some* purpose to it, even if he didn't understand the details.

"Get me out of here," he said, then the spikes withdrew themselves from his skull and after a disconcerting moment when he felt like he existed in two different places at the same time, he found himself back in the ship.

Unclipping his belt, Cal hurried off the bridge and along the corridor. He stopped at the hatch, leaned against the wall to support himself, then took a deep, steadying breath.

The blob of goo was still partly on his shoulder, but mostly oozing down his front. He tried scooping it back up again, but it was practically liquid now, and seeped through his fingers like long strings of snot.

"Oh, buddy," he whispered. His voice cracked.

Curling his fingers until the nails dug into his palms, Cal shook his head, straightened up, and strode down the ramp. Habit made him pull together a smile, but it was a thin and unconvincing thing, and it fell away just as quickly as it had appeared.

Miz and Mech stood with Soonsho and Tim. Of them all, it was only Mech who was able to meet his eye. He nodded at Cal, just once, his eyebrows raised in something like an apology. Cal returned the nod, then continued to where Dorid was standing.

His teeth gritted.

His fist drew back, apparently of its own free will.

Cal managed to wrestle the urge to punch the old man in the face to something of a draw. Rather than right-hook him to the ground, he instead delivered a solid thump to his upper arm that was probably more shocking than painful.

"H-hey!" Dorid protested.

"You did this!" Cal roared. "You killed Splurt."

"I didn't mean to," Dorid replied, gingerly rubbing his arm. "It was an accident, an experiment gone wrong. No-one else was even supposed to be here."

"And what would you have done if we hadn't been?" Cal demanded. "Huh? What would you have done then? Let it kill you? Kill Soonsho? Whatever the fonk else lives on this shizzhole planet?"

Soonsho's electronic tones came from somewhere behind him. "It wasn't his fault. It was my idea."

Cal spun. "Yeah? *Yeah*?" he demanded. His expression and tone forced Soonsho back a step in fright. Cal felt his momentum stutter then collapse. "Well, it was a stupid idea. You know, whatever it was."

He stood there for a while, waiting for his blood pressure to return to normal, and feeling increasingly guilty for his outburst.

"I may have accidentally killed all your clones," he admitted.

Dorid winced, but then put a brave face on it. "That's fine. Apology accepted."

"I wasn't apologizing," Cal told him.

Mech appeared beside them. He cleared his throat. "Uh... You do realize...?" he said, pointing to the ground.

Cal looked down and discovered he was standing in a puddle of green goo. "Aw, shizz!" he groaned, quickly picking his way back to dry land. He stopped by Mech, and they both watched Cal's footprints slowly smooth over until they were no longer visible.

A hand touched Cal stiffly on the back. He could feel the claws even through his jacket. Mizette said nothing. She didn't have to.

"I know, Miz," Cal said, nodding at some unspoken truth that had passed between them. "I know."

"I feel like it's partly my fault," Mech said. "If he hadn't been coming to catch me..."

Cal shook his head. "You shouldn't think like that, Mech. It isn't partly your fault."

"Thanks, man."

"It's *mostly* your fault," Cal said.

"*What?*"

Cal managed a smirk. Just a small one, but it was a start. "You made that too easy."

"Yurk!"

They all looked back to see Loren skidding in a pile of Splurt, her eyes wide in panic, her arms flapping frantically as she tried to stay upright.

"Like, have some respect," Miz told her.

"I didn't mean to— Erk! Fonk, this stuff's slippy."

The others all faced front again and waited until she eventually arrived beside Mech.

"I mean... Can he die?" Miz wondered. "Because, like, I totally didn't think he could."

"Everything dies," said the Time Titan. He stood on the other side of the puddle, his hands crossed respectfully in front of his smock.

"Wait. You," said Cal. He pointed across the puddle. "You can bring him back. You can rewind his time line, or whatever you do. You can fix him!"

"I'm afraid I can't," said Tim. "I said before there was something unusual about it."

"*Him,*" Cal corrected. "About *him.*"

"Sorry. Yes. About him. It wasn't until I saw him change size that I realized what it was."

"He's, like, a shapeshifter," said Miz.

Tim shook his head. "No, not that. Shifting shape is one thing, but growing the way he did. Increasing one's mass to such an extent. Well, that defies reason. And physics."

"I said that," Mech announced. "Right? I said that before. How does he grow? It don't make sense."

"One of the few advantages of my role is I can see things that others cannot," said Tim. "And what I saw when it... when *he* grew... Well, I've never seen anything quite like it."

Cal was in no mood to beat around the bush. "How?"

"He borrows from himself," Tim explained. Although 'explained' what quite a generous description of it.

"He what?" asked Loren.

"Not from his current self, but from past or future versions of himself. He borrows matter *through time*."

"Borrowed," Cal said. The matter-of-fact way in which he said it surprised even him. "He borrowed matter through time."

"Oh. Yes. Well..." said Tim, but he didn't really go anywhere with it. "The point is, there's nothing I can do."

A hot, oppressive sort of quiet fell. Nobody knew quite what to say, and it fell to Loren to break the silence.

"So, what do we do with him?" she asked. "Do we bury him? Launch him into space?"

"Keep him in a jar..." Miz suggested. It was hard to tell if she was being entirely serious or not, but she certainly appeared to be.

"It'd have to be one fonking big jar," said Mech, indicating the puddles all around them.

"We wouldn't have to keep all of him," Miz explained. "Just, like, a handful, or whatever. We could scoop some of him up and—"

"We're not keeping him in a jar," Cal said. "No-one's scooping him up."

"Well, like, what then?" Miz asked.

Cal squatted down. "I don't know," he admitted.

"Because we can't just—"

"I don't know!" Cal said, more firmly this time. He could almost hear Miz's hackles rise, but he didn't care. So what if she was angry? It didn't matter. Nothing much of anything mattered now.

Cal made a cup shape with his hand and picked up some of the gooey puddle. He watched it drizzle like snot between his fingers.

"God, we'd been through so much, you know?" said Cal. "How many times did he save me? Did he save all of us?"

"A lot, man," said Mech.

"And now he's a fonking puddle," Cal said. He exhaled slowly. "I can't believe I'm not going to see that face again. Well... I mean, not *face*, exactly. Eyes, or... You know what I'm trying to say."

"Yes," said Loren. She put a hand on his shoulder. "We know."

Cal placed his own hand on top of hers and their fingers interlocked. He looked up to the sky and closed his eyes for a moment, composing himself.

"Splurt, buddy," he began, then the puddle of goo erupted upwards like a drowning swimmer breaking the surface for one final frantic breath. It spun upwards into a tumbling tangle of slimy tendrils, whipped at the air for several frenzied seconds, then compacted together with a gloopy *kurschlopp*.

A green blob, a little smaller than a basketball, plopped

onto the ground at Cal's feet. Two eyes gazed up at him, unblinking on account of having no eyelids to speak of.

Cal and the others all gazed in disbelief. After a moment, Cal flicked the slimy residue from his fingers. "Ew," he muttered, then: "*Splurt!*"

Snatching up the little guy, Cal held him at arm's lengths, spinning around and around, tears and laughter and snot and surprise all ejecting themselves through various parts of his face in turn. He pulled Splurt in close then, and they sort of danced together on the spot, cheek to blobby cheek. Admittedly, it was Cal who did most of the dancing, but it was obvious that Splurt was enjoying himself if you knew what to look for.

"Don't you ever do that to me again!" Cal told him. "You hear me? Don't you ever almost sort of die on me again."

"Should've known he'd be back," said Miz. She reached over and gave Splurt a half-hearted pat. "Between you and now Splurt, seems like no one on this team ever really dies."

"You'd better believe it," said Cal, his grin coming back broader than ever. "Although I do now feel even more guilty about killing all those clone guys. Is that weird?"

"You flattened dozens of people with a monster," Mech pointed out. "No, feeling guilty ain't weird. In fact, I'd say it's pretty fonking mandatory."

He half-smirked, then gave Splurt a gentle *dunt* with a metal fist. "Glad you're OK, little guy."

Splurt's eyes shook from side to side with the impact but they still somehow managed to look grateful, nonetheless.

Cal deposited Splurt on his shoulder. The little blob grew, just a fraction, as he sucked up the smear of goo that had been keeping his spot warm for him.

Turning, Cal addressed the rest of the group. "Well,

all's well that ends well, I guess. Another Space Adventure is over, and we've once more..."

He faltered.

"Wait. What did we do?"

"We ain't done nothing yet," Mech said.

Cal raised his eyebrows. "Seriously? Nothing? Because it feels like we've done quite a *lot*." He began to count on his fingers. "So, getting old, coming here..." He clicked his tongue against the roof of his mouth a few times. "Actually, I guess that's pretty much it. Jesus, we have done nothing. We need to hurry this up. What's the plan?"

"Well..." Loren began.

"Time bomb! That was it!" said Cal. He looked to the others for confirmation. "Right?"

"We identified the location of a Quanturum deposit," confirmed Tim.

"There we go!" Cal said. "I mean, I don't exactly know what – if anything – we're actually going to do with that information, but it's a start."

"We should go check it out," said Mech. "Maybe there'll be, you know, clues or something."

"Boom! Yes! Thank you, Spacelock Holmes," Cal said. He smiled, quite proudly. "You like that one? Because, like, *Space Sherlock Holmes* is too much. It's overly complicated."

"I don't know who that is," Mech pointed out.

"No, I know, but... Spacelock Holmes," Cal said again, mostly just because he liked it. He shrugged. "Anyway, clues. We should go check out the Quantrus thing."

"Quanturum," Tim corrected.

"And that. We'll check that, too."

Skipping across to Soonsho, Cal gave her a hug. "You know you can come with us, right?"

"I know," she replied. "And thank you. But I'll stay. For now."

"Fair enough," said Cal. "But you shout if you need us. Chances are we'll hear you even if we're on the other side of the galaxy."

He moved on to Dorid. "Sorry for the dead arm. And, you know, for killing all those others yous. And partially destroying your castle."

"All my own fault," Dorid assured him. "Well, maybe not the arm..."

"We'd stay to help you rebuild, but..." He reached for a suitably diplomatic end to the sentence, but came up short. "I don't really want to."

Dorid chuckled. "Thank you for your honesty."

"Hey. Any time."

Once the others had said their goodbyes, Cal bounded up the ramp ahead of them. "Come on, we haven't got all day," he said, hurrying them on. "Places to go, clues to find, galaxies to save."

Soonsho and Dorid retreated a few paces, picking their way over a mound of rubble, then watched as the *Untitled*'s landing ramp raised and its take-off thrusters ignited. It was quite breathtaking, really. The ship rose gracefully, churning the dust up in great clouds below it as it took off into the—

CLUNK. It hit the semi-transparent dome protecting the castle, scraped upwards along it for about forty feet, then plunged almost all the way to the ground. Even through the ship's hull and over the roar of the thrusters, they heard Cal's screams.

A moment later, a speaker on the underside of the ship crackled and Loren's voice emerged. "Uh, could you lower the shield, please?"

Dorid fumbled in his pocket until he found a palm-sized remote control. He pressed a button and the shield shimmered away into nothing.

"Thanks!" said Loren, then the *Untitled* rocketed upwards and became just another far-off star in the darkening evening sky.

FOURTEEN

Cal stood in the *Untitled's* kitchen, alternating between flattering and punching the shizz out of the food replicator.

"Look, I know you can hear me," he told it. "Surely you can't be *completely* empty? What about, like, one jelly bean? A single jelly bean, color of your choosing?" He thumped himself on the chest a few times, psyching himself up for the several seconds of unpleasantness the machine put him through whenever he asked it for something new. "Do it. Let's go, you beautiful big bamston."

The replicator's lights pulsed faintly. They had been pulsing faintly since it had produced that tiny banoffee pie slice, though, so this didn't bode well for anything exciting being about to happen.

"Come on!" Cal yelled, raining hammer-blows on the machine for almost a full second before it became too painful, then just shaking it for a while instead. "One fonking jelly bean. Is that really too much to ask?"

"Apparently so, sir," Kevin intoned. "The Mush supply is entirely depleted. Perhaps you should have asked to borrow some back at the castle."

Cal's jaw dropped. "Son of a... Of course we should have done that. Why didn't you suggest it then?"

"Was that while I was being buried under debris, or while you were all mourning the loss of Master Splurt, sir?" Kevin enquired. "Or perhaps while we were battling a monstrous mutated clone that could've killed us all at any moment? I mean, there may have been a *slight* window of opportunity between all those, but to be honest I'm not sure if—"

"OK, OK, I get it," Cal told him. He turned away from the replicator, then attempted to surprise it by spinning and slapping it hard on its side. This hurt his hand quite a lot, and he decided to stop hitting the thing now, before he did himself any real damage. He settled for shooting it an indignant look that he hoped would have a devastating effect on the fonking thing's self-confidence.

That done, he left the kitchen and joined the others up on the bridge. The view screen was filled with space. Lots and lots of space, moving quite quickly. He did his best not to look at it for too long, and slumped into his chair.

"Replicator's still broken," he announced.

"It ain't broken. You just used it all up," Mech replied.

Cal waved a hand. "Look, let's not argue semantics. It isn't working. That isn't anyone's fault."

"It's your fault," said Loren.

"OK, but what does 'fault' even mean, anyway? Right?"

Kevin made a sound like a throat being cleared. "According to the dictionary..."

"Rhetorical question, Kevin. We all know what it means."

Cal spun his chair until he was facing Tim. The Time Titan sat in one of the chairs positioned along the bridge's rear wall, holding onto his seat belt like his life depended on it. Which, with Loren flying, it probably did.

"But it's not a problem," Cal said. "I know how we can get our Mush back. Tim can rewind it."

At the mention of his name, Tim tore his eyes away from the screen. His lips, which had been muttering a silent prayer ever since the ship-meets-shield incident outside the castle, pulled into a downward curve.

"Sorry?"

"The Mush. The stuff that makes the replicator, you know, replicate. You could do your time magic on the bag, fill it back up, and problem solved."

Tim shook his head. "What? No. No, I'm afraid not. I can't do that."

"Can't?" asked Cal. "Or won't?"

"Both. Either," said Tim. "Time isn't as straightforward as that. I can't just wave a hand and rewind something back on itself. Well, I mean, I could, but there would be repercussions. Perhaps lethal ones."

He gestured to Cal's stomach. "If I was to refill the machine, where does it all come from? If I'm reversing its timeline then every piece of the stuff you ate will be *un*eaten. You might be able to feast today, but it won't matter, because you'll have starved to death a month ago. Or been so light-headed with hunger you didn't see something about to leap at you from the shadows." Tim gestured to Miz. "Or she couldn't move fast enough to save you from something." He continued on to Loren. "Or her time line changes so she crashes due to sheer calorie-deprivation, killing you all."

"Like, is that why you keep doing it, Loren?" Miz wondered. "Are you hungry all the time?"

"I cannot rewind something in isolation is my point," Tim concluded.

"You rewound me," Cal reminded him.

"Because you had side-stepped into a different flow of time, and therefore your actions had no – or few – repercussions on this time line. You see?"

"Not really," Cal admitted. He puffed out his cheeks. "So, quit beating around the bush, Timbo. Cards on the table time. What are you saying? Are you going to magic us up some Mush or not?"

"No. No, I'm not," said Tim.

"Well, why didn't you just say so?" Cal asked. He crossed his arms over his belly and rocked in his chair, making it squeak. "Man, I am fonking hungry. Is there, like, a Pizza Hut or whatever on the way to where we're going?"

"One, no. And Two, we have no money," Loren reminded him.

"We stole this spaceship. Pretty sure we can steal a pizza," Cal reasoned.

"Anyway, it's too late," Loren said.

There was a collective '*Wargh*!' from everyone on the bridge as the *Untitled* stopped with Loren's usual spine-shattering level of abruptness.

"We're here," she said, her voice becoming a slightly awestruck whisper.

Cal coughed his testicles back out of his lower abdomen and blinked rapidly until colors no longer swam before his eyes. He drew his gaze across the viewscreen from left to right. There, in front of them, was space. Lots of space, and yet no more space than was probably normal.

"We're where?" he asked. "There's fonk all here."

"We've entered Gooramy Space," Loren said. "That's where Dorid's co-ordinates point to."

"They point to the middle of nowhere?" Cal groaned. "So, what are you saying? That creepy son-of-a-bedge stitched us up?"

"No. They point to a planet *within* Gooramy Space," Loren said.

"Then let's go there," Cal said, rocking in his chair and gesturing ahead. "Come on. Chop chop. Drive, or fly, or whatever. Let's go to the planet and get on with finding clues, or... God, I don't even know what we're supposed to be doing. Tell me someone else knows."

"We can't," said Mech. "Gooramy Space is sacred. We can't go any further without their permission."

"Come on, no one will know!" Cal said. "Look outside, there's nobody here."

"They'll have picked up our approach," Loren said. "They'll be on the way."

Cal sighed and slouched back in his chair. "Miz, what do you think?"

"About what?" Miz asked, flicking her eyes up.

"This whole Gooramy Space situation."

Miz shot the view screen a look that bordered on contempt, then shrugged. "I have no opinion."

"See? Miz agrees with me," Cal said.

Mech scowled. "What? No she don't."

"OK, well she does, obviously, but I'll be the bigger man here and you and I will just agree to disagree on that one," said Cal.

"How come we have to bring him anyway?" Miz asked, flicking her head in Tim's direction.

"Because we have no idea what we're supposed to be doing," Cal said.

"No, I mean, how come he can't just, like, teleport or

whatever? Like he did before when he was the giant baby thing."

Cal creaked his chair around. "That's a point. Couldn't you just beam yourself over to the planet, check it out, then beam back?"

Tim shook his head. "As I said earlier, I am the Time Titan, not the Time and Space Titan. I was only able to travel to the *Odyssey* via the chronal disturbance itself. I traveled through its cracks, if you like."

"Oh. OK. That makes sense," said Cal. He leaned in Mech's direction and whispered. "That does make sense, right?"

"Fonked if I know."

"Meh. Sounds plausible enough," Cal said. "You know, compared to everything else that's ever happened to us." He sighed again, louder this time, and rotated his chair back to the front again. "Who are these Gooramy guys, anyway? Are they the orange ones with nipples for eyes?"

Everyone turned to look at him. Even Splurt lowered himself down from the ceiling a fraction to join in.

"Wait. No." Cal made a switch-around motion with his fingers. "I mean eyes for nipples. Nipples for eyes would be horrifying."

"Oh. No, those are the Groonkshuks," said Loren.

"Right. Right, yeah. Groonshuks," said Cal, over-enunciating the word for reasons he wasn't really sure of, but which he quite enjoyed all the same. He tapped his armrest and thought. "Are the Gooramy the porcupine guys with the cute little bunched up faces? You know? Their faces are all..."

He screwed up his face, but failed in his attempt to make it particularly cute.

"Like that. All bunched up. They sing all the time.

Remember?" He gave a half-hearted performance of a tune that no-one recognized, and that probably didn't exist. "Always with the singing. Is that them?"

"I don't know what the fonk you just described. But for their sake, I hope I never meet one," Mech said. He brought a hand to his waist and indicated some invisible line there. "The Gooramy are half fish, half... you know, person."

"Come on, Mech. I'm sure they're *all* person," said Cal. "We're not living in the dark ages here. Just because someone's half-fish, doesn't make them any less of a..." He drew in a gasp so sharp and sudden that a little oxygen warning light flickered briefly on Loren's console. He moved to stand up, but the seatbelt had other ideas and slammed him back down. He didn't notice.

"SPACE MERMAIDS!"

"Say what?"

"We have those! On Earth!" Cal cried. "Except not space ones. Normal ones."

Loren and Mech exchanged puzzled looks. "You have Gooramy on Earth?" Loren asked.

"Yes! But we call them Mermaids. And they're entirely fictitious. But *yes*!" Cal gushed. He put his hand to his waist, just as Mech had done. "So, half fish, half human, right?"

"Human*oid*," Loren said. "But yes. That's sounds like them."

"And they're in *space*? What are they doing in space?"

"What are any of us doing in space, sir?" Kevin asked. "I often ask myself that same question while everyone else is asleep, and I'm sitting here all alone in a cold, endless void."

"Uh, OK," said Cal.

"In case you're wondering how I know you're asleep, it's because I watch you," the AI continued. "Closely."

"That's... good to know," Cal said.

"Just joshing, sir. Don't be concerned," Kevin said. "I don't watch *that* closely."

"Right," said Cal, dragging the word out.

"On an unrelated note, I thought you might like to know there are a number of ships approaching from over that way."

The crew all held off from saying anything while they waited for the penny to drop.

It didn't.

"Again, can't see you pointing there, Kevin," Cal said. "Maybe you could help us out here?"

"No need," said Loren. On screen, four smallish fighter ships and one cruiser appeared one by one in the space ahead of them. "They just dropped out of warp."

"Yes, that's the ones, ma'am," said Kevin. "Gooramy short-range fighters, I believe, supporting what appears to be a diplomatic vessel of some description."

"Any life signs?" Cal asked.

Mech looked back over his shoulder. "Of course there's life signs. Why wouldn't there be life signs?"

"I don't know," said Cal. "You were all saying cool things, so I wanted to say something, too and oh good God, that ship has a penis."

On screen, a long flexible tube was extending from beneath the largest of the ships. It hung limply below it, swaying gently left to right as if buffeted around on some unseen space breeze.

"It's a boarding tunnel," said Mech.

"It's a what now?"

"They'll connect it to our airlock," Loren explained. "Then either they'll come here or they'll tell us to go there."

Cal glanced around the bridge at the dirty coffee cups

and assorted other trash that was all within arm's reach of his seat. "They're coming here? Should we tidy up?"

"Attention, unregistered vessel."

The voice was slightly damp, a little rough around the edges, and gargled its way through the letter R. The words spat from the speakers, apparently having bypassed the usual communications procedure altogether. At least, Cal hadn't noticed the little blinking icon on the screen, or seen anyone press one of the many different buttons that seemed to answer it.

"You have entered Gooramy Space. State your intent."

It took Cal a moment to realize all eyes were on him. He shifted in his seat, then pointed his face vaguely in the direction the voice had come from.

"Uh... rocks."

Mech scowled. "Rocks?" he whispered. "What the fonk does that mean, 'rocks'?"

"I mean, we're here to look at some rocks." He shrugged at Mech and silently mouthed, "Is that better?"

The expression on Mech's face made it pretty clear that it wasn't.

"Which rocks?" asked the voice.

"Quannum," said Cal.

"Quanturum," Tim corrected.

"That one. What he said. We just want to take a look at it. We'll be, like, five minutes, tops."

There was silence for a moment. Only Miz could make out the faint mumbling of the Gooramy discussing how to respond.

On screen, the snaking white boarding tunnel curved out of sight around the *Untitled*. A moment later, a *clang* shook the ship.

"We shall negotiate face to face," the voice on the speaker commanded. "Join us aboard our vessel."

"OK!" said Cal, relieved he wouldn't have to put the dirty dishes away. "We'll be right there."

"And no funny stuff," the voice warned.

"Deal."

"Or we'll mess you up."

"Gotcha," said Cal. "Oh, do you guys have anything to eat? You know, like a sandwich? Like a ham sandwich. Or maybe a tuna sand... No, not tuna. Shizz. Sorry. Like just something to eat?"

The only reply was dead air.

"Hello? Damn it. They're gone."

Cal stood, remembering to first unclip his belt this time. "Looks like we're going to negotiate with the space mermaids," he announced, and the idea of it seemed to delight him. "I know I don't need to say this, guys, but we should probably leave the talking to me."

Loren snorted. "We definitely shouldn't."

"They asked you a question, and you literally just said the word 'rocks' at them," Mech added.

"They caught me off guard. Next time, I'll be ready." He pointed individually to everyone on the bridge. "Loren, you stay here with Tim. Mech, Miz, you come with me."

Miz tutted loudly. "How come I have to go? What do you need me for?"

"Are you kidding me?" said Cal. "You're my right-hand girl. You think I can trust this pile of bolts to protect me?"

"Fonk you, man."

"See? I need you with me, Miz," Cal continued. He winked. "What do you say?"

Miz tried her best to look mind-numbingly bored by

everything Cal had said, but the twitching of her tail gave her away.

"Fine. I'll come," she conceded. "But it better not be just people all standing around talking. I hate that."

"I doubt they'll be standing," said Cal. "They're space mermaids. But I take your point. Tell you what, if the conversation seems to be dragging on, we'll shoot someone."

"Don't you dare!" Loren warned.

"Relax, I'm kidding!" he told her, then he turned to Miz and mouthed, "Totally not kidding."

Miz's snout curved into a smirk, then she padded after Mech toward the door. Cal had barely taken a step when Splurt drooped down in front of him like a long drip of snot.

"Not this time, buddy," Cal told him. "I can't risk you getting obliterated again. OK? Hang here. Recover. Get back in shape. You know, metaphorically speaking. Your shape's fine as it is."

Splurt rippled. His eyes widened.

"Don't guilt trip me, mister," Cal told him. "I need you here to make sure Loren doesn't fly off without us."

"Don't tempt me," said Loren.

"You hear that, buddy?" Cal said. "You keep an eye on her for me, OK?"

The bulbous part of the Splurt-drip became a single staring eyeball and swiveled in Loren's direction.

"God, that's unpleasant," Cal muttered. "But good job, pal. We'll be back soon."

With a final finger-to-forehead salute at Tim, Cal left the bridge and joined the others by the airlock. The white tunnel was attached like an umbilical cord to the outer door. Cal peered into it, but saw nothing except the ridged plastic walls where they curved off in the direction of the Gooramy ship.

"Is it safe?" he asked. "Should we bring space suits?"

"It's safe," Mech confirmed. "It's fully sealed at both ends and pumped full of air. It's even got artificial gravity. We can walk straight aboard their ship."

"Well alright, then! Let's do this!" said Cal. He hit the button that opened the airlock doors and stepped into the mouth of the tunnel. "Let's go meet the space mermaids!"

FIFTEEN

FORTY MINUTES LATER, they were still walking.

The first five minutes had been pretty enjoyable. They were setting off on a new adventure, Cal was going to meet some space mermaids, and there was a generally positive vibe within the group. Even Miz wasn't complaining, which was something of a miracle in and of itself.

The next twenty minutes were less fun. Although, in hindsight, they now felt like the glory days of the expedition. They'd settled into a comfortable stride by then, and Cal had passed the time asking countless questions about how mermaids coped in space.

How did they get around on their ship, for example? Wheelchairs? Little hovercrafts? Did they swim in zero gravity, using their tails to flick them along? That would've been the coolest, he decided, but the others were already pretty much ignoring him by then, so they neither agreed nor argued the point.

Every minute that followed since then had been excruciatingly tedious. The problem wasn't the distance, exactly, as much as the fact they couldn't tell how much of said distance was left to go. The boarding tunnel was always slightly curved, meaning they couldn't see more than twenty or thirty feet ahead of them before the bend got in the way.

Mech knew how far it was, but he'd stopped answering Cal's *Are we nearly there yet*s roughly twelve minutes into the journey. Now he just plodded on, muttering quietly to himself, his weight shaking the tunnel with every step.

If Mech was getting impatient, though, it was nothing compare to Mizette.

"Eurgh. How much further? We've been walking for, like, forever!" she groaned, flapping her arms dramatically, then shoving them straight down by her sides.

"It's got to be close, right?" said Cal. "I mean, we must be halfway across the fonking galaxy by now."

"I should totally have stayed on the ship. I knew it. I should have, like, totally stayed behind."

Mech muttered some more.

They walked on. Seconds bled into minutes.

Cal began to whistle.

"Don't," said Mech. It was the first full word he'd said in a while, and the way he said it made Cal's lips unpurse themselves all on their own.

They walked on.

Cal had an idea.

"I spy with my little eye..."

He looked around them.

"Something beginning with..."

"It's tunnel," Mech grunted.

"T."

"Tunnel," guessed Miz.

"Bingo. Miz gets it, because the round hadn't officially

started until I said the letter," Cal said. "Sorry, Mech, you jumped the gun. What can I say?"

"You could say nothing at all," Mech told him. "I would like that very much."

"OK, Miz, your turn," Cal said.

Mizette's eyes darted around. "I—"

"Tunnel," said Mech. "It's tunnel. There's nothing but fonking tunnel."

"He's right," said Miz. "And I totally hate this game, anyway."

"How about a sing-song?" Cal suggested. "You know, to keep the spirits up?"

"Sing and I'll punch your mouth loose," Mech warned him.

"Fair enough," Cal said.

They walked on.

Six seconds later, Cal began to beatbox.

Mech stopped. "What did I just say?"

"I'm not singing," Cal said. He spat a couple of *dum-dums* and a *tssh* in Mech's direction. "I'm laying down a sick beat. Or a banging tune. Or, you know, whatever the kids say these days."

"Guys!" said Miz. She hadn't bothered to stop as that, paradoxically, would've taken more effort than simply continuing on. She was a dozen feet ahead of them now, her tail flicking side to side in the first flush of excitement. "I can see the door. We're here!"

"Thank you, Jesus!" Cal cried, thrusting his hands in the air. His voice rolled off along the tunnel in both directions, then bounced back at them off something solid up ahead.

Cal began to run, which bounced the others around inside the flexible pipe. They all half-jogged, half-bounced the final short distance to the tunnel's end, then stumbled onto the solid floor of the Gooramy ship's airlock.

"We made it. We actually made it," Cal wheezed. "I'll be honest, I didn't think we were getting out of that tube alive for a while back there."

"You almost didn't," Mech mumbled.

Behind them, the outer airlock door slid closed. Cal straightened up, pushed his shoulders back, and took up a position at the inner door, which led into the ship. Unlike on the *Untitled*, there was no window built into this one, so Cal had no idea if anyone was on the other side. Still, better to look as impressive as possible, just in case.

"OK, so we leave the talking to me, remember?" Cal told the others. "I'll explain the situation, we'll have a few laughs, they'll probably make us a picnic, and we'll be on our way."

There was a *bleep* from the other side of the door. Cal smoothed down his shirt, ran his fingers through his hair, then fixed on a grin. "Space Mermaids," he said. "This is going to be so awesome."

The door slid open.

Cal screamed.

Instinctively, he lashed out, catching the abomination on the other side of the door with a right hook that knocked it off its feet and sent it sprawling onto the deck.

"What the fonk are you doing?" Mech barked, grabbing him before he could throw another punch.

"What the Hell is that thing?" Cal yelped.

"It's a Gooramy!" Mech said. "They're half fish. I explained that."

"I didn't think you meant *top half* fish!" cried Cal, indicating the fallen figure's armless torso and grotesquely bloated fish head. "They're supposed to be bottom half fish!"

"Bottom half fish? How the fonk would that work?" He shuddered. "That'd just be nasty."

"*And that isn't*?" said Cal, gesturing down to the figure on the floor. Its lack of arms was hampering its attempts to stand up, and it sort of flapped around, its bulbous eyes wide with panic, its mouth snapping open and closed.

"Shizz. Help me get it up," Mech said.

"I'm not touching that thing!" said Cal. His whole body convulsed, ejecting an involuntary but entirely heartfelt, "Uyeeurgh!" from his mouth.

Mech shoved Cal aside and stepped out into the corridor. As soon as he did, a long trident-like weapon was jammed against his metal ribcage. Mech convulsed as electricity tore through him.

"Ow! What the fonk?" he spat, turning and knocking the weapon aside.

Two more of the fish-people had been waiting on either side of the door. Unlike the first, these two had four robotic limbs attached to their armless torsos. They each held identical trident weapons, pointy ends primed and ready to stab.

"Get back!" warned the guard that had attacked. "You dare assault a diplomat of the Gooramy!"

"Hey, I didn't assault no one," Mech said. He shot an accusing look back into the airlock. "My... companion here reacted in surprise, for which he apologizes. Right?"

"Uh, right," said Cal, bending forward until his head appeared through the door. "Totally apologize. I was expecting bottom half fish," he said, as if that somehow excused the fact he'd punched a diplomat to the ground. He gestured to the guards' heads. "This... Well, it caught me by surprise." He shuddered out a, "Bleeurguh!" then forced his mouth into a welcoming smile. "Anyway, great to be here, thanks for having us aboard."

Stepping fully out of the airlock, he put his hands on his hips, then looked off along the corridor in both directions.

"Do you guys have, like, a snack bar around here?" he asked, then the butt of a trident *crunched* across the back of his head, and everything slipped silently into darkness.

CAL WOKE UP KICKING, punching and shouting something less than complimentary about Tobey Maguire. His knuckles *clanged* against Mech's leg, and pain stabbed through his hand and up his arm.

"Ow! Watch it," he protested.

"You fonking punched *me*," Mech pointed out.

Cal rubbed the back of his head and groaned. He could remember very clearly where he'd been hit, but couldn't feel any lump. It didn't hurt, either, which was a blessing. If they were being held prisoner by wrong-way-round Mermaids, the last thing he needed was a headache.

He was sitting in an armchair that smelled quite strongly of fish, in a room that also smelled quite strongly of fish. Two Gooramy – Gooramies, maybe? He'd have to check – stood by the door, tridents clutched in their robotic hands, heads turned so one bloated eye could keep watch on the room while the other watched the entrance. Their scaly bodies shimmered in the glow of several round lights on the wall that shone like portholes facing the sunrise.

"You OK?" asked Miz. She was slouched in a chair on his left, while Mech stood on his right. "They hit you pretty hard."

"I'm fine," said Cal. "They just caught me by surprise, that all. But how did they take you guys down?"

Mech and Miz exchanged glances. "Uh, they didn't," said Mech.

Cal frowned. "Huh?"

"They just knocked you out, asked us nicely if we'd follow them, and we agreed."

"You agreed?!" Cal spluttered. "Why didn't you avenge me?"

"You did kind of hit one of them first," Miz reasoned.

"Well, *yeah*," Cal said. He began the sentence in a way that suggested there was a follow-up point to come, but it didn't materialize. He sighed. "Tell me you at least looked like you were following them begrudgingly."

"Oh, totally," said Miz.

"Yeah, man. We complained the whole time," Mech said.

"That's a lie, isn't it, Mech?" Cal asked.

Mech smirked. "Yeah. Yeah, it is. They're actually pretty nice."

"They gave us lunch," Miz said.

Cal sat bolt upright. "They gave us lunch?!"

"They gave *us* lunch," Mech said. "But we ate it."

"You *ate* it? What, *all* of it?"

"Uh-huh."

"But you don't even have to eat!"

Mech shrugged. "Seemed kind of rude not to. Besides, it was delicious. I mean we're talking *top five things I've ever tasted* delicious."

Cal's stomach rumbled in protest. "Oh come on! You didn't keep me *any*?"

"Nope," said Mech. "And we also spoke to their diplomats and straightened everything out."

"What? No! I thought we agreed I'd do the talking."

"Well, you were kind of unconscious, so I took over," Mech said. "We got permission to go where we need to go. They just want you to do something first."

There was something about the look on Mech's face that made Cal's whole body go tense. It was that slight flaring of the nostrils and curving of the mouth that suggested the cyborg was fighting back the urge to laugh that worried him.

"What? What do they want me to do?"

"I said 'no way'," Miz told him. "Like, there's no way it was happening, but it was the only way they'd even talk to us."

Cal looked from Miz to Mech and back again. "What? There's no way what was happening?"

"We had to agree. It was the only way," Mech said. His voice cracked, spreading his smirk further across his face. "Also, I thought it was the funniest fonking thing I'd ever heard, so there's also that."

"What did you agree to?" Cal demanded. "Guys? What do they want me to do?"

Before either of them could answer, the door to the room slid open. Cal visibly recoiled as another of the fish-headed creatures entered. This one had something not unlike a band-aid covering a spot just above one of his gills, and Cal guessed it was the same guy he'd floored earlier. The resentment burning in his bulging eyes helped to back this theory up.

"It is time," he announced in an authoritative gargle. "The Shoal Queen awaits in her chamber."

Mech snorted.

"It is time for the mating ritual to begin."

"The...? Wait, the...? No." Cal was suddenly on his feet. "No. God, no! No way. Not happening."

"Arrangements have been made," the diplomat insisted. "The deal has been done."

"Well it can be fonking well *un*done! Because there is no way I'm screwing a fish-person," Cal said. "I mean... *maybe* if it'd had been the other way around. But even then."

"If the agreed arrangement is not undertaken, we shall have no choice but to destroy your ship and class you all as prisoners," the diplomat continued. "The boarding tunnel is still connected. We could deploy an explosive that would bypass your shielding and detonate inside the ship itself. Anyone on board would be killed instantly."

His bulging eyes swam as he considered this. "*Almost* instantly."

Cal shot Mech an accusing look. "I thought you said they were nice?"

He exhaled forcefully, just in case anyone could be in any doubt about how unhappy he was about this whole situation.

"Seriously?" he groaned. "With the big eyes and the gills and everything?"

"Just don't look at her face," Mech suggested.

"They're *all* face!" Cal pointed out. "They're legs, fishy body, then boom. Face."

"You could close your eyes," said Miz.

"But then there's the smell," Cal protested. "So much smell." He tutted. "Do we even need the ship? Will it really be that much of a loss? The guys would understand."

"Just go mate with the damn fish queen," Mech told him.

"Fine. Know what? Fine. I can do this. It's not a problem," Cal said. He strode over towards the waiting diplomat, got halfway, then about-turned. "No. Jesus. No, this is not happening."

Two robotic arms grabbed him by the shoulders. A trident jabbed into his back, buzzing its electricity across his skin. "Guys! They're taking me!" Cal yelped as he was dragged backwards towards the door.

Mech waved, his metal mouth smiling more broadly than Cal had even known was possible.

"Try to be quick," Miz called after him.

"I fonking hate you guys!" Cal managed to blurt, before the guards dragged him out of the room. The diplomat nodded curtly to Mech and Miz.

"It is a great honor to be chosen for the mating ritual. He should be pleased."

"Secretly, I think he's delighted," said Mech. "He just doesn't want to show it."

The diplomat gave another nod, then retreated backward through the door. "Someone will come to attend to you shortly," he told them, then the door slid closed, leaving Mech and Miz alone in the room.

Miz chewed anxiously on her bottom lip. "Think Cal's going to be OK?"

"Huh? Oh, yeah. Yeah, he's gonna be fine," Mech said. He chuckled. "Physically, I mean. Psychologically? That shizz is gonna stay with him for a loooong fonking time."

SIXTEEN

Cal was dragged through a number of doors as he was carried through the ship. He grabbed for a few, digging in with his fingertips until one of the robotic arms pulled him free, but it was only delaying the inevitable.

Finally, they reached an imposing set of double doors fashioned from a metal much shinier and more expensive-looking than any Cal had seen elsewhere on the ship. There were ornate symbols carved into each door. The translation chip in Cal's eye started to decipher them, but he was too terrified to read what they said.

"Look, guys, let's talk about this," Cal began, but then the doors slid open and a single shove sent him stumbling into the beckoning gloom.

He skidded several feet along the ground, then scrambled upright and made a dive back in the direction of the exit. The doors slid closed before him, trapping him inside. Cal hammered a fist against them, shouted a few desperate pleas for help, then stopped when he heard a slow, lumbering *squelch* and the *pup-pup-pup* of a fishy mouth flapping open and closed from somewhere close behind him.

"Oh God," he whispered. "This is it."

He didn't want to turn. It was pretty much last on his list of priorities, in fact, but he knew he had no choice. Steeling himself, he shuffled around in a half circle.

Something from a nightmare stood before him.

Somewhere around fifteen years previously, Cal had been flicking through TV channels one night, when he'd come across a documentary about fish. Specifically, it was about the Lumpfish – a creature the program makers had deemed to be the single ugliest thing living in the ocean, and which resembled an overfilled colostomy bag with fins and a face.

The thing wheezing in front of him now reminded him of it a lot, although admittedly the one he'd seen on the show hadn't been wearing a knee-length skirt with stylish strappy shoes.

Cal flattened himself against the door, as if he could somehow seep right through the metal and out into the hallway beyond. Mood-lighting candles flickered around the room, casting flickering shadows across the Gooramy's slimy scales and reflecting in her hideously bulging eyeballs.

Even her legs – the one part he thought he could rely on to take his mind off the whole horrifying experience – had let him down. He'd been praying for supermodel legs. Or just model legs. Or just *vaguely attractive woman* legs. Instead, she had two thick poles of meat that went straight up and down with no hint of a curve, and were decorated all over with dots of stubble.

Still, at least the *Discovery Channel* had never made an hour-long documentary about them, so they were still a step-up on the rest of her.

Cal realized he was staring wide-eyed at the queen. Not as wide-eyed as she was, obviously – that would've taken a serious thyroid condition and a foot pump – but pretty wide-eyed all the same. He also realized he hadn't said anything, although his brain was currently running around screaming inside his head, so he thought he could probably be forgiven for his temporary lack of manners.

"Hey... *you*," he managed, his voice croaking out of his throat on the third attempt. "I should probably warn you, I have a headache."

"Here. Now," the Gooramy commanded, pointing to a spot right in front of her. For an alien fish-queen, her accent was surprisingly Russian-sounding. "Stand before me."

Cal fumbled his fingers along the wall by the door, hoping to find some control panel or emergency exit button there, but he was out of luck.

"I do not have all of day," the Gooramy snapped. "Here. Now. Before me."

Looking back, Cal didn't remember moving. He certainly made no decision to move, but his legs must have got together and planned it on their own, because the next thing he knew he was standing in front of the... he felt 'monster' was probably too harsh a word, but his mind kept bringing him back to it.

"You must be cleaned."

Cal swallowed. It was partly through nerves and partly to push back the feeling of nausea brought on by the Gooramy's overwhelming fish-stench.

"I had a shower yesterday," he said, leaving out the fact that fifty or more years had passed since then.

"Not enough. You must be Gooramy clean before you are permitted to see Shoal Queen."

Cal blinked. "Huh? Wait... You mean you're *not* the queen?"

"Ha! No. I am but servant, not Shoal Queen. Though you will wish I was."

"I doubt that *very* much," Cal said.

"It is true. Trust me. Shoal Queen has many deformities. Physically. You will find her upsetting to look at. She will make you sick," the fish-woman said, really selling the idea by dry-heaving a few times. "Like this."

Cal's brain started doing panicky laps again. He was about to throw himself at the fish-woman's mercy and beg her to either help him escape or kill him quickly when she spat a gush of stinking salty liquid in his face. The force of it knocked him back several steps. He coughed and spluttered out a mouthful of briny sea water, blinked several times, then yelped as the big Gooramy appeared behind him and used her bulk to bundle him towards another door that had been hidden in the shadow near the back of the room.

"Now you are Gooramy clean," she said. Cal tried to side-step clear, but her weight and momentum shoved him through the door just as it opened. It *clanged* closed so quickly he felt the wind of it at his back.

Several spotlights illuminated high on the wall in front of him and he hissed, blinded by their glow. Shielding his eyes with one hand, he tried to size up the room he'd landed in, but his night vision had been all-but obliterated, and everywhere he looked he saw nothing but the imprint of the spotlights on his retina.

"Hello?" he said in a low, throaty whisper. "I, uh, I think there's been a mistake. I'm just here to fix the refrigerator, and somehow ended up in here. So, if you could..."

"Silence."

The voice came from somewhere in the darkness ahead. Several feet higher up, too. Fonk, how big was this thing?

It was smoother and markedly less Russian than the servant's voice. There was something snake-like about the way she dragged out the *s* sounds – *ssssilenccce* – that didn't exactly make Cal feel any more confident about his current predicament.

"You wish to see me?" the voice asked.

Cal swallowed. "Not really."

"I will dance for you."

A spasm of horror shuddered through him. "That's a lovely offer, but really not necessary," he said. "Just point me towards the busted refrigerator and I'll—"

A low, pulsating beat throbbed from the walls and up through the floor. It was slow, steady and almost tribal - the sort of tune the residents of Skull Island might hammer out when summoning King Kong, Cal reckoned. This thought, too, did little to make him feel better about the whole situation.

A shape moved in the dark gaps behind the spotlights and Cal made himself as flat as possible against the door.

"Oh Jesus," he whimpered. "Here we go."

The spotlights swung down, sweeping their glow across the floor until they picked out the bare feet and ankles of the Shoal Queen and continued on up her legs.

Cal screwed his eyes shut in horror. A moment later, after his scrambled brain had processed the data it had been given, one of the eyes opened again.

The Shoal Queen stood on a raised stage at the opposite end of the room. She was a little taller than Cal, and boasted the supermodel legs he had been praying for.

To his surprise, she also boasted the supermodel torso,

arms, head and face. She was human. Or mostly human, at least.

Her hair was long, green and told tales of the ocean. Her skin was immaculately smooth. Colors danced across its silvery sheen as she gyrated sensually in the eyes of the spotlights. She wore a skimpy swimsuit of seaweed and shells that clung to her impeccable curves as she rolled her hips and curved her arms and performed for her would-be mate.

As the Shoal Queen turned, Cal noticed she had a set of small gills on the side of her neck. Meh. He could live with that.

"Uh... You're..."

"Does my deformity scare you?" she asked, weaving her mesmerizing frame a step closer.

"No. Well, I mean, I'm sure I can soldier through it," Cal said. "It's what's inside that counts, right?"

The Shoal Queen giggled with delight. It instantly catapulted itself into Cal's top three favorite sounds.

"Thank you. None has ever been able to look beyond my grotesque appearance before," she said, twerking another step closer. "You shall be my first."

Cal swallowed again. It was a very different swallow to any of the others he'd done in the past ten minutes.

"Your first?"

"Hmm-mm," said the Shoal Queen, biting her copper-colored bottom lip. "You do not mind?"

Cal laughed. It was quite a high-pitched and slightly hysterical laugh, and it lasted just a fraction of a second. "No. No, I don't mind. I mean... someone's got to do it, right?"

The beat of the music had replaced Cal's heartbeat

now. He could feel it resonating through them – through them both – as the Shoal Queen closed in.

Fonk, she was beautiful. And not just in a *she doesn't have a giant fish head* kind of way. Genuinely, by any available standard, bona-fide gorgeous.

"Then we shall be joined," she said, sliding the seaweed strap of her swimsuit over one perfect shoulder. "Together. Here and now."

"OK. Well, obviously it's under protest, but..." He reached for his belt buckle, and had just started to undo it when the door behind him was torn open and he fell out into the other room. "What the fonk?!" he yelped, then he found himself looking up at an all-too familiar metal jaw. "Mech?"

"We couldn't let you go through with it," Mech said, grabbing Cal and hoisting him to his feet. "Sorry, man. We should never have agreed to this."

"What? No! I mean... you made a deal."

"And now we've *un*made it," said Miz. She stood over the unconscious form of the weirdly Russian Gooramy woman, claws extended and ears pricked up for danger.

"Is that wise?" Cal asked. "I mean a deal's a deal, right? This is going to make us look bad. We don't want to get a reputation for going back on our word!"

Mech hoisted Cal over his shoulder. "You can thank us later. For now, we need to get back to the ship."

Cal grabbed for the Shoal Queen's door, but Mech was already off and running. "Seriously, it's fine!" Cal insisted. "I'll take one for the team!"

"There's no *way* we're letting you do that," said Miz, bounding along beside them. "Like, no *way*." She bumped him gently on the arm. "We've *totally* got your back."

Cal could only watch as the door to the Shoal Queen's chamber got further and further away. He caught a glimpse of her outline – her perfect, *perfect* outline – silhouetted against the spotlights, and just managed a, "Call me!" before a blaster bolt exploded against the wall ahead of them, forcing Mech to take a detour into a different hallway.

"Shizz. They found us already," Mech grunted.

"Just take me back. Seriously, I couldn't live with myself if anything happened to you guys because of—"

More blaster fire screeched past them. Up ahead, the corridor was filling with robot-armed fish-people. It was hard to read their boggle-eyed expressions, but from the way they pointed their guns, it was safe to assume they weren't happy.

"Hold on!" Mech warned, then he thrust out an arm and charged through a wall, collapsing it as if it were made of cardboard. Two guards on the other side reacted in surprise, turning and raising their trident weapons just as Mech came barreling through.

A metal fist took one of them out. A succession of claw swipes cut down the other.

"Sorry!" Cal called back to the fallen fish-people as he was carried on. "Tell the queen it wasn't my fault!"

Another wall came up. Another sound like thunder rolled along the corridors as Mech charged straight through it.

Angry shouts spat at them along the passageway. Mech spun his top half around, making Cal simultaneously scream and throw up in his mouth. Six pulsing laser blasts streaked from the cyborg's arm, driving back the Gooramy soldiers.

"We need to get back to the ship," said Mech.

"If, like, they haven't already blown it to bits," Miz pointed out.

Mech shook his head. "Nah. That guy was bluffing. They wouldn't," he said. "I mean, I have nothing to base that on, I guess, but here's hoping."

Another wall loomed ahead. This time, Mech fired a couple of shots at it, blowing it outwards before they reached it. Alarms screeched through the ship now, and the sound of running feet filled the corridors.

"Do you even know where you're going?" Cal asked.

"Yes. Hold on," Mech said.

"I *can* run, you know?!" Cal yelled, but Mech ignored him. A set of security doors snapped closed ahead of them, blocking the corridor. A volley of blasts from Mech's arm cannon bounced harmlessly off the barrier, barely scorching the metal.

"Hold on," Mech grunted.

"Will you *stop* telling me to hold on?" Cal cried. "I'm fonking holding on!"

Most of his sentence was lost to the thunder of rending metal as Mech shoulder-barged the wall beside them and crashed straight through it into a room filled with insanely complicated looking equipment.

"What's this stuff?" Cal asked.

"Comms relay," Mech said, hurrying for the door – the actual door this time, not a hole in the wall – that led out of the room.

As he reached it, he stopped. He thought for a moment, then his upper half spun a full one-eighty, whipping Cal's arms and legs out. Mech opened fire, turning the equipment into a tangle of burned spaghetti.

"That should stop them reporting back for a while," he

said. "Should buy us enough time to get off here, find the Quanturum and—"

"Quit fonking monologuing!" Cal cried, watching the first of a platoon of Gooramy clamber through the hole in the wall. "And run!"

The next few minutes were a blur of sharp turns, screaming gunshots, and exploding walls. When they finally reached the airlock, they found it guarded. Not well guarded enough to stop them, or even slow them down, but guarded all the same.

Miz took out three of the soldiers, while Mech dealt with two more. Even Cal managed to knock one of them out when Mech turned too sharply and his flailing feet connected with a fishy head. It was entirely accidental, but he was claiming it, all the same.

The outer airlock door was locked. This didn't prove too much of a problem. One punch-and-pull from Mech ripped it out of its housing, exposing the white plastic boarding tunnel beyond.

"Great. This again," Miz groaned.

"Still, got to be more exciting this time, right?" said Cal. "You know, what with us running for our fonking lives, and everything?"

Mech raced into the tunnel. Every step he took on the less-than-solid floor bounced him up towards the top of the tunnel, where Cal's head was then *clunked* against the plastic ridges.

"Ow. Ow. Ow," Cal complained. "Mech, put me – *Christ!* – down."

With a shrug, Mech launched Cal several feet along the tunnel ahead of him. Miz caught him before he could land and helped turn him around so he was facing the right way.

"Thanks," he wheezed, but she was already pulling

ahead, bounding along on all fours and disappearing around the tunnel's curve.

Cal glanced back over his shoulder. Mech was thundering along behind him, but the cyborg's size and the fact he clearly wasn't built for speed meant he was already starting to fall behind.

"Hurry up!" Cal urged.

"You watch what you're doing, and I'll watch what I'm doing," Mech bit back. "Go on. I'll catch you up."

"OK, see you back at the ship," Cal said.

"What? You're actually fonking going?" Mech barked. "You're actually going to run off and leave me behind? After I saved you from fonking the fish-queen?"

"I had that *fully* under control!" Cal retorted. "There was no save necessary."

Mech had just started muttering something about gratitude when a *clank* from the airlock shook the tunnel.

"What was that?" Cal whispered.

There was a sound not unlike a rocket igniting. "Nothing good," Mech said. "Go! Run! They're launching the missile."

"They're launching the missile?! You said they were bluffing!"

"Well, what do I know?" Mech said. "Go. Move!"

"It's miles! We'll never outrun a fonking missile," Cal said. "Unless..."

He stopped running and pointed to Mech's forearm. "You can talk to Loren through that, right?"

"Yeah. Why?"

"Call her up. Now!"

Mech tapped his arm. "Channel open."

"Loren! You there? Pick up!"

"Cal? Everything OK?"

"We've had better days," Cal admitted. "Drop the ship."

"What?"

"Drop the fonking ship! Go down. Keep the tunnel attached, but drop the fonking ship!"

"OK, but..."

The whooshing of thrusters igniting grew louder behind them. "Just do it!" Cal hollered, then he and Mech stumbled on, clambering awkwardly through the tunnel as it shook and trembled around them.

The floor ahead of them became a shallow incline leading downwards. Cal whooped. "She's doing it. She's doing it!"

"You're crazy," Mech told him. "You're fonking crazy."

"Better crazy and not blown to pieces than sane and... *woooooah*!"

The shallow incline became a steep drop. Cal's momentum carried his top half forward, throwing him head-first into a plunge. Up ahead, he heard Miz cry out in confusion. Behind him, he heard Mech's arms *whirring* as he, too, began to fall.

And further back still, he heard the roar of the missile as it was launched into the tunnel.

Cal plunged almost straight down now, his arms held in front of him like Superman, the stifling air of the tunnel slicing upwards past him and whistling through the gaps in Mech's metal parts.

"Why didn't we think of this last time?" Cal shouted, but his rate of descent meant the words were shoved back down his throat.

They fell for a good couple of minutes, Cal expecting the missile to catch up with them at any moment. Mech would probably take the brunt of it, but that came as little consolation, as even with his limited knowledge of what he thought of as 'science stuff', Cal reckoned the explosion would tear the plastic tube in half, immediately sucking him out into space. He was by no means an expert but – again, from his understanding of 'science stuff' – he felt sure this would be bad.

With some effort, Cal managed to turn his head and call back to Mech. "Are we nearly there yet?"

From up ahead, there came the *crunch* of Mizette hitting the *Untitled*'s inner airlock door.

"Never mind!" Cal said, then he was spat from the mouth of the tube, propelled across the airlock, and slammed into Miz.

"Ow. Fonk. That hurt," he grimaced.

His body told him to give it a second to check for any serious injuries. His mind, however, became rather insistent that he move, taking pains to point out the huge cyborg currently hurtling towards him like a high-speed projectile.

Miz recovered first. She kicked her legs and launched them clear just as a flailing Mech was ejected from the tunnel mouth. The subsequent impact buckled the inner airlock door, but stopped short of punching a hole straight through it.

Spinning, Mech raised both arms and fired up through the outer airlock, severing the tunnel with a series of small explosions.

"Kevin, shut the airlock door!" Cal commanded.

"It's already closed, sir," said Kevin.

"The other one!"

"Oh. You should've specified. Apologies, sir," Kevin intoned.

The door snapped closed just as an explosive warhead emerged from the mouth of the tunnel.

"Kevin, go!" Cal cried.

The *Untitled* lurched forwards, throwing all three of the occupants of the airlock against the back wall. They braced themselves for the explosion, but the missile had skimmed past the ship's tail end and was tumbling harmlessly off into space.

"We did it!" Cal said. "I can't believe we did it! We escaped without being blown to bits!"

A torpedo detonated against the shields, tossing them all around violently.

"Wait, no. I take that back."

"Those fighters are attacking," said Loren, her voice coming clipped and urgent over the speaking system. "What the fonk did you guys do up there?"

The outer airlock door shuddered halfway open. Mech shoved it the rest of the way, and they all bundled through.

"Long story!" Cal replied, darting onto the bridge and sliding into his seat just as a volley of cannon fire *thumped* against the shields.

"Cal almost banged a fish-lady, then we ran away," said Miz.

"OK. Apparently not that long," Cal said.

Loren turned in her seat. "He almost *what*?"

"Spaceships, spaceships!" Cal warned. "Judge later. Fly now."

"They're shooting at us!" announced Tim from his chair at the back. "Those ships, they're shooting at us."

"Well observed, Timbo," Cal told him. "Yes, they are. Hold onto something, this might get a little..."

The *Untitled* banked suddenly upwards into a spinning corkscrew, and whatever word Cal was about to say was lost in a chorus of his panicky squeals.

"What was that?" he demanded, once his stomach had dropped down from around his ears.

"You told me to fly. I'm flying!" Loren snapped.

"That's not flying, it's..." He struggled to find a witty analogy, then more or less gave up. "Something that's like flying, but different and much worse."

"Incoming!" Mech announced.

"On it!" Loren slammed the sticks sideways, but too late to avoid a torpedo exploding across the front shields. The flare lit up the bridge, temporarily blinding everyone aboard.

"Which part of it were you 'on', precisely, ma'am?" Kevin asked. "From where I'm standing you appeared to be very much 'off it'."

"Shut up, Kevin!" Loren hissed.

"We should send me back over," Cal suggested. "You know, like a peace offering? I think me and the queen could broker a deal. Really thrash it out, you know?"

A scything beam of red energy carved across the top of the *Untitled*, filling the bridge with heat and smoke and panic.

"You know we're *totally* on fire, right?" Miz said, barely glancing up from her nails.

"Splurt! See what you can do about that!" Cal called. Up in the vents and pipes at the ceiling, Splurt became something heavy and fire-retardant, and set to work.

"Why are they doing this?" Tim called. "They're still shooting."

"We noticed!" Loren replied. She shoved the sticks forward, plunging the ship into a diving maneuver that flattened Cal's tongue against the roof of his mouth and raised him a couple of inches out of his seat.

The evasive action failed. Another torpedo detonated on the underside shielding, and reams of warning text rolled upwards across the screen.

"Shields at thirty per cent," said Mech. "Lower deflector array almost gone."

"Shizz!" Loren spat. "Why is no one shooting?"

"They are shooting," Cal said.

"I meant why aren't we shooting back?"

Cal blinked. "Shizz. Kevin!"

"You screamed hysterically for me, sir?"

"Shoot these guys!" Cal ordered. "Take out the fighters. Leave the big ship."

"Very good, sir," Kevin intoned. "Might I assume Ms Loren has no moral objections on this occasion?"

"Don't know, don't care!" Cal replied, raising his voice to drown out any reply from Loren. "Either they blow up or we do. I know which one I'm choosing."

"Too late!" Mech roared. He turned away from the view screen, covering his head with his hands, the part of his face that was still human knotted up in panic.

There, dead ahead, were four torpedoes, racing straight towards the *Currently Untitled.* The first would take out what was left of the shield, clearing the path for the other three to rip the ship apart.

In the time it took Cal to even think that, the first missile found its target. The shield flickered, then seemed to evaporate off into the darkness of space.

An alarm screeched. A crew braced.

And three explosive warheads rocketed through outer space.

SEVENTEEN

It stopped.

If pushed, that's how Cal would describe it. Stopping.

Not the torpedoes. Or not *just* the torpedoes. Everything. The *Untitled*. The fighters. The oncoming warheads.

Not the screaming – at least, not right away – but everything else. Stopped. Dead.

The *Untitled* hung motionless, the three torpedoes blurred by their proximity to the ship's view screen.

Cal was pretty sure he could move, but didn't dare to in case a gesture from him would somehow kick-start the universe into motion again, whereupon they'd be immediately obliterated by fire and loud noises.

Everyone else on the bridge was equally motionless, based on what he could hear. He could only see Loren, but the way her shoulders heaved with each deep, gulped breath told him she wasn't frozen, just too afraid to move.

Slowly, using just his feet, Cal turned his chair around until it was facing the back of the room. Tim had his eyes closed and the tips of both index and middle fingers pressed together in front of his face.

"I'm going to assume you played some part in this?" Cal whispered.

The Time Titan kept his eyes closed, but nodded. "I don't like to interfere, but I wasn't left with a lot of choice."

"Loren's fault," said Miz.

"No one's fault. Just circumstance," said Tim. A bead of sweat formed on his brow, and Cal realized it was taking a lot of effort to keep everything frozen.

"What do we do?" Loren asked. She tried adjusting her controls, but they were solid and immobile. "We can't move. As soon as you restart time, those torpedoes are going to hit us head on, right? And we have no shields."

Cal leaned forward in his chair and gazed out at the galaxy beyond the incoming warheads. The stars had stopped twinkling. He felt less like he was looking out at space, and more like he was admiring a high-resolution photograph of it.

"How far does it go? The time freeze thing?" Cal wondered.

"Everywhere," Tim said.

Mech *clanked* around in a half-circle. "You froze the whole system?"

"Whole universe," Tim corrected. He spat out a yelp of pain and forced his fingertips more tightly together.

Cal whistled quietly. "And I thought the giant space baby was impressive."

"Hold onto something," Tim hissed. His whole body was trembling now, his fingers vibrating as something did its best to force them apart. Gritting his teeth, he moved his pinkie fingers closer together until their tips touched.

The universe skipped a beat. The torpedoes, which had been firmly making their presence felt on the screen, were gone. The fighter ships were still there, but their position had changed – not by much, but enough to be noticeable.

"Like, what just happened?" Miz asked.

"I skipped us f-forward three seconds," Tim wheezed. "We bypassed the moment of impact, meaning the torpedoes are now b-behind..."

Something inside his head went *pop* and a spurt of blood colored his moustache directly below one nostril. As he slumped sideways, time roared back into normal speed. The sensors showed three torpedo-sized dots streaking away from the *Untitled*, their on-board guidance systems scratching their heads in confusion.

"Loren, get us out of here!" Cal instructed.

"Punching it," Loren replied.

The stars stretched into a tunnel of flickering light, and the *Currently Untitled* leapt to warp speed, leaving the Gooramy fighters far, far behind.

A MINUTE OR SO LATER, once Cal had adjusted enough to the relentless inner-ear assault of warp speed to be able to stand, he hurried to the back of the bridge and peered down at the Time Titan. Tim was slumped forward in his chair, the seat belt the only thing preventing him falling forward onto the floor.

"Is he dead?" Loren asked.

"I don't know," Cal said. "Hold on, I'll check."

He kicked the old man on the leg – not hard enough to hurt, but enough to get his attention, assuming he had any attention left to give.

"Hello?"

They waited.

"No, he's dead," Cal announced.

"Check properly," Loren said. "Take his pulse."

"I'm not touching him. He's dead!" Cal protested. "I'm not touching a dead guy."

"He totally isn't," Miz said, her ears twitching in the Time Titan's direction.

"He is. I checked!" said Cal. He bent down, bringing his mouth closer to Tim's ear. "Hello? Timbo? Are you alive? Blink once for yes, do nothing for no."

He did nothing.

"See? He's all the way dead," said Cal, then he screamed as Tim threw back his head and gasped in a spluttered breath. Cal's misguided survival instincts kicked in and he drove a panicky right hook across the old man's face, instantly knocking him out again.

"Man, that was cold," Mech said.

"Accident! Total accident!" Cal said, holding his hands up as if in surrender. "He took me by surprise. Not my fault."

Tim jerked upright. Cal cracked him across the face with an open-hand slap, snapping his head around and plunging him back into unconsciousness.

Cal stared at his hand in horror.

"Jesus, what is *wrong* with me?"

"Get the fonk away from the man," Mech said. "Before you beat the poor son-of-a-bedge to death."

"Alright, alright. Backing away," said Cal, raising his hands again. He stopped several feet away and crouched down. "Timbo? Timbo, you still with us?"

The Time Titan gave a sleepy sort of snort, and Cal breathed a sigh of relief. "He's still alive."

Wincing, Tim raised his head. He *cricked* his jaw around, and rubbed the side of his face. His beard had helped protect him, but part of a hand-shaped red imprint was visible on his cheek.

"What happened?" he groaned.

"A number of terrible accidents," Cal said, jumping in before anyone else could answer. "But let's not get bogged down by the details. The important thing is you're OK. The other important thing is nobody is to blame, and none of us should ever speak of it again."

Tim dabbed at the bloody stain on his moustache, then regarded the smear on his finger with a mix of concern and curiosity. "I'm getting too old for all this," he muttered, before shaking his head and making an admirable attempt at pulling himself together. He gestured with a frail arm toward the view screen. "Where are we?"

"We're headed for the co-ordinates Dorid gave us," Loren explained. "Didn't see much point waiting for permission, since we're now apparently at war with the Gooramy for reasons nobody has bothered to explain yet..."

"I told you," said Miz. "They wanted Cal to bang a fish-lady."

"A fish-*queen*," Cal corrected. "Let's not undersell it here."

Loren kept her gaze on her controls. "And did you?"

Cal returned to his seat. "Why? Do you care?"

"Of course I do."

Cal's eyebrows raised. "You do? Seriously?"

Loren turned, visibly agitated. "It got us shot at. We almost died. If you're putting us in danger, then of course I care."

"Oh. Yeah. Right," said Cal. "I mean... No. I didn't. That's why they were trying to kill us."

"Well... maybe you should have," said Loren.

"That's what I told these two," said Cal.

Loren's eyes narrowed. "You did?"

"I mean... I didn't want to, obviously, but for the sake of the mission, or whatever, I thought..."

He found himself talking to the back of Loren's head.

"But I didn't. And that's the main thing," he concluded.

"Good for you," Loren said.

Something about the tone of her voice triggered something in Cal's memory. He'd heard her use that exact tone recently. It was something he'd meant to ask her about. Something he...

Wait.

"You won't miss this."

Loren's fingers stopped midway to one of the switches on her console.

"That's what you said. You're not going to 'miss shizz like this'. Back at Dorid's place, that's what you said."

"Did I?" said Loren. "Heat of the moment. Ignore it. Forget I said anything."

"No, I mean you must have meant something, right?"

"Like I said, heat of the moment. It's nothing."

"Loren...?"

"Cal, just... Just leave it, OK?" she replied. Something *bleeped* softly on her console. "We're closing on the location. I'm taking us out of warp."

"Fonk. OK. Everyone hold on," Cal warned. He barely managed to cup his hands over his crotch before the ship decelerated with Loren's usual pelvis-shattering levels of style and panache. Splurt rocketed from his hiding place in the ceiling, thudded into a fried-egg-shape against the view screen, then plopped to the floor.

An asteroid *clunked* off the hull, filling the bridge with the creaking of damaged metal. Another solid chunk of stone, roughly the size of a football, slammed into the ship's nose, making the screen flicker.

Before them, stretching out like a vast wasteland, was a cloud of tumbling rocks.

"Is this the place?" Cal asked. The *Untitled* shook as a rock the size of a family car hit the underside then scraped all the way along it to the back. "I've got to say, not what I was expecting."

"It's gone," said Loren. "This was supposed to be a planet, but... it's gone."

"What do you mean 'it's gone?" Mech asked. "How can it be gone?"

"Death Star?" Cal suggested. "That could do it."

"What's a Death Star?" Miz asked.

"A moon with a gun," Cal explained. "They made, like, twelve of them, I think." He shook his head ruefully. "Never fonking learned."

"OK, I'm just gonna go ahead and ignore whatever the Hell he's talking about," Mech said, while working the controls in front of him. "Scanners show a lot of rocks and not a whole lot else. This is what it should've looked like."

A star chart was overlaid in a window on the right of the screen. It showed a star with what seemed to be a single planet in orbit around it. Cal tried to read the name.

"Nmnem... Nyimim... Mnumem..."

"It's pronounced Nmiminimbe," said Loren.

"That's what I said. Nmumimum," Cal replied. "And we're sure we're in the right place?"

A chunk of rock *thunked* off the front of the ship.

"It's the right place," Mech confirmed. "Nmiminimbe is gone. The whole planet's been completely destroyed."

The full enormity of what had happened finally hit Cal.

"Jesus," he said, and a silence made up of shock and disbelief fell over the bridge.

It went on for quite a while.

Cal glanced at the others, wondering if it was appropriate to speak yet. It wasn't like they had friends living down on Mnimi... Mimin... on whatever the fonk it was called.

Or did they?

Shizz.

This could get delicate.

"Such a shame," he said, clicking his tongue against his teeth in disapproval. "Such a tragic waste. I mean, all those people..."

"It was uninhabited," Loren said.

"What? Then why are we all sitting here moping about it?" Cal asked.

"A whole planet has been destroyed," Mech answered.

"A big rock became lots of smaller rocks," Cal countered. "Boo-hoo. The way you were all acting, I thought it was a fonking orphanage or something."

The Time Titan cut in, stopping the conversation before it could descend any further into bickering. "The Quanturum. I should be able to detect it at this range, but... There's nothing."

"Sensors aren't picking any up, either," Loren confirmed.

Cal gasped. "So that means..."

He waited.

"I was hoping one of you were going to fill in the rest," he said, once it was clear no one was going to. "What does that mean?"

"It means it's gone," said Loren. "This planet was the only known source of Quanturum, and now it's all gone."

She looked across to Mech. "You think someone blew up the whole planet to get it?"

Mech shrugged. "Maybe. I mean, planets don't just blow up on their own. Not without good reason, anyway." He motioned to the screen. "Nothing showing this place was unstable. Had to be deliberate."

"Like, why would someone blow up a whole planet just to get some rocks?" Miz wondered.

Tim's voice trembled around the edges. "What if what happened aboard the *Binto Odyssey* was a test?" he said. "A proof of concept."

Loren turned in her chair. "They're building another bomb."

"I fear so."

"How big a bomb are we talking?" Cal asked. "I mean, how much did they use in the last one?"

Tim moved his hand vaguely. "Perhaps a piece the size of a teshuk. Or a little larger. But smaller than a noomf."

Cal moved his eyes from Tim to the others. "Is that a lot? I have no idea what those things are."

"They're fruit," said Loren. She made a gesture with her hands and indicated a size a little larger than an apple."

Cal mimicked the gesture. "Couldn't you just have said 'that size'?" he asked Tim, but the Time Titan was gazing at the newly formed asteroid field ahead and wringing his fingers together in worry. "OK, so if they did make a bomb out of all this stuff, just how screwed are we?"

"Eight," said Mech.

"Is that *eight out of ten* screwed, like a normal person would do, meaning we have some leeway to do some heroic save-the-galaxy shizz, or *eight out of eight* screwed, like you do?"

Mech turned back and met his eye. "Out of five."

Cal's lips moved silently as he calculated. "So we're, like, a hundred and forty per cent screwed? Is that what you're telling me?"

Mech shook his head. "No."

Cal relaxed a little. "OK, good."

"We're a hundred and *sixty* per cent screwed. And not just us, the whole fonking galaxy. If what the old man's saying is right, I mean."

All eyes went to Tim. He had undone his seatbelt and now walked slowly across the bridge towards the screen, his smock *swishing* around at his ankles.

"You're correct," he said. "If the builders of the first device have scaled it up to use a whole planet's worth of Quanturum, the damage could be insurmountable. What we saw on the *Odyssey*... what you experienced... those were fractures. Cracks in time which disrupted the natural ebb and flow."

He reached the screen and stopped. The light of the distant sun danced through the debris field, casting moving shadows across his face.

"A weapon of this scale wouldn't just fracture time, it would obliterate it. The time stream would collapse. Not all at once, but the damage would quickly spread throughout the galaxy – throughout the universe – until..."

His voice tailed off. He placed a hand on the screen, supporting himself.

"Until what?"

"I don't know," Tim admitted.

"What? I thought this was your whole thing?" Cal said. "Time. I thought you knew all about that sort of stuff?"

Tim sighed. "You know about water, yes? You can manipulate it – cause ripples in it with your fingers, pour it into drinking glasses. That sort of thing."

Cal wasn't sure if he was supposed to answer the question, but fortunately Tim continued before he had to make a decision either way.

"Now imagine you take one of those filled glasses and you drop it. You know what will happen – it will break."

"Not necessarily," Cal muttered.

Fonking Smashdown Day.

"Assuming it does," Tim continued. "Can you predict where the liquid will go? With any degree of accuracy, I mean? Could you draw the outline of it on the floor before it happened?"

"Depends. Is it a carpet floor? Because then I'd need a special pen."

"My point is, this is like that," Tim continued. "Only instead of a glass of water, it involves the entire fourth dimension. So, can I tell you precisely what will happen? No. Do I know it will be catastrophic? Yes. That I can promise you."

Cal conceded the argument. "OK, you've convinced me. It's eight out of five. But we can still do something about it." He looked around the bridge. "Right?"

"I'm open to suggestions," said Mech.

"Trace the time rocks," Cal said, pointing enthusiastically at the control panel in front of Mech. "Use the scanners or whatever and trace where the time rocks went. Then we just follow the trail."

He crossed his arms quite smugly and wriggled back in his chair, getting comfortable. "Problem solved. You're welcome."

"Can the scanners do that?" Miz asked.

"No. No, they can't," said Mech.

"Of course they can. They do it in movies all the time," Cal said. "Kevin?"

"You hollered, sir?"

"Have the scanners track the time rocks for me, would you?"

"Very good, sir. One moment."

Cal's smug expression became even more so. He winked at Mech. "Have the info for you in a sec."

"I've made the request to the scanner array, sir," Kevin intoned.

"Great job."

"But it's looking at me rather blankly."

"It's what?"

"Oh! Hold on. I'm getting some data coming through from it now, and... Ah."

"What's it say?"

"Nothing complimentary, sir. It's dismissing your suggestion as something of a nonsense."

"Oh."

"And questioning your intelligence."

"Right.

"And your parentage."

Cal uncrossed his arms. "So, what we're saying is the scanners *can't* track the time rocks?"

"That would certainly appear to be the case, sir."

Puffing out his cheeks, Cal slapped his hands on his thighs. "OK, well it was a solid idea, but... Anyone else?"

Before anyone could volunteer a suggestion, a ripple of light passed through the debris field ahead of the ship. It seemed to emanate from the point where Tim's hand was pressed against the screen.

"OK, what was that?" Cal asked, leaning forward. "Timbo? You OK there?"

The old man's mouth was moving, a murmur of sound

burbling deep down in his throat. Cal hopped out of his chair and joined the Time Titan up front.

"Tim? Everything... Ooh, fonk. Look at his eyes. That's awesome. They're all swirly."

Outside, the cloud of rocks became filled with flickering gray shadows. They were barely visible against the blackness of space, and flowed and ebbed like smoke, but Cal thought he could make out familiar shapes in there. Ships. People. Weapons, or maybe tools.

The planet reformed as a haze of dark vapor. Cal saw it as both enormous and tiny at the same time, like he was watching some spectacular live event through the screen of a phone camera.

"What's he doing?" Miz wondered.

"I think he's watching a rerun," Cal said. He beckoned to Splurt, who was still on the floor by the screen. The little blob oozed up his leg, then clambered onto his shoulder. "I think he's seeing what happened here."

"Correct," Tim confirmed, and the voice that emerged from him was that ship-shaking deep rumble they'd first heard back on the *Odyssey*. "Observe."

Cal and the others watched, though it was hard to tell what they were watching exactly. A lot seemed to happen in several different patches of space, most of it too wispy and insubstantial to make out clearly.

If Cal had to guess the story unfolding in front of them, he'd say a couple of large spaceships had arrived, then several figures had descended to the surface of Mnimim... of the planet in smaller ships.

There had been mining involved – huge industrial tools that burrowed deep beneath the planet's crust. A lot of material – the Quanturum, presumably – had been taken back to the bigger ships, but the equipment had been left behind.

The ships had barely left orbit when the explosion tore through the planet, sending pieces of it spinning off in all directions through space, and completely covering the tracks of whoever had carried out the raid.

One figure, in particular, kept rearing up through the fog. Cal saw him giving out orders, directing the drills, and overseeing the planting of the explosives. Each time he appeared, he was more substantial than the last time, as if the image was becoming stronger through sheer repetition.

"Who is that?" Cal asked. He stepped closer to the view screen, his eyes fixed on one of the three versions of the figure currently out there in space. It was a man. Two arms, two legs, facial features all roughly where you might expect.

The image was boarding a wispy spaceship, preparing to leave the planet, when his features solidified enough for Cal to make out the detail.

"Holy shizz. Freeze frame. Hold it there!" he said.

Tim cocked his head a little. The smoke ships and vapor figures all stopped moving.

Cal leaned closer to the view screen until his nose was practically touching it. Even that close-up, the resolution was so high Cal could've sworn he was looking through a window.

And there, looking back, was a face Cal recognized.

"Sweet fonking shizzmas," Cal said. "Is that who I think it is?"

EIGHTEEN

THE MORE CAL STARED, the more convinced he became of the smoke-figure's identity.

"I know that guy. *We* know that guy. That's Dave. Or whatever his real name was," Cal said. "That's the guy from the clown planet who was trying to steal the big ball dude."

The swirling pattern in Tim's eyes turned a milky white, then faded. He sagged, and the shadow-figures outside evaporated.

"The 'big ball dude?" he said, his breath rasping from the effort of whatever it was he'd just done.

"No, he didn't *have* big... I mean, he was trying to steal a big ball from a prison. It had a bad guy inside it." Cal clicked his fingers a few times as he hunted for the name. "Geronimo."

"Geronimus," Mech corrected.

Tim's eyebrows raised. His face paled. "Geronimus *Krone*?"

"That's the guy," Cal said. "Dave there, although that's probably not his real name, now that I come to think about it, he tricked us into helping him steal the space prison that Krone was locked up in. The big ball thing."

"Geronimus Krone," Tim said again. He stumbled a little until he fell against Mech, then held onto the cyborg's arm for support.

"Yep, Dave wanted to free him. Presumably to do bad shizz. Didn't pay too much attention to the details," Cal said. "Good news is, Dave's dead – we blew him to pieces – and old Geronimo is still safely under lock and key. Or, I don't know, retina scanner and eye, or whatever."

"Where?" Tim demanded.

"Zertex put him somewhere. Not sure where, but it's fine. They don't want him free any more than we do," Cal said. "Or, you know, we assume so. We're like ninety-five per cent confident."

"We need to check," Tim replied. "Geronimus Krone must not be free. Must *never* be free."

"You know the guy?" Mech asked.

"I know *of* him," the Time Titan said. "Him, I never personally had to deal with. His generals? Them I met, although not a day goes by when I wish that I hadn't."

"I know a few people like that," Cal said. "Naming no names." He coughed loudly. "Mech."

"Fonk you, shizznod."

"Guys, shut up," said Loren. "Let him talk."

Tim smoothed his smock down with one hand, and his beard with the other. "The generals, they served Krone during his reign of terror, leading his armies across the galaxy and crushing all who dared stand against them. Men, women, children. They didn't care. They were monstrous. Darkness and corruption made flesh. They called themselves the Four."

Cal snorted. "Jesus, they must've been up all night

thinking of that one. I mean, talk about obvious." He frowned. "Unless, you know, there were only two of them, in which case, I take that back."

"The Four what?" Miz asked, leaning forward in her chair in a way that suggested she was taking at least a modicum of interest, which was possibly a first for her.

Tim peered along his nose at her. "Greyx, correct? I believe your people knew them as the Four Blights," he explained.

"Yeah. Yeah, I've heard that story," Miz said, and from her expression it was not one that had a particularly happy ending.

"They feature in the myths and legends of most civilizations," Tim confirmed. "In some stories they arrive in great space ships. In others, they travel by sea, or on wings..." He flicked his eyes to Cal. "Or on horseback."

Tim gave Cal a moment to take that in, before continuing.

"The legends of the Omparo people say they stride purposefully. The Rikkitiks believe they come on pogo sticks. The Maggashakai record-keepers insist they all come standing on one another's shoulders, wearing a very long coat," he said. "The details are slightly different, but the core of it is the same. Four individuals, ushering in death and destruction and the end of all things."

"The Space Four Horsemen!" Cal gasped. "No. Hold on. The Four *Space* Horsemen. The Four Horse *Spacemen*?" He shrugged. "Fonk it. One of those. Yeah, I've heard of those guys. Real end of the world shizznods."

"What happened to them?" Loren asked. "Where did they go?"

"The other Time Titans and I..." Tim began, then his voice betrayed him and he was forced to take a moment to compose himself. "We went against our code and agreed to intervene."

"Wait, wait, wait. *Other* Time Titans?" said Cal. "I didn't know there were others."

"There were twelve of us. Now there is only me," Tim said. His eyes shimmered in the light of the distant sun, but this time there was nothing supernatural about it. "My brothers and sisters and I, we stood against the Four and their armies. We took time and we turned it into a weapon to be used against them."

"Alarm clock in a sock?" Cal guessed. He mimed swinging something around his head. "Because that's gonna hurt."

"We collapsed the fourth dimension on top of them," Tim said, his voice becoming a whispery hiss as he recalled the memory. "We tossed them in a temporal hole and we poured time itself into it until we had buried them alive."

"Sounds pretty awesome," said Miz.

Tim shook his head. "Necessary. Far from 'awesome'," he said. "Eleven of us died that day, our energy spent. I alone survived to carry the burden of what we had done."

"Saved the galaxy," Cal said.

"Betrayed time itself," Tim said, punctuating the sentence with a sob. "We went against all we are supposed to stand for. All we are supposed to be."

He closed his eyes and turned his head away for a moment. When he turned back, there was a strength to his voice that hadn't been there a moment ago. "But we stopped them. We damned the Four and their armies to exist in an eternal loop. Aware – endlessly aware – but trapped forever in the wrinkles of time."

"Sounds firm but fair," said Cal.

"We thought so," Tim said. "The entire army – all those

countless soldiers and ships – are now in a bubble the size of a pinhead, locked away in a vault on the prison moon of Ka'Reth, reliving the same second over and over and over again."

"Wait a minute, wait a minute," said Mech, a frown troubling his brow. He ratcheted his dial around a notch or two, cranking up his brainpower. When he continued, his voice was half an octave higher. "So, let me get this straight. The human, who for want of another name we shall continue to refer to as 'Dave', attempted to free Geronimus Krone from the prison planet on which he was being held. Correct?"

He glanced impatiently at the others.

"Sounds about right," Cal said. "So?"

"I'll get to the 'so' momentarily," Mech continued. "We also now know that the very same 'Dave' stripped this entire planet of its Quanturum. Enough Quanturum to – as the Time Titan himself puts it – 'obliterate time itself'."

"Still waiting on that 'so', big guy."

"*So* as 'Dave' has already attempted one break-out, can we surmise that his motivation for obtaining this much Quanturum is so he may use it in *another* breakout attempt? Specifically, the breakout of 'the Four' from their makeshift prison within the folds of time."

Cal blinked. "Was there a question in there? I kind of tuned out," he admitted.

Loren leaned back in her chair, deep in thought. "He's saying Dave wasn't just looking to break out Geronimus Krone, he was going to break out his generals and his army, too."

"Then it's a good job we blew him up," said Cal. "I'd actually been feeling kind of bad about that, so this has perked me right up. I mean, in a way, by blowing him up we actually saved the galaxy twice."

"And you're sure he's dead?" Tim asked. "You saw his body?"

Cal nodded. "Yep. I mean, no, we didn't see his body, because there was no body left to see. We blew up his ship, though, so that was pretty definitive. Then we caught Geronimo's big ball thing before it could smash open, and we gave it to Zertex to look after."

Tim nodded slowly. "Zertex being...?"

"The space government. Formerly *evil* space government. Well, the jury's still out," Cal explained.

"They're not evil," Loren chimed in. "Not anymore."

"Like, how don't you know what Zertex is?" Miz asked.

Tim shrugged. "Governments come and go. When you get to my age, you sort of lose track."

"So... what are we saying here?" Cal asked, looking to the others. "Everything's fine? That's the conclusion? Dave's dead, his evil plan is thwarted, and everything's fine?"

He shrugged, forcing Splurt to cling onto his neck to avoid falling off. "I mean, don't get me wrong, I love a happy ending, but it feels kind of anti-climactic, don't you think?"

"I'm not complaining," said Loren.

"Yeah. I guess not," Cal said. He turned and headed back to his chair. He had almost reached it when he stopped. "Unless..."

He shook his head. "Nah."

"Unless what?" Miz asked.

"Nothing. Doesn't matter," said Cal.

Mizette tutted. "Fine. It's not like I even care."

Cal turned. "Kevin?"

"Yes, sir?"

"You remember the clown planet, right?"

Silence.

"We landed on the platform and you had to wait up there while we went down to the surface in the big elevator thing."

More silence.

"We almost got killed by clown robots. Whole planet turned out to be a giant prison. There was a big dinosaur thing? No? Any of this ringing any bells? It was, like, a week ago."

"I vaguely recall something, sir," Kevin told him. "Didn't we arrive to find the planet had been destroyed?"

"No, that's... that's this planet," Cal said, indicating the debris field outside. "That's what's happening now. The thing I'm talking about happened *before*. Like, you know, previously?"

"Oh, you mean Funworld. Yes! I recall it, sir. What of it?"

Cal somehow managed a smile. "Great! This kind of feels like a stupid question after the conversation we just had, but do you happen to remember if there were any other ships in the area around the time we were fighting Dave's ship?"

"Oh yes, I remember, sir."

They all waited.

Loren was the first to break.

"Then can you tell us?" she asked.

"Oh yes. Of course, ma'am. There were no other ships around."

Cal let out a breath he hadn't realized he was holding. An itch somewhere near the center of his brain suddenly felt as if it had been scratched.

"OK, great. Thanks, Kevin," he said, turning back to his chair.

"Well, *basically* none."

Cal stopped.

Cal turned.

"Basically? What do you mean 'basically'?"

"There *had* been another ship in the landing bay. A Funworld maintenance vessel. Nothing to write home about. It departed the docking platform shortly after the ship you engaged with did. Surprisingly nippy for such an old pile of junk."

Cal sat down, his mind racing. There was something wrong. Something he couldn't yet put his finger on.

"We blew up the ship. We caught the ball. We gave it to Zertex," he whispered.

"Cal, what is it?" Loren asked.

Cal didn't answer. "Even if it was the wrong ship, we still caught the ball. We gave it to Zertex. They locked it up."

He knew the answer. He'd known it for several seconds now, but the part of his brain that wanted to spare him the worry was doing its best to protect him from it.

But it couldn't hide the truth forever.

"We caught *a* ball," he realized. "That fonking shizznod set us up!"

Miz scowled. "What are you talking about? Who set us up?"

"Dave!"

"The guy we killed?"

"The guy we *thought* we killed," Cal corrected. "He's alive, and he's got Geronimo."

"Geronimus," Mech said.

"Jesus, OK, whatever his fonking name is! Dave has got him. They're both out there."

"But, like, we blew up their ship."

"They weren't on it. They were on the Funworld ship."

Loren frowned. "So... if that's true – if they're both out there..." Her blue skin paled, just a fraction. "Then what did we deliver to Zertex?"

And with that, Cal's brain let rip with the full terrible truth.

Of course. It all made sense. Somehow, against all odds, it was Cal who finally understood *exactly* what was going on.

Worse than that, he had a pretty good idea of what was going to happen next.

"Oh God," he groaned. "Oh God, do we have a problem."

NINETEEN

Miz sighed. It was not one of her most emphatic sighs, but it was up there.

"So, like, is everyone else following this? Because I have *zero* idea what's going on right now."

"No time. Explain later," Cal said. He jabbed a finger to the screen. "Loren, call Zertex. Find a way to get in touch with President What's-Her-Name."

"Valtrax," said Mech. He'd turned his dial back dead center, and was back to barking out his usual gruff tones. "And how the fonk are we supposed to get through to the damn president? Ain't like we got a direct line."

Loren gently cleared her throat. "I might have."

"You do?" Cal asked. "How come? Since when?"

"Haska... President Valtrax, she gave it to me."

Mech frowned. "Haska? You on first name terms now?"

"Look, do you want me to call her or not?" Loren asked.

"Do it," Cal said.

Loren's fingers flew across her controls. A moment later, the face of President Valtrax appeared in a window on screen. With her short white hair, scaly skin and complete lack of oily smarm, she was practically the diametric opposite of the previous Zertex president, Sinclair. Cal approved of this, what with Sinclair having been such a total shizznod.

"Teela. This is a surprise," Valtrax said. "Are you calling to accept my offer?"

"No," Loren blurted. "I mean, that's not why I'm calling. We have a possible situation." She turned in her chair and almost flinched when she saw the suspicion and betrayal in Cal's eyes. "Cal? You want to fill her in?"

Cal blinked a few times, as if coming up from a hypnotic trance. "Uh, yeah. Yeah." He raised his eyes to the screen. "That big ball we gave you. With the bad guy inside. Where is it?"

"It's safe. As agreed," the president replied. "Why do you ask?"

"We think it's a bomb," Cal said. "A very special kind of bomb. You need to tell us where it is."

An expression of surprise flitted across Valtrax's face, but was gone before anyone could register it. "It is stored in a vault that is quite blastproof. Even if it is a bomb, any explosion will be contained."

"Not this one," said Tim.

Valtrax gestured at the old man. "New recruit?"

"Just a friend," said Cal. "Tim. He commands time. Long story."

"Influences, not commands," Tim corrected.

"Whatever. That ball you have locked away, it's a Time Bomb."

"What, with the clock on the front?"

"You'd think so, but no. It'll literally destroy time."

President Valtrax took a moment to get her head around this. "I don't know what that would involve."

"Fonked if I know, either," Cal admitted. "But it's bad. Universe destroying bad. So you have to tell us where it is."

Valtrax's gaze went to Loren. "Is this true, Teela?"

"Uh, yeah. Yeah, as far as we know," Loren replied. "We really do need to know where it is."

The president nodded curtly. "Very well. Please hold a moment while I find out."

The face was replaced by the Zertex logo, and a silence descended over the bridge.

"This is awkward," Kevin muttered.

"Her 'offer'?" said Cal. "What offer?"

"Nothing, it's..." Loren's voice tailed off. She sighed, but kept facing front, unable to look at the others. Not yet. "She offered me... a position. Within Zertex."

"She's giving you your job back?" Cal gasped.

"Tell me you said yes," Miz said, brightening and sitting upright in her chair.

"Not my old job. A new job," Loren said. "I'd be working alongside her to make Zertex... better. To fix the problems Sinclair caused."

"Wasn't just Sinclair," Mech pointed out. "That whole fonking organization is filled with bad dudes."

"And I'd be helping clear them out," Loren said. "I'd be doing a good thing."

"And... what? You'd just go? Leave us?" He added the 'Leave me?' silently in his head. "You're our pilot!"

"The ship doesn't need a pilot. Kevin can fly it."

"Yeah, but Kevin's creepy and weird," Cal said. "No offence, Kevin."

"None taken, sir."

"No-one flies like you do, Loren."

Miz snorted. "You can say that again."

"Unlike Miz, I meant that in a good way," Cal said, shooting the wolf-woman daggers.

"We could all go," Loren said, finally turning. "I could get us all jobs there."

"I ain't working for Zertex," Mech said.

"We have no food!" Loren pointed out. "We have no money. We're bouncing around in space doing... what, exactly?"

"We're helping people," Cal said.

"Who? We destroyed half a city yesterday. You were ready to shoot down the cops who – rightfully – came to arrest us for it. Who were we helping then, Cal?"

"OK, I'll give you that one," Cal said. He pointed to the screen. "But we're stopping a Time Bomb."

"A Time Bomb that we handed over in the first place," Loren pointed out. "I love you guys – I mean, I don't necessarily *like* any of you a lot of the time, but... I don't know. We can't go on like this. This isn't a life. Not a real one."

President Valtrax reappeared before anyone could answer. "Apologies for the delay," she said. "I have the location of the... object you entrusted to us."

Cal jumped in before she could continue.

"Prison moon of Ka'Reth."

Valtrax looked momentarily taken aback. "Why, yes. Yes, how did you know?"

Tim took a stumbling step backwards and almost fell onto Miz. "Hey, watch it, you old weirdo."

"Oh no," the Time Titan whispered. "Oh no. What have they done?"

"Oh... shizz," Loren whispered, as the penny finally dropped for everyone else on the bridge, with the exception of Miz. And possibly Splurt. "He played us. He knew we'd give you the bomb. He knew exactly where you'd put it."

"He's got Krone, and now he's going to break out his whole fonking army," Mech realized.

Cal stood up. "Pres, you want to prove Zertex are the good guys? Then you have to... You have to..."

He turned to Tim, his voice faltering. "What do we do? I don't know what to do."

Tim's mouth sort of flapped open and closed in a way that suggested words should have been coming out, but weren't. He shook his head. "I don't... I'm not..."

Well, he was no fonking help.

Cal turned back to the screen. "We need to get that bomb as far away from that moon as possible," he instructed. "Or a lot of people are going to be a lot of dead very quickly."

"What is going on?" the president demanded.

"Look, you're going to have to trust us on this," Cal told her. "Get that bomb away from that moon."

Valtrax tilted her head, just a fraction, but it was enough to put Cal on high-alert. "What is it? What aren't you telling us?"

"We tried to contact the administration on Ka'Reth a moment ago. They have failed to respond."

Cal shot a questioning look to Tim. "The bomb?"

"N-no." The Time Titan shook his head. "I would have felt it."

"OK, then we still have a chance," Cal said. He pointed to the screen. "You. Start evacuation of any systems close to that prison. We need to get those people as far away as possible."

"I'm *sorry*?" Valtrax said, her nostrils flaring in something not unlike amusement. "I'm the President of Zertex, Mr Carver. You cannot bark orders at me."

"You want to prove your good enough for our friend to

come work for you? Then do what I tell you," Cal said. He grinned, and made it one of his better ones. "Please. Pretty please. Get those people to safety. You're the only one who can."

Valtrax seemed to chew over her response before letting it out. "It will take time."

"Then you'd better get started," Cal said.

"And what about Ka'Reth? What about your bomb?"

"We'll deal with that," Cal said. "I mean, I haven't put it to a vote yet, but we've got nothing else planned for the afternoon. We might need back-up, though. Have some of those annoying little fighter ships of yours on standby, but make sure they keep their distance until we tell them to, or until the shizz has clearly hit the fan."

This was a step too far for the president. Her scaly features pulled into a scowl of disapproval. "Who do you think you are, exactly, telling me what to do? I'm the president of half the galaxy."

"We're Space Team," Cal retorted. "And if you still want there to be a galaxy to be president of, then you'd better get your fonking skates on."

They held each other's gaze across the vast chasm of space, neither one ready to back down. It was Tim who broke the deadlock.

"I believe your people know them as the Four Outrages," he said. "They arrive upon great storm clouds to cleanse your world of everything innocent and pure. They take the children first, make their parents watch as they do... things. Such terrible things."

President Valtrax's face tightened. "What is he talking about?"

"That's who's coming," Cal said. "That's what's going to

happen when that bomb goes off. We can stop it. We can stop it happening. But we need your help."

Valtrax's eyes narrowed, and Cal could practically see her running through her options in her head. "We'll begin the evacuation," she said. "But you will keep me informed. I expect full transparency."

"You got it, space pres. And have those ships ready. Screen off."

There was an awkward pause.

"Sorry?" said Valtrax.

"Oh. I thought... That was supposed to be a signal for someone to end the call," Cal explained.

"I see. Rather abrupt, wasn't it?" Valtrax asked. "I mean, 'goodbye' would have been traditional."

"OK, OK. Goodbye," said Cal. "Jesus. Now can someone end the—"

The Zertex symbol appeared on screen, then the communications window disappeared. "Did she end the call? I wanted to end the call."

"Does it matter?" Mech asked.

"Well, I mean, it just would've been nice if I'd been the one to end the call. That's all I'm saying. More, like, authoritative, or whatever. It just would've been nice."

"Do you want me to call her back up so you can end the call?" Loren asked.

Cal bit his lip. "Should we? Or would that look weird?"

"Yes, it would look weird! I was kidding," said Loren.

"OK, fine! It's not a big deal," Cal said. "I just would've liked to—"

"Will you shut the Hell up about who ended the motherfonking call?" Mech barked.

Cal tutted and leaned forward in his chair. "I was just

saying, that's all," he mumbled. "OK, Loren, plot a course for—"

"Already done it," Loren said, then she pushed forward on a thruster stick and the *Currently Untitled* became a blur of warp speed among the stars.

TWENTY

To DESCRIBE the Ka'Reth system as 'a shizzhole' would be to do a grave disservice to other shizzholes across the galaxy. For starters, the planet was a rather alarming shade of red that either suggested danger, or that the four orbiting planets were populated entirely by prostitutes, and they were all touting for business.

The planets themselves ranged from 'I wouldn't go there if you paid me' to 'is that even a fonking planet?' with the hazy gaseous ball that was Ka'Reth falling firmly into the latter category.

The prison moon orbited worryingly close to the planet below, skirting the very edges of its opaque atmosphere. It looked as dead as anywhere else in the system, aside from a domed metal building that rose from the dark side like a blister.

"Is that it?" Cal asked.

"That's it," Loren confirmed.

Miz swung her legs off the arm of her chair and sat up a little straighter. "Shouldn't there be, like, defenses or whatever?"

"Girl's got a point," said Mech. "Whole sector should be teeming with patrol ships. This place is supposed to be protected."

"The moon does appear to be equipped with some rather heavy duty shield technology," Kevin announced.

"OK. That's more like it," said Cal, relaxing a little.

"However, it's currently switched off," Kevin continued.

"Fonk. OK."

"Would you like me to scan for life signs?"

"Do it," Cal said.

"I'm afraid I can't, sir. The roof's too thick. Probably shouldn't have offered, really. Rather got your hopes up there, didn't I?"

"You really did, Kevin," Cal said, then he spun in his chair. "Tim. Can you...?" He looked around. "Where's Tim?"

From further back in the ship, there came the sound of a toilet flushing.

"Oh," said Cal. He leaned on an elbow, drumming his fingers on his arm rest while he waited.

"Should I take us in to land?" Loren asked.

Behind her, Miz pulled on her seatbelt.

"Hmm? No, let's wait to see what Tim has to say first."

They waited.

The toilet flushed again.

"The Time Titan appears to be having some difficulty, sir. Should I activate the power flush?"

"We have a power flush?" asked Cal. "Then yeah. Do that."

"Very good, sir."

There was a sound like thunder. The *Untitled* shuddered violently, forcing Loren to grab the yoke until her knuckles turned white. Tim screamed, but the roaring of the power flush mostly drowned him out.

"Power flush completed, sir. That shifted it."

Cal straightened in his chair. A moment or two later, the door to the bridge opened and an ashen-faced Tim shambled in, drying his hands on his smock. He stopped when he saw everyone watching him.

"What?"

"We're here," Cal said. "Can you sense anything?"

"Hmm? Oh." Tim glanced up. "No. Nothing."

He sat down.

"Sorry."

"Well, that was worth the wait," Cal muttered, turning back to face front. He puffed out his cheeks. "Should we call them? Or just arrive unannounced and keep the element of surprise?"

"The element of surprise? When *she's* flying?" Miz snorted. "Because, like, they'll be *totally* surprised when we come crashing through the roof."

"To be fair, they probably would find that surprising," Cal pointed out. "I mean, I know you were being sarcastic, but that *would* be pretty surprising. From their point of view, I mean. Depressingly predictable from ours."

He tapped a fingernail against his teeth as he started out at the prison moon. "Let's put it to a vote. All in favor of calling ahead?"

No-one raised a hand.

"OK, then. Looks like element of surprise it is."

"I already called ahead, sir," Kevin said.

"What? Why?"

"I wish I knew, sir," Kevin admitted. "Sometimes I just

do things without thinking. It's probably a form of mental illness."

"Fonk. Fine. OK, did they respond?"

"It was an automated menu and queuing system."

Cal shifted in his seat. "Jesus. This place is worse than I thought."

"I'm still trying to navigate through the options," Kevin continued, and there was a slightly hysterical edge to his voice that was hard to miss. "None of them seem to quite match our reason for calling. I rather feel like I'm going around in circles."

"Then hang up!" Cal told him. "We didn't want you to call them in the first place."

"Oh, thank you, sir," Kevin sobbed. "*Thank* you."

It had taken under two hours to reach the Ka'Reth system, and the team had dedicated the time to coming up with a plan. As they had no real idea what they were walking into, though, the plan they had eventually settled on was, "Fonk it, we'll wing it, and see what happens," which had been proposed by Cal and quickly seconded by Mizette.

Miz had seemed more enthusiastic than usual, although this was not exactly saying much. It was the girl, she explained. The little girl back on the *Odyssey*, frozen forever in time, her life never to be lived. In a rare display of openness and emotion, Miz had told them that what had happened to the girl, "totally, like, sucked," and vowed to take a bloody and violent revenge on whoever turned out to be responsible.

Cal hadn't been able to bring himself to speak to Loren about her leaving, and had instead spent the rest of the trip torturing himself. This he did by imagining some of his favorite foods, while his stomach grumbled angrily in protest.

Even now, with the prison moon of Ka'Reth looming larger on the screen, and the fate of the galaxy almost certainly resting on his shoulders, he could murder some M&Ms.

"And we're sure there are no defenses still active?" Cal asked.

"Don't seem like it," Mech said. "Looks like everything's been powered down except life support, gravity and the vault locks."

Cal chewed his lip. It didn't feel right. Then again, a lot of things didn't feel right these days. He mostly just put it down to being in outer space, and generally thought no more about it.

Something felt specifically wrong about this, though. He'd gone over everything they knew – or thought they knew, at least – a hundred times on the trip here, and couldn't shake the feeling that there was something they were missing. Something that didn't quite fit.

Dave had faked his death. He had either already freed or was working on freeing Geronimous Krone. The ball Cal had thought contained Krone was actually a bomb, designed to obliterate time and, by extension, the time prison holding the Four Horsemen of the Spacepocalypse.

That all fit. It all made sense.

And yet, there was something not quite right, he was sure of it.

"How are the shield repairs coming on, Kevin?"

A pause followed. "I'm sorry, sir?"

"The shield repairs," said Cal, looking up at the speaker. "The repairs to the shields. How are they coming along?"

"I thought master Mech was doing that, sir?"

Mech turned, scowling. "What? No. I been standing here the whole time. You were doing it."

"Was I, sir? Since when?"

"Since I said, 'Kevin, fix the shields,'" Cal told him.

"Sorry, the *shields*? Yes, they're all fine now. I fixed those," Kevin said. "I thought you were asking how the 'field' repairs were coming along."

"Why the fonk would I ask...? What fields?"

"Well, I mean, I didn't know, sir. That's where the confusion was stemming from," Kevin explained. "I did think it rather odd."

"Jesus. OK. So we have shields. That's good," said Cal. He clicked his tongue against the roof of his mouth. "Then I guess we go down there and put a stop to all these shenanigans. Everyone agreed?"

"Totally," said Miz. She flicked her fingers, popping out her claws. "I can't *wait* to get at these guys."

"I like that energy, Miz. Keep it up," Cal encouraged. "Everyone else should follow Miz's example. Positive. Enthusiastic."

Miz tutted and sunk back into her chair. "Whatever."

"Short-lived..." Cal concluded. He nodded to Loren. "OK, let's get this over with. Take us down."

Mech shifted on his metal feet. "Why do I have a bad feeling about this?"

"I don't know, but I've got it, too," said Cal, then he forced himself to brighten up. "Still, just another day for the brave men and women of Space Team, right?"

Splurt lowered from the ceiling and shot Cal quite an accusing look. "Brave men, women, and shapeshifting goo blobs," Cal corrected, which seemed to satisfy the little guy. Splurt flopped down into Cal's lap, transformed briefly into an adorable space kitten, then *squelched* up onto Cal's shoulder as a gelatinous green ball.

"There's a ship on one of the landing pads," Loren said, indicating a spot on the roof of the building currently growing larger on the screen. "Doesn't look like a prison ship."

"Is it from Funworld?" Cal asked, but Loren shook her head.

"Looks like a TNK class fighter," said Mech, zooming that section of the screen into a separate overlay.

"It obviously is. You just have to look at it to see that," said Cal. "Also, what's a TNK class fighter?"

"They're like mini battleships. Slow and hard to maneuver, but can take a ridiculous amount of punishment," Loren explained.

"Anyone on board?"

"Don't seem to be," said Mech, checking the ship's scanners. "Whoever it is, they must be inside."

Cal pointed to another area of the screen. "Is that another landing pad?"

"It is," Loren confirmed. "It's a big one. Probably used for supply ships."

"Big enough that you could land on it?" Cal asked.

"I could land on the smaller one," Loren insisted.

Cal nodded. "Oh, of course! I know you could. I mean, past evidence doesn't exactly support it, but I absolutely know you could do it. I just think that one will be better."

Loren looked back over her shoulder. "Why?"

"Why?" Cal laughed, but only briefly. "Why what?"

"Why would that be a better one to land on?"

"Well, because... I mean..." He looked to Miz and Mech. "Guys?"

"Because we might not die on impact?" Miz suggested.

"Because we might not overshoot it and, like, crash into that planet way over there?"

She sat up and her snout curved into a smirk. "Ooh, I *like* this game."

"Because there's a separate entrance next to that pad, which means we might be able to get inside without anyone noticing," Mech said.

Cal clicked his fingers and pointed at the cyborg. "That one. That's the one I was thinking of, not the mean stuff Miz said, which I totally disagree with."

Loren sighed, then adjusted the controls. The angle of approach shifted, bringing the larger landing pad towards the center of the screen.

"Smoothly done," Cal told her.

"Yeah, yeah," Loren said. She raised her right hand at him and extended her index finger.

"Wrong one," Cal said. "But I get the idea, so points for effort." He leaned forward in his chair and studied the approaching pad. "And you're sure you can land on it?"

"I could hit it with my eyes closed," Loren insisted.

"We don't want you to 'hit it,'" Cal replied. "That's literally the last thing we want you to do."

Loren tutted. "You know what I mean."

"OK, then let's get down there, get inside, and we'll figure out the rest as we go. Everyone happy with that?"

He swung around in his chair, looking from the crew to the Time Titan sitting up at the back. "Happy, Tim?"

"Far from it," Tim said. "But what must be done must be done."

"Great words of wisdom there, Timbo. Real profound. With your permission, I might get that put on a t-shirt," Cal said. "You know, assuming the universe doesn't get destroyed in the next fifteen minutes. In which case, I probably won't bother."

"I have a bad feeling about this," Mech reiterated.

Cal leaned back in his chair and watched the landing pad grow larger on the screen. "Me too, big guy," he muttered. "Me too."

TWENTY-ONE

The landing went surprisingly smoothly, although Cal did insist that Loren keep her eyes open, and had Mech watch her to make sure she didn't shut them to try to prove a point.

The moon's atmosphere was thin, but breathable. It smelled like burnt toast and nipped angrily at the edges of Cal's eyes, but he could cope with it long enough for them to reach the hatch entrance leading into the prison below.

Mech had spent a full minute raining firepower on the circle of reinforced metal, but had barely left a mark. He had just cranked his dial two-thirds of the way towards 'Hulk-mode' when Loren had turned the hatch's handle and it had immediately slid open.

"Go on, say it," Mech said to Cal.

"Say what?"

"Whatever smart-ams shizz you're about to say."

Cal widened his eyes in mock surprise. "I resent that, Mech. You did your best and that's what counts. Whether you failed spectacularly and embarrassed yourself or not is irrelevant. You tried and that's the main thing."

"I hate you, man. Have I ever told you that?"

Cal grinned. "You may have mentioned it."

The gravity was a little heavier than Cal had been expecting, and by the time they'd made it down the ramp that led down from the hatch, his thighs felt like they were burning.

He'd been allowed to bring a blaster pistol on the strict understanding that he didn't accidentally shoot any of them with it, and while he'd enjoyed holding it out in front of him like a cop on a TV show for a while, his arms had quickly begun to kill him, and he'd now tucked the gun into the back of his pants for safe-keeping.

Splurt had slung himself across Cal's shoulders like a backpack, distributing his increased weight more evenly. Cal hadn't asked him to do this. He wasn't even aware of consciously thinking it, but the little blob had picked up some subconscious niggle, and adjusted himself accordingly.

It was kind of him, Cal thought. Granted, it would've been kinder still if he'd just grown legs and fonking walked, but it was a nice gesture all the same.

The prison complex was pretty much exactly what Cal had expected. It reminded him in many ways of the prisons he'd spent time in back on Earth, although this one was a little more... What was the word he was looking for?

Spacey.

It wasn't that anything was particularly high-tech or futuristic-looking. Quite the opposite, in fact. The metal walls were pitted with rust. The floor was scuffed and lined with the deep grooves made by heavy objects being dragged through the place every day for decades.

It was the little differences that made the place seem alien: the symbols on the wall that his translator chip took a few seconds to decipher; the weirdly-shaped doorways that were clearly built to accommodate people twice his size; the alien corpses lying dismembered on the floor.

Especially that last one, in fact.

"What happened to them?" Loren wondered, as they tip-toed around a small ocean of blood with an island of mutilated flesh somewhere near the middle.

"Nothing pleasant," Cal said, tearing his eyes away from the ravaged face of a uniformed young woman. Her mouth was open. Her throat, even more so. "Miz, you getting anything?"

Miz shook her head and flared her nostrils. "Just blood. Walls are too thick to hear anything except us."

"Same problem here," Mech said, indicating his scanners. "Damn walls must be sensor-shielded. I got no idea what we're walking into."

"Come on, we never have any idea what we're walking into," Cal pointed out. "That's what makes it exciting."

A sound crackled from Mech's arm. Cal screamed and grabbed for his gun, but recognized Kevin's voice before he could open fire.

"Hello!" the AI called through the speaker. Mech frantically stabbed at the buttons.

"Shh! Shut the fonk up!"

"Sorry, sir? Having some difficulty hearing you," Kevin said, raising his voice to a shout. "Can you hear me? Hello? HELLOOOOO!"

"Yes! Jesus, Kevin, we can hear you," Cal hissed. "Keep your voice down."

"Apologies, sir," said Kevin, dropping his volume down to a more natural speaking level.

They waited for him to say more, but he volunteered nothing.

"What do you want?" Mech demanded.

"Oh. Yes. I called you, didn't I?" Kevin said. "I made a rather interesting discovery I thought might be of interest."

"I hope it's something related to our current situation, Kevin, and not about how high cows can jump or your favorite color," Cal warned. "Because now isn't the time for that stuff. Although, mine's blue, by the way. Sort of baby blue."

"It's about the Mush, sir," Kevin replied. "You'll get a wry chuckle out of this, but I've just discovered we *do* have more aboard. It was in the Mush locker of all places."

Cal's lips thinned.

"What?"

"The Mush, sir. The substance for the replicators? We've got some. Too much of it, if anything. I just thought you'd like to know."

"I know what it is. You're telling me we have a Mush *locker*?" said Cal. "That's just, what? Full of Mush?"

"Jammed to the gunnels with it, sir," Kevin confirmed. "We probably should've looked in there, in hindsight."

"We didn't know it existed," said Loren.

"Didn't you, ma'am?" Kevin's tone became slightly accusing. "Perhaps you should've asked."

Loren opened her mouth to reply, but Cal waved her into silence. "OK, good job, Kevin. Load it up for us and we'll have a feast when we get back."

"*If* you get back, sir," Kevin corrected.

"Thanks for the vote of confidence, pal," Cal said. "Now shut the fonk up before anyone hears us."

The next corridor had just two or three corpses in it. It was hard to be any more accurate without close forensic examination, and none of them had either the time nor inclination to do that.

The next room was a dining hall. There was no point trying to figure out how many bodies were in there, since the only way of picking most of them up would be with a wet-vac and mop.

"Still got a bad feeling about this, Mech?" Cal whispered.

"Yes! Of course I do. I've got a *worse* motherfonking feeling than I had when I said it."

"It does seem kind of excessive," Cal said, skirting around the edges of a quivering flesh blancmange. "Like whoever killed these people didn't just kill them, they fonking *killed* them."

"Krone," said Tim from the back of the group. "This was Krone's doing."

Cal whistled quietly between his teeth. "OK, in that case I say Mech takes on Krone, the rest of you deal with Dave and anyone else he has hanging around, and I'll shout words of encouragement from the sidelines. You know, like, 'Woo! Go guys! Give him Hell!' Everyone cool with that?"

He stopped.

"Wait."

"What is it?" asked Loren, her eyes darting around for signs of trouble. "What's wrong?"

"Why is Krone here?"

"Cause they're breaking out his army," Mech said. "We know this."

"No, but why is he *here*?" Cal asked. "If I'm going to detonate a bomb, I'm going to make sure I'm not standing in the blast radius first."

"Aw, fonk," Mech grunted. "So you're saying..."

"It's a trap."

The voice that emerged from the speaker on Mech's arm was not Kevin's.

"And he finally figures it out! I'll be honest, Cal, I was starting to think you'd never get there. Congratulations. You're not as dumb as you look. Although, that's hardly an achievement."

"Dave," Cal said.

"Well, no. As I think I explained, that's not my real name," the voice continued. "It's Ethan."

"I'm going to call you Dave," Cal said. "We're all going to call you Dave."

"Fine. I mean, it'll be you who looks stupid, but... do what you like."

"OK, Dave," Cal said. "Now, are you going to show yourself, or are you going to keep hiding like a big Davey-Dave?"

"Who said I was hiding?" the voice drawled. "Nice ship you have here, by the way. You must tell me where you got it."

Cal broke into a run. "Mech, shut that shizznod off. Get me Kevin."

"I can't," Mech said, jabbing furiously at his arm as he tried to silence the sound of fake-Dave's laughter. "He's overriding the comms control. I can't shut him up."

"This is fun, isn't it?" Dave sniggered. "I can keep talking and talking and talking at you and there's nothing you can do about it. Nothing you can do about it at—"

Mech shot himself in the forearm and Dave's voice died in a screech of feedback. "Laugh now, shizznod," he grunted.

"That was, like, totally insane," Miz said, gesturing to the blackened screen on Mech's arm. She raised her eyebrows salaciously. "I love it."

"Splurt, Tim's struggling," Cal said as they skidded through a puddle of prisoner guts. "Help him keep up."

Dropping off Cal's back, Splurt rolled into a ball, waited for the Time Titan to draw near, then wrapped around the old man's legs like an exo-skeleton.

"Oh, I say!" Tim gasped, as the robotic limbs pistoned beneath him, powering him after Cal and the others as they raced up the ramp that led to the open hatch.

Cal raised his blaster, ignoring the ache in his shoulders. "What do we think? All guns blazing?" he whispered.

"Play it cool," Loren urged. "We don't know what we're running into."

"Uh, no. We should totally go up there and rip them apart," Miz replied.

"We can hear you, you know?" called Dave or Ethan or whatever he was called. "We can hear you quite clearly, and if you want to survive the next few seconds, I'd advise you all to listen to Ms Loren. Just saying. Fact of it is, it doesn't bother me either way."

Cal sighed. "God damn it," he said, then he lowered his gun and led the way up onto the landing platform.

Dave stood in front of the *Currently Untitled,* flanked on both sides by parallel lines of black-visored stormtrooper types. A short, unassuming looking older man stood a little behind him, his hands folded behind his back. He wore a coat with long tails, an equal parts hilarious and adorable miniature top-hat, and had the shiniest shoes Cal had ever seen. He looked quite dapper. Totally fonking ludicrous, but dapper with it.

Unlike last time they'd met, Dave was also dressed to impress in a sharp dark blue suit with paler blue shirt below. He wore a tie, but casually, the top button of the shirt undone. It rode up a little when he held out his arms and smiled.

"Hey there, fellow Earthman! Fancy seeing you here."

Cal ignored him. "Kevin, you OK?"

"My apologies sir, I didn't notice them coming," Kevin replied through the ship's speaker system. "I had my head stuck in the Mush locker. Metaphorically speaking."

Splurt deposited Tim on the landing pad beside the rest of the team, then returned to blob-form and rolled to Cal's side.

"Nice bomb you've got there," said Cal, gesturing to the metal sphere standing roughly halfway between him and Dave, and a little over on Cal's left. "I have to admit, I'm impressed. Switching ships, making us think we were handing over old Geronimo. You played us good."

"Geroni*mus*," Dave corrected.

"Yeah, yeah. Whatever. Where is the evil shizznod, anyway?"

Dave bowed, just a little, and stepped aside. The dapper little gent behind him took a step forward. He regarded Cal with a mix of curiosity and apathy. It was not an even mix, and the curiosity evaporated almost at once, leaving behind just a cold, dead-eyed stare.

"Wait, that's the most dangerous man in the universe? That's Geronimus Krone?" Cal snorted. "I thought he was your accountant."

Cal gestured with his gun to Krone's head. "I like your hat. What did you do, mug a leprechaun?" he asked, then Krone waved a finger and a scream burst on Cal's lips as his leg snapped across the shin bone, dropping him to one knee.

Miz's legs twitched. Her claws extended, her teeth baring.

"Don't!" Dave warned. He gestured to the assembled henchmen on either side of the group. They all had weapons, and they all had them trained on Cal. "Move and they shoot him. And I assure you, everyone who works for my organization is an *excellent* shot. They will not miss."

Mech slowly raised a hand, gesturing for Miz to stay where she was. Loren moved to Cal's side, but a blaster bolt exploded on the ground at her feet, forcing her back.

"Don't help him!" Dave warned. "Stay back. That goes for the blob, too. Any of you try to attack us, he dies. Any of you try to help him, he dies. Anyone gets on my nerves, he dies. Is that clear?"

"Hey man, you OK?" Mech asked.

"Meh," Cal said. He hissed as another jolt of pain tore through his broken leg. "How does it look? Does it look bad?"

The others made a series of non-committal noises.

"Shizz. OK, how bad, exactly? Out of eight?"

"Shut up!" Dave said, stepping forward and drawing a blaster of his own. He and Krone kept walking until they stood beside the metal sphere, bringing them to within a few feet of Cal. Dave raised the blaster and took aim between Cal's eyes.

"I'd like to shoot you now," he said. "That would give me immense pleasure. You have no idea."

He lowered the weapon. "But I also want you to see what happens. What you helped make happen. You see, none of this would've been possible without you, Cal. Without *all* of you."

He took another step closer and squatted down in front of Cal. "Did you figure it out yet?" he asked. "I know it must've been niggling at you. That feeling that something was missing. That there was something you hadn't quite figured out. Did you get there? Did you work it out?"

"Of course I did," Cal said. "But how about you explain

it to the others for me, and I'll occasionally chip in with intelligent comments?"

Dave snorted. "Imbecile," he said, then he ruffled Cal's hair and stood up. "It was obvious. The *Binto Odyssey*. The Time Bomb. How could it have been a test?" He jabbed a thumb in the direction of the ball. "We'd already built the bomb. It was already in place. Sort of late to be messing around with prototypes, don't you think? What would we have been testing?"

Tim gasped. "Not a test. A lure."

"Ding! Congratulations, Mr Time Titan! That is the correct answer!" Dave cried, pointing to Tim as if he'd just won a top gameshow prize. "We weren't testing anything, we were getting you guys' attention! This whole thing, right from when I first stole your money, this whole thing has been leading you to here. To now. With us."

"Why?" Cal wheezed. "Why did you want us here?"

Dave stepped closer until he stood over Cal. His voice, which had been becoming increasingly hysterical, now dropped to a matter-of-fact monotone. "Because I wanted you to see. Because I knew your pathetic hero complex would make it impossible for you to resist."

He shrugged. "But mostly because I knew you'd bring *him*."

Tim yelped in fright as some invisible force caught him by the smock and dragged him across the landing pad towards Geronimus Krone. Mech moved to intercept, but the clattering of blaster rifles being aimed more emphatically at Cal's head stopped him.

"Yes, I wouldn't," Dave told him. "Unless you want his death on your conscience. And his brains on your shoes."

"I don't wear shoes, shizznod," Mech said.

Dave looked momentarily confused, then raised one eyebrow. "Well... touché."

Down on the ground, Cal was experiencing something interesting. Not the searing pain in his leg, or feeling or utter helplessness and rage – although he was definitely experiencing those, too. This was something else. Something different. A tingling across the break in his shin that made the pain feel better and worse at the same time.

It was almost like...

Oh.

Oh Tim, you beautiful old bamston.

Cal kept his head down and his mouth shut, and tried his best not to let on.

Tim, meanwhile, was having an experience of his own, although his was less 'interesting' and more 'underwear-wettingly terrifying'.

He had stopped just ahead of Geronimus Krone, his arms held firmly at his sides like he was bound with invisible ropes. Krone's dull, dark eyes gazed up at him from beneath the brim of his little hat.

Krone raised a hand and extended an index finger as if pointing to Tim's shoulder. The Time Titan tried to look to see if something was there, but his head was held firmly by the same supernatural force as his arms.

"What? What is it?" he whimpered, then he shrieked in pain as Krone's finger became an elongated sliver of steel and stabbed cleanly through his upper arm.

"Hey, leave him alone!" Loren said, but all those guns aimed at Cal's head made a point of aiming more accurately.

"You see... the bomb?" said Dave, gesturing to the ball. "The bomb was a MacGuffin. You know about MacGuffins, right Cal? An object with no real purpose designed just to service the plot? Hitchcock? No? Doesn't matter. The point is, the bomb isn't important. The bomb, spectacular as it is, was never going to go off. What would be the point? It'd destroy everything, and no-one wants that, right? The bomb was just to get you all here. I mean, we had to make it, because we didn't know whether or not your Time Titan friend could sense it. But there's no detonator. It was never going to blow up."

He clicked his fingers and one of his armored henchmen broke ranks. This one didn't carry a gun, and instead held a goldfish-bowl sized glass ball with a speck of light no bigger than a Peanut M&M floating in the center.

God, Cal wanted some M&Ms.

"Do you know what this is?" Dave asked.

"Is it all the charm and charisma you had surgically removed?" Cal guessed. "Because it's bigger than I'd have expected."

"It's the Four. Horsemen to us, but they have all kinds of names. Geronimus's generals, trapped in a little nugget of time," Dave explained. "And more than that, even. It's his armies. Vast legions of warriors. A thousand thousand battleships, all condensed into that one tiny dot."

"A thousand thousand ships?" Cal said. "That's, like... how many? Wait, don't tell me, don't tell me."

He narrowed his eyes and calculated. "So, *ten ten* ships would be... what? A hundred ships?"

Dave rolled his eyes. "It's—"

"Wait! Psssht! I'm getting it," Cal said. "So... OK. A thousand thousands would be..." His lips moved as he whispered his working out. "Ten, then take the zeroes..." He looked up. "Ten hundred thousand ships? Is that right?"

Dave didn't appear impressed. "And what's another way of saying ten hundred thousand?"

It took Cal a moment. "A hundred ten thousand?"

"A million!" Dave snapped. "A million. Jesus *Christ*! It's a million ships."

"Are you sure?" Cal asked. "That seems a lot. A thousand *times* a thousand..."

"Shut up! It's a million!"

"You could've just said, like, 'We've got a million battleships,'" Miz pointed out. "That would've avoided any confusion. To be honest, I'd have found it way more impressive. Say you've got a million ships and I'm like, 'No way, that's *so* awesome.' Say it's a thousand thousand and I'm like, 'Huh? How come this guy's counting like such a total tool?' You know what I mean?"

Mech and Loren both mumbled their agreement.

"She has a point," Cal said. "You did sound like a total tool."

"All of you shut the fonk up!" Dave barked. "My point is—"

"Yeah, what's your point, Dave?" Cal asked.

"Shut up! My point is, we were never going to use the bomb."

"You said that part," Cal told him. He looked back over his shoulders at the others. "He said that part, right?"

"Yeah, he said that part," Loren confirmed.

"I thought so."

Cal turned back to Dave to find the blaster pistol aiming at his head. "Say another word. Go on. I dare you," Dave growled.

Moving slowly, so as not to gets his brains blown out, Cal mimed zipping his lips shut.

"We wanted the Time Titan," Dave said, keeping the gun up. "We've always wanted the Time Titan. That's all we needed."

He shuffled aside a little, giving Cal an uninterrupted view of Tim's back. The Time Titan was held several inches above the ground, hanging from the metal finger-spike through his shoulder. From the limp way he dangled, Cal guessed he'd passed out. Probably for the best.

Krone's finger retracted slowly, pulling Tim towards him. Cal couldn't see exactly what ol' Geronimo was doing, but it involved him clamping his hand over the Time Titan's face, and then a lot of sparkly stuff shimmering in the air around them.

"What's he doing?" Cal asked.

"I don't know the details of how it works, exactly," Dave admitted. "But I do know it won't be something your friend enjoys, and I also know what the end result will be."

He pointed in the direction of the glowing time nugget in the goldfish bowl and grinned. "Pretty cool, huh? The Four Horsemen and all their armies born anew."

"Oh God. What is it with you people and your evil schemes? Can't everyone just get along?" Cal asked. He puffed out his cheeks. "You know what happened to me today?"

"You had your leg broken?" Dave said, smirking.

"Fifty years. That's what happened to me today. Fifty fonking years."

For a moment, Dave seemed confused, but then the realization dawned. "The *Odyssey*? Tell me you fell into a crack!"

"Yep."

Dave erupted with laughter. "Oh... Oh, wow. That's too perfect. Fifty years? Seriously?"

"Fifty years," Cal confirmed. "With just Splurt and a whole lot of monsters for company."

"Oh. Oh, that's made my day," said Dave, wiping his tears of mirth on the sleeve of his suit. "That is too funny."

Cal shrugged. "Meh. Joke kind of wore thin after the first decade and a half," he said. "There was a while there – maybe twenty years or so – when I didn't even speak."

"You?" Dave snorted. "Didn't *speak*? I find that very hard to believe."

"Man, I would have liked to have seen that," Mech muttered.

"It was interesting," Cal said. "And I learned a lot about communicating with Splurt. You know, non-verbally?"

Dave's eyes flicked to the green blob pulsating beside Mech.

"I also learned about patience, you know? I was never patient before. Always rushing in. But now? Now I know how to wait for just the right moment."

Dave's eyes flicked back to Cal. His finger tensed on the trigger of his blaster. "Do you?"

"You'll also notice, that I'm young again," Cal said. "See, Timbo there – the Time Titan – he restored me. Brought me back to my prime."

Dave shot a withering look along the barrel of his gun. "This is you in your prime?"

"I know, it's not much to look at," Cal admitted. "I can't run very fast, I'm not all that strong, I have mild incontinence issues when traveling at warp speed. But there's one thing about my prime that *will* impress you."

"Oh?" said Dave, raising an eyebrow. "And what's that?"

"I heal crazy fast," Cal said, then he launched himself upwards, knocked aside the blaster, and exploded Dave's nose with the top of his head.

TWENTY-TWO

Splurt lashed out, his blobby body becoming two elongated plant-like tendrils that scythed the legs out from under the gunmen on either side. Mech raised both arms in opposite directions and let rip with his wrist cannons, obliterating most of the men in mid-air.

Half-blinded by blood, snot and tears, Dave swung the butt of his gun at Cal's head, but Cal had been expecting that. He ducked, drove three rapid punches into Dave's stomach – bam-bam-bam – and finished with a thunderous knee to the balls.

"God, I've missed fighting Earth guys," said Cal as he watched Dave fold like a broken puppet to the ground. "You always know where their nuts are."

A sudden wind whipped up from where Krone stood with the Time Titan. Tim's head was bent back, and Cal could see Krone's fingers had become thin tubes that entered Tim's head via his nostrils and mouth. Krone's eyes had changed, too. Where before they had been dark and glassy, they now swam with the same sparkling colors that filled the air around both men.

Time slowed. At least, it felt that way. Whether it actually slowed or not, Cal couldn't say, but a lot of major events seemed to occur before his eyes, and there was very little he could do to stop any of them.

The glass container with the glowing M&M inside exploded. Cal saw the ripple pass through the transparent walls, then watched each individual piece fall lazily to the ground – with the exception of all the pieces that embedded themselves in the armor of the guy who had been holding the thing. And, judging by his screams, *through* the armor in places, too.

He watched the little ball of light become a slightly bigger ball of light.

By the time he'd processed that it was growing, it was already the size of a tennis ball, its edges fizzing and crackling like a sparkler on 4th of July.

It became a soccer ball.

Then a basketball.

Then a howling vortex filled with mind-bending shapes and colors and sounds.

It was only when the first figure appeared inside it that everyone snapped out of their daze. He, she – or possibly it – was dressed in an outfit comprised almost entirely of spikey bits. Its mask was a grimacing skull with two curved metal horns forcibly inserted through the temples. Orange eyes glowed behind the mask. Cal swore he could feel them boring deep into his soul.

"You're too late," Dave coughed. "They're coming. They're coming!"

"We need to shut this shizz down!" Cal said. "We need to get Tim away from that fonk."

He felt the wind of Loren running past him, her blaster raised.

"On it. Cover me," she urged, spraying fire towards the spikey-armored newcomer as she ran. The bolts seemed to accelerate as they raced towards the hole, then froze in the air just beyond its edges.

"Loren, wait, don't!" Cal yelped, setting off in a run after her.

Time slowed.

He saw Krone's eyes flick towards Loren.

He saw the villain's free hand fold into a point, becoming a long metal blade.

"No!"

A fast-moving shape charged past him from behind, sending him spinning to the ground.

Cal heard the sound as he landed. He knew, in that moment, it was the worst sound he would ever hear.

It was the sound of metal tearing through flesh and shattering bone.

Time stopped.

Cal couldn't move. Couldn't turn. Couldn't look to see what had happened.

He heard Mech. The cyborg's voice was different. More hollow, somehow.

"No. Aw, no."

Time resumed.

Cal turned. Cal looked. And all the air left his body as if he'd been kicked in the stomach.

Loren was on the ground halfway between Cal and Krone, half-sitting up, her blaster raised.

Beyond her, an inert shape lay in an expanding puddle of blood.

An inert *hairy* shape.

Mizette.

"No. No, no, no, no," Cal whimpered, the word tumbling out of his mouth on a loop he couldn't stop.

Geronimus Krone raised his blood-soaked blade and met Cal's eye. "Down, doggy," he said, and his mouth twisted into a harlequin smile.

Krone tossed Tim aside, the Time Titan's purpose now served. The hole was widening now, and three other figures had appeared behind the first, each one more terrifying than the one before. If Hell ever staged a thrash metal festival, these guys would be top of the bill.

"Splurt! Get Miz and Tim back to the ship!" Cal cried.

A many-tentacled thing rolled across the ground, snapped its arms around Mizette and the Time Titan, and hurriedly yanked them clear.

Cal couldn't bring himself to look at the way Mizette's body hung down so limply in Splurt's grip. Instead, he reached for his blaster, took aim at the most dangerous man in the universe, and fired over and over and over again.

Mech and Loren fired, too, until the air was filled with the scorching screams of blaster fire. They fired like that for a full minute, hammering Krone with concentrated bolts of fire.

He was still smiling when they stopped. They hadn't killed him, hadn't hurt him. They hadn't even knocked off his hat, and Cal had aimed several shots at it specifically for that purpose. They had achieved nothing, and the hole in time was getting bigger.

"There's nothing you can do to stop this, you know?" said Dave, limping past Loren as she kicked backwards and got to her feet. He stopped just in front of Krone. "My organization has spent a long time planning this. I personally have invested years making sure everything worked out just the way we wanted it to. Then, all we had to do was wait for a predictable hot-head to come along, and here we are."

Dave chuckled. "Of course, I had no idea you'd be from Earth. That's just a bonus." He looked Cal up and down. "We're the last of our kind, Cal Carver. It's going to be such a shame when I—"

The blade severed his head with one clean strike, slicing through his neck like it was a stick of warm butter. Blood fountained upwards from the stump, then fell like drizzle on Geronimus Krone, who was revealed when Dave's body slumped sideways.

Four seconds later, his head *thumped* down beside the rest of him.

"He talked too much," Krone said. His voice had an odd sing-song tone to it, like he was always midway through telling a joke that he personally found hilarious.

The hole was not a hole now. Cal wasn't sure what it was, exactly, but 'hole' didn't really do it justice. It was more like a painting of a hole layered on the fabric of space itself. Inside it, Cal could see those four terrifying figures, but there was a moving sky behind them now, too, filled with ships. A thousand ten hundred ships, to be exact.

"Your universe is mine," Krone told them. "Your choice is how you die. On your knees, like cowards. Or in some pointless act of heroism, like your dog."

Cal felt rage twist him from the gut upwards, but it was met by a sinking feeling of helplessness coming the other way.

There had to be something he could do. Some way to stop this. But what? He had no idea. He wasn't smart enough. If he was, he could've done something clever. Something that could snatch victory from the jaws of defeat, save the galaxy, and wipe the fonking smirk off this shizznod's face.

But he couldn't think of anything clever.

So, he did something dumb.

"Kevin! Open fire!" he commanded.

Geronimus Krone sighed. It was an amused, patronizing sort of sigh that somehow managed to make Cal hate the man all the more.

"Your ship's blaster fire won't hurt me," Krone said.

"Yeah, don't aim at him, Kevin," Cal said. He pointed to the enormous metal ball right beside the villain. "Aim at that."

"Very good, sir," Kevin chimed, then the *Untitled*'s cannons erupted.

Krone made it to the first letter of the word, "No," before the ball burst open in an eruption of fire and metal and time. The hole that had been painted on space fragmented like shattering glass. The figures inside it became deformed, their limbs contracting and elongating even as the ships behind them dripped like liquid down the sky.

"Ooh, this may have been a mistake," Cal said, and his words alternated between lengthy drawn out-drones and high-speed chipmunk chirps that sparkled as they spiraled from his mouth.

Geronimus Krone was frozen down his right side, while his left arm and leg jerked furiously around like they'd been stuck on fast forward.

Loren was a statue at Cal's side. Mech was a blur. And time continued to unravel around them.

Cal felt himself speed up and slow down simultaneously. His heart thrummed in his chest like one constant tone. His feet were lead, and fixed to the metal roof of the prison, which ebbed with blooms of expanding and contracting rust patterns.

Color and noise and some bastard offspring of the two crashed down on Cal and the others like a tidal wave. Cal felt his bones shatter, his flesh decay, his atoms scatter on the wind.

And then he felt something wrap around him, holding him, pulling him back together. The colors became a blinding white that filled the whole world and all the worlds beyond it.

When it cleared, an elderly man in a blood-stained smock stood before him, his hands twisting as if wrestling with thin air. Tim's eyes spun with all the shades and colors of time.

"That was stupid," he said, and his voice boomed like it had when they'd first met him. Cal couldn't see them, but he got the impression of another figure towering over the Time Titan. A giant space baby, weaving its arms in time with the much smaller figure before it.

The wind rushed in, howling towards the collapsing time hole with a hurricane's fury. Geronimus Krone, still half-frozen and half-flailing, was sent tumbling into the abyss. Cal enjoyed a fleeting moment of triumph, then his feet were pulled out from under him and the wind carried him towards the point of no return.

A green tendril wrapped around his wrist, jerking him to a stop. Cal managed to raise his head enough to see Splurt hooked around the front landing leg of the *Untitled*, holding him and Loren in place. Cal could no longer see Mech anywhere, but he could feel him like a buzzing at the base of his skull.

He twisted around until he could see Tim. "Where's Krone?" he hollered. "Where did he go?"

"Lost in time," Tim replied. "Exactly where and when, let us hope we never find out."

"You can stop all this, right?" Cal cried.

"What? No! Of course I can't stop it," Tim replied. "It's... it's too much. The damage is too great. I'm too old."

"Bullshizz!" Cal shouted back. "I watched you stop time across the whole universe. You've totally got this, Timbo."

Tim glanced up and around them at the damage. The splinters were invisible, yet Cal could see them clearly. Dust motes swirled in some, hung motionless in others. Smoke formed solid jagged blocks where it passed through some time lines, but evaporated into nothing in those directly adjoining them.

"There's nothing I can do from out here," Tim said. He pointed to the rapidly closing time hole. "But perhaps from in there."

"OK, great! And then you can come back out?"

Tim smiled sadly at Cal, and in that look Cal found his answer.

"Then that's a bad plan!" Cal said. "There's got to be another way."

"It's the only way. My time was always going to run out. Sooner or later," Tim said. "I can think of no better way to go."

His feet lifted off the ground, his smock whipping and snapping as it was pulled by the wind.

He stopped in the air beside Cal. "It has been interesting. I'll give you that much," he said, then he raised his arms to his side and surrendered to the pull of the time schism.

Cal watched the Time Titan tumble inside, his hands weaving furiously in the air, spots of color swarming around him like flies. For a moment, the old man's face was knotted up in concern, but then he smiled beneath his beard, and *whooped* loud enough to be heard over the roaring gale.

The hole closed. The wind dropped. And the fractured fragments of time were once again made whole.

"What the...? What happened?" Loren gasped, jumping back to life.

"A lot!" Mech said. He staggered to a stop between Loren and Cal, his eyes wide and staring. "A lot fonking happened."

"He stopped it," Cal realized. "He fixed the break."

"I been standing here for eight months," Mech continued, "watching you slow-moving motherfonkers try to get your—"

"Miz!" Cal said, stumbling to his feet and racing for the *Untitled's* landing ramp. He was inside in a heartbeat, frantically searching through the ship's rooms. "Miz? *Miz*? Kevin, where is she?"

Kevin's voice was uncharacteristically somber. "Master Splurt laid her to rest on the bridge, sir."

"Laid her to rest? What do you mean, 'laid her to rest?'"

"I'm so terribly sorry, sir."

"No. What? No."

Cal slapped a hand against the wall, fingers splayed, supporting himself as his legs staggered him along the corridor.

She lay on the floor in front of her usual spot, arms by her sides, eyes open but seeing nothing. Cal wasn't sure why, exactly, but he noticed her tail, and the way the hairs splayed out against the floor, making it look much larger than it actually was.

The rest of her, though, looked smaller somehow. Like what was in there – what was Miz – had already vacated the premises.

"No, no, not happening," Cal said, dropping to his knees beside her. He interlocked his fingers and placed them in the center of her chest, but as he pumped more blood seeped out from behind her, running into the valleys and indents in the metal floor.

"Loren! Mech! Help me!" he cried. "Somebody help me here!"

He shook her. He didn't know what else to do. "Miz! Miz! Come on, sexy Chewbacca! Don't you do this. Don't you fonking do this! Please don't do this!"

"Cal."

Loren's hand was on his shoulder. He shrugged it away.

"No! She's going to be OK! She's going to be OK! You hear me, Miz?" His voice became a series of angry sobs. "You'd better be OK, young lady, or you are in *so* much trouble! You said it yourself, no-one dies on this team. No-one dies."

"It's too late, man," Mech said. "She's gone."

"No! N-n—"

The rest of the word choked him. Cal rocked forward on his knees, burying his face in Mizette's damp fur, his shoulders shaking in big silent sobs.

Splurt rolled to his side and nuzzled up against his leg. Mech and Loren stood behind him, both wanting to say so much, but neither one knowing just the right words to use.

Loren wiped her eyes on her sleeve. "She saved me. I thought she hated me, but she saved me."

"She did hate you, ma'am," Kevin said. "Emphatically."

Loren sniffed, closed her eyes tightly, then looked up at Mech. What she saw there took her by surprise.

"Hey, I didn't know you could cry," she said.

Mech brushed his metal fingertips against his flesh cheek. "Huh. Me neither," he said.

They waited in silence until Cal finally straightened.

"You OK?" Loren asked.

"I told her mom I'd protect her. I told her she'd be safe with us," he said. "Now what do I tell her?"

"That's she dead, sir?" Kevin suggested.

"Rhetorical question, Kevin!" Mech barked.

"I wasn't finished," Kevin said. "Tell her that she's dead, but that she died saving *everyone*. The Greyx. The Symmorium. Those weird ones with the fish heads. She gave her life that others may live. She died as she lived: Like, totally fonking awesome."

Cal snorted out a bubble of snot. "*Totally* fonking awesome," he agreed. He made no attempt to wipe away his tears. There were too many for that now.

"We should get her off the bridge," Loren said. "Put her in her bedroom."

"I'll do it," said Mech, but Cal stopped him.

"No. I'll do it," he said.

He scooped an arm beneath her shoulders, cradling her head, and slipped his other arm beneath the small of her back. "I got you, kiddo," he whispered, then he tried to stand up. Something in his lower back went *twang*. "Fonk. No, she's way too heavy. Jesus, what was I thinking? Mech, you do it."

"I got her," said Mech, crouching.

"But gently."

"You got it," Mech said, then he slipped his metal arms beneath the lifeless body of Mizette of the Greyx and carried her – gently – through to her room.

CAL SAT IN THE KITCHEN, idly pricking his fingertip

with a space fork and watching the wound immediately close over again. Outside, the stars streaked past as the *Currently Untitled* hurtled towards Greyx Prime, bringing Mizette home.

"You know the food replicator's working again, sir?" Kevin said.

"Hmm?" Cal looked up. "Oh. Yeah. I know. I'm not hungry."

"Are you thinking about Ms Miz, sir?"

"I am, Kevin, yes."

"Would you like me to call her mother and let her know we're coming?" Kevin asked. "I could drop a few hints as to why. You know, so it doesn't come as a complete shock."

"What? No!"

"I could say, 'Remember how you *had* a daughter?' Well—"

"Kevin, if you do that I will rip your circuits out with my bare hands," Cal warned him. "No calling ahead. No calling anyone. Do you understand?"

"I understand, sir," said Kevin. "And I apologize. I was only trying to help. To be honest..."

Cal flicked his eyes up at the speaker. "To be honest what? Did you call her? Is that what you're going to tell me, because I swear..."

"No, not that, sir," said Kevin. "To be honest... I am having difficulty."

Cal leaned back in his chair. "What kind of difficulty."

"I feel like there's... a hole, sir. Like there's a piece of me missing that I'll never get back. Like something that was there is now lost. Do you understand what I mean?"

"I do. I understand exactly what you mean."

"Also, Mizette is dead," Kevin said, sounding a little

surprised, like he'd only just remembered. "So that's put rather a downer on everything, too."

Cal puffed out his cheeks. "It has. Can't argue with that."

He stood up. "Anyway, great talk, Kevin. I'd better go... somewhere else."

"Are you going to check how things are going on the bridge, sir?"

"Yes! Yes, I'll do that," Cal said.

Leaving the kitchen, Cal paused outside Mizette's door and brushed his hand against it. With a nod, he moved on up to the bridge and sat in his chair. Splurt had cleaned the blood off the floor while the others were through in Mizette's room, although Cal wasn't quite sure how, and wasn't convinced he wanted to know.

As soon as Cal had sat down, Splurt flopped down from the ceiling and landed on his shoulder.

"Loren, you called Zertex yet and told them 'thanks for nothing'?" Cal asked.

"I've tried, but we're getting no reply," Loren said.

"Guess they're keeping out of our way," Mech grunted.

"Good. Let's hope it stays that way," Cal replied.

They sat in silence, watching space roll by ahead of them. Loren opened her mouth to speak a couple of times, but then closed it again. On the third time, she finally said what was on her mind.

"Miz spoke to me. After Krone... After she got hurt. She spoke to me."

Cal and Mech both turned to her. "She did?" Cal asked. "What did she say?"

"She said that I was a terrible pilot."

Cal nodded. He glanced at Mizette's empty chair. "Yeah, that sounds like her."

"And then she told me not to leave," Loren continued. "And then she reiterated that I was a terrible pilot."

Cal's chair *creaked* beneath him. "And?"

"And I don't think I'm *that* bad."

"Not about the pilot thing. About leaving."

Loren stared ahead for a while, then half-turned in her chair. "Of course I'm not leaving," she said. "I belong here with you guys. Besides, I've had enough of arguing with Miz. I guess it wouldn't hurt to give her the last word this one—"

"About to crash into Greyx Prime," Kevin announced.

"What?! Fonk!" Loren spun in her chair, frantically hammered a series of controls, and the ship screeched to a stop. They all pretended not to hear the *thump* of something heavy hitting the wall in Mizette's room.

"Sorry. My fault!" Loren said.

"I don't think anyone needed that pointed out to them, ma'am," said Kevin.

"It's OK. No harm done," Cal said, although from the wheeze in his voice it was possible this wasn't entirely true. He gestured down at the planet below. "Is that Greyx Prime?"

"Yeah," said Mech.

"Does it look different?" Cal wondered, then a crackling filled the screen and the view of the planet was replaced by the surly sneer of a grey-furred wolf man.

"Unidentified vessel, you are in violation of Greyx Space," the guy barked. Pretty much literally. "Leave this sector or face the penalty."

"Uh, hi. We're here to see Queen... Uh, Miz's mom," said Cal.

"You have five seconds to vacate the sector," the Greyx

continued. "Or you shall be put to death in the name of the King."

Cal shook his head. "Wait. Hold on, what? You don't have a king. He died. You have a queen."

"Not the Greyx king, *the* king," the wolf man snarled. "The King of All Space. The High Emperor of the Galaxy."

Cal flicked his eyes to Mech. "What the fonk's he talking about?"

"I got no idea," Mech said.

"What's his name, this King of All Space?" asked Cal.

"Do not toy with me," the Greyx spat. "You know his name. The Universe knows his name. He has ruled us for generations, and we have been grateful for his guidance."

Cal leaned forward in his chair. "Remind me."

"King Krone," said the Greyx, bowing his head in a show of deference and respect. "The High Emperor, Geronimus."

The words rained like punches around Cal's head and chest, driving him back into his chair. *Lost in time and space*, that's what Tim had said. Krone had been cast adrift in the time stream.

Somehow, he'd found his way out.

"Loren, get us out of here," Cal said.

"On it," Loren replied, her fingers already flying across the controls.

"Mech, can you do, like, a space scan and try to pick up TV transmissions? Is that a thing?"

"Yeah, that's a thing," said Mech. He tapped at his controls as the *Untitled* jumped to warp speed, leaving Greyx Prime trailing in its wake.

"Getting something," Mech said. He gestured to the view screen. The top left corner was replaced by what looked like some news footage showing Krone standing before a vast rally of people.

Another image appeared, this time showing the spikey-armored general they'd seen in the time hole striding through the burning wreckage of a ship.

"No," Cal whispered.

More clips flashed up. Krone's face on a palatial building. A group of placard-carrying protesters being torn apart by space wolves. People begging, people bowing, people dying.

And ships. A thousand thousand of them, advancing across the galaxy, obliterating all those who stood against them.

"We sent him back in time," Loren realized. "He's been building up. That's why I couldn't reach Zertex. There *is* no Zertex."

"Man's made himself the King of Space," Mech said. "We thought we'd stopped him, but this is worse than ever."

Loren turned away from the screen until she faced Cal. "What do we do?" she asked.

Cal's gaze flicked from each video feed to the next, the swirling light patterns reflecting in his eyes.

"Cal?" said Loren, trying but failing to hide the shake in her voice. "What do we do?"

What should he say to her? What should they do? Something clever, probably. But then, clever was never his strong point.

Something dumb, then.

Cal stood up. He looked around the bridge until his eyes finally fell on Miz's empty chair. He spent a moment saying a silent goodbye, then he turned back to face front and grinned. He wasn't sure why, exactly, but he grinned.

"We're gonna need a bigger team."

Printed in Great Britain
by Amazon

60002341R00170